BILLION DOLLAR REVENGE

SHARON WOODS

For those who dream big, find someone who will help turn that dream into reality. Don't settle.

CHAPTER 1

CHELSEA

I STARE AT MYSELF in the floor-length mirror, admiring how well my new black bustier and straight blue Levi jeans fit my body. With my long legs and athletic frame, my outfit gives the illusion that I have more curves than I actually do. It's my 27th birthday, and I'm eagerly waiting for my boyfriend of nearly two years to come pick me up so we can celebrate together.

I try to smile as I arrange the flowers in the vase on my nightstand, but my heart aches knowing they weren't from him. That doesn't matter, though, because we are going to have some time together tonight at my favorite restaurant. At least, that's what I keep telling myself.

He should be here any moment. I finish my inspection of myself, quickly painting my lips with my favorite creamy mauve lipstick and running my fingers through my bangs. Grabbing my purse, I throw my phone and lipstick inside, then head down to show Summer——my friend and roommate——my outfit.

As my black heels click against the living room floor, my best friend whistles from her well-worn spot on the sofa, and I break into the widest of grins.

"You look hot. I wish you had a real man to show all this off to," she says in a curt tone. I know she's trying to be happy for me, even though she's voiced her concerns about Bobby being a flake. But I love him, and I know how hard he works. Being a full-time employee at Lincoln Media while navigating the New York City traffic daily is no easy task.

I check the time on my phone. "He should be here any minute."

She nods but remains silent.

He's probably running a few minutes late——he always is. I made the reservation for eight o'clock to make it easier on him. He stays late at work to impress the CEO because he wants a promotion. He told me he needs to fulfill extra duties until he gets the job. However, a very small part of me hoped he would've made an exception for my birthday.

"Come sit while you wait," Summer offers, lifting a side of the cream throw blanket.

Our favorite movie, *Love Actually*, is on. I can't say no; it's better than staring at the door. I move toward the sofa, take a seat, and lay the throw blanket on my lap. My phone is in my hand, waiting for Bobby to text me, saying he's outside.

He won't knock on our door, or come inside; he says he doesn't like spending time at my place because I have roommates. But I haven't told them, because how could I? It would give them even more reason to hate him. I know Bobby hasn't been the best boyfriend in their eyes. It's starting to irritate me too, but I'm sure it's just a rough patch. All relationships go through them. Well, that's what I tell myself.

The emotional moment in the movie comes, and my chest aches. It's a scene that reminds me love isn't easy, or always reciprocated, but can still be beautiful in its own way. *"To me, you are perfect."* I sigh, sinking farther into the soft fabric of the sofa. I'm a hopeless romantic, obsessed with love. I adore this feeling, and I want to experience it in my own life. Even if Bobby has said he loves me, he's never the one to initiate it. When I say, "I love you," he says, "Me too."

Some people show affection in different ways, and I guess that's not his style. And that's okay. I imagine us getting engaged, married, and having kids. I just need to wait a little longer for him to see I'm mature and ready. My parents don't show a lot of affection to each other either; no hand holding, no PDA, so I don't expect our relationship to be any different.

The movie ends, and I hold back the tears in my eyes so they don't ruin my makeup.

Blinking rapidly, I look for my phone that's slipped off the sofa and landed on the floor. I grab it and realize it's been half an hour. Our reservation is for...*now*, and if we are more than ten minutes late, they will give the table away. With a sense of unease, I pick up the phone and dial him. His phone doesn't ring; it goes straight to voicemail.

My heart feels like it's shrinking. Where is he? A moment later, my phone chimes.

> **Bobby:** Sorry, I'm in a meeting. I won't be able to come to dinner. Celebrate with your friends.

I stare at my phone, as my chest grows tight, restricting my breathing. But it's my birthday...Surely, his boss doesn't require him to stay this late. He wouldn't have chosen this. No, there's no way. I type a quick response, hoping to change his mind.

> **Me:** Really? It's my birthday. I told you I'll drive and we can just go for an hour.

> **Bobby:** No, I can't. I have a long night ahead of me. I've told you my job comes first. This is important to me.

Me: *And I'm not important to you?*

I lower my head and sag into the back of the sofa, feeling suddenly nauseous.

"He's not coming?" Summer asks in a clipped tone. I forgot for a moment she was beside me. Her hand touches my arm, and I wince. Pulling her hand away, she lifts the blanket off her, revealing her comfy green sweats. "He's such a dick. But fuck it. It's your birthday."

I tilt my head and look at her in confusion.

"I'm going to go with you! I'll text Nova, and she can meet us after dinner."

My mouth falls open slightly, heart swelling with gratitude.

"Sounds good," I say, pulling myself together.

Having fun with my friends, even if for a few hours, might be all I need. Summer runs to her room, and there's a lot of banging around. When my phone chimes again, my breath hitches. I read the new message.

Bobby: *You are. I'll make it up to you next week.*

The cloud of disappointment lifts slightly as Summer walks into the kitchen, grabbing her keys and winking. "Let's go, birthday girl."

Her dark blue jeans and black long-sleeve top hug her curves perfectly. With her brown hair wavy and parted to the side, she doesn't have any makeup on except for mascara. Naturally flushed cheeks from rushing around the room show off her natural beauty.

Bobby's favorite kind.

He always says he wishes I didn't wear so much makeup. I have reduced the amount I wear since we began our relationship, but he always looks at me funny if I go bold with my lipstick or draw too much attention to my eyes with a wing liner...but I love makeup. I can be creative with it and that makes me feel good.

"You don't need all this makeup," he would say, and most of the time I take it as a compliment. Maybe if I was more like her...No. I can't do this tonight. I don't need to compare myself to anyone.

I get up and follow her to the kitchen, determined to have a good night. My best friends, Nova and Summer, are more than enough.

As I swallow the lump of pain, I hear Summer say, "There are some promises you shouldn't make."

I feel a little piece of me break inside at her words. Because what can I say other than, "I know."

"Nothing a glass of wine or three can't fix." She winks, making me laugh as she loops her arm through mine, and even though I'm taller at five-nine, compared to her five foot frame, I lean into her.

"Thanks."

Just then, my phone rings. Bobby's name flashes across the screen, and I stare at it.

"Is that him?" Summer asks.

I nod, hoping he has changed his mind.

I quickly hit the answer button, ready to say hello, when I hear a female's voice.

"I thought you were busy tonight..." a sweet, unfamiliar female voice speaks.

My heart races as I sit up, press the speaker button, and lower the phone to the table between us. Neither of us makes a sound. I'm even holding my breath, waiting to hear his reply.

"I'm not," Bobby replies.

"Mmhmm," she purrs.

"I was supposed to have dinner with Chelsea," Bobby explains.

"Then what happened?"

"She said it was her birthday."

"I thought you said you two weren't serious."

"We aren't. She's deluded. My parents were trying to force it."

Stomach sinking, my hand covers my mouth, and the backs of my eyes sting from his words. *Asshole.*

"So we're good?"

"Of course, baby."

He never called me anything other than Chelsea...

"Good, because I don't share."

"I love——" Summer hits the *end call* button, and we sit in silence. Neither of us knows what to say. We both heard Bobby flirting with someone else. He said we weren't serious, and yet with her, he was about to say words I've been desperate to hear.

I'm trying to get out of my head, but I can't help but hear his words on repeat.

"What a dickhead," Summer snaps.

I'm unable to move for a moment, shocked. My eyes still stare at the phone as tears run down my face, but I'm not sad, I'm humiliated.

Have you felt the walls close in when everyone stares at you, feeling sorry for you? That's how I'm feeling. I just want to run and hide.

I deserve it. People warned me. Family, friends, even co-corkers.

Summer pushes my hair out of my face, wiping away tears, offering to go over there and tell him off. "He's a dick. I'm going to kill that cheating bastard."

"He's not worth it," I say in a broken whisper.

"You're going to be fine," Summer says.

My head tilts to her. I find her eyes dull and sad. "I know, I just wish I hadn't wasted so much time."

"Don't waste your time wishing you could change the past," Summer says, walking me to the sofa.

"I know. Still wish I could, though." I drop my chin and type a quick text, my fingers trembling with anger and heartbreak.

> **Me:** *You lying, cheating bastard. We're done. Don't fucking ever contact me again.*

Sitting down, I pull the cream blanket over me and think about how I ignored his horrible behavior because I was scared that if I was alone, I'd never find someone again. And being alone terrifies me, because then I'll never get married or have children like I so desperately want.

I'm getting older, and Bobby would remind me of that constantly. As if I needed to be told exactly why I needed him. He played on what I wanted the most, only to end up hurting me.

I'm more angry and upset at myself that I let him treat me this way. But it wasn't like this at the beginning. He was sweet and charming. It started as a gentle comment about what to wear when we went to dinner, or how beautiful I was with less makeup, or how smart I looked in corporate clothes. I heard compliments, but now I can see how he was just trying to control me. In the more recent months, he turned it up, making me fear my life without him.

"You're going to get through this," Summer says in a soothing tone, wrapping her arms around me.

"I know I will," I whisper through the tears rolling down my cheeks.

Unfortunately, I still replay every word he said in my mind for the rest of the night.

CHAPTER 2

EVAN

THERE ARE NO WEEKENDS at my newspaper company, The New York Press. I'm in my office, approving the breaking news about the new Royal wedding scandal involving the princess and her bodyguard.

All hands are on deck for this story. Normally, Shyla handles all the work-related articles, but I haven't had a major scandal like this in years, so I'm taking the lead on this one.

I've been at work since four a.m., and I'll be here until I head to my brother Oliver's for poker at seven.

I stare down at the article that needs finalizing in the next two minutes so it can go to print on time.

As I examine the picture and the article, I immediately hate the layout. The picture isn't right; it seems blurry, and their faces need to be clearer.

I pick up my phone and dial my personal assistant, Gabby. She worked with my dad before I took total ownership of the company five years ago. Whenever I'm here, she comes into work, although she doesn't have to. I give her a nice bonus every year as a thanks. I appreciate her long hours and dedication to help me.

"Hi, Mr. Lincoln."

"Gabby, can you call the photographer and editors? I need whoever's in up here now."

"Sure, Mr. Lincoln."

Hanging up, I lower my hands, resting them on either side of the paper. After another long inspection, I come to the conclusion that it's definitely the wrong picture.

A moment later, there's a knock at my door.

"Come in," I say with urgency.

My head lifts, and I stand straighter when I see the photographer Bobby and new photographer Callum.

"Come look at the article that will go to print. Tell me what's wrong with it," I say.

They walk briskly to me, their eyes cast down to the papers sprawled on my wooden desk.

"It looks fine to me, Mr. Lincoln," Bobby replies, standing back from the article, arms crossed over his chest.

Callum mumbles how he thinks it's fine too, but he's a new hire, so he naturally agrees with his colleague.

I grind my teeth as my eyes roll inside my head, my frustration mounting. "Bobby, 'fine' isn't good enough. Do you have another image we could use?" I ask, my voice tight and strained.

Bobby runs his hand through his short brown hair, clearly deep in thought.

"We don't have time to think. This article needs to go to print now," I bark, losing my patience. He wants a promotion to photo editor. This position would give him more creative control, responsibility, and the opportunity to change the layout of the newspaper. But this article is proof he's not ready yet. Why did I have to point out the blurry image? He should have been all over it. He doesn't push himself beyond what's necessary. I'm looking for staff who push their limits. I'm here now because I did that very thing. I worked overtime for my dad for years, learned every department, and came up with new ideas to help grow the company.

It's Callum who speaks. "We do."

My eyebrows furrow and then release as I focus my attention on the new guy. "Can I see them?"

"Sure," he says in a higher-pitched voice, avoiding my gaze. Clearing his throat, he reaches into his suit pocket for his phone but clumsily drops it. Shaking out his hand, he quickly bends down to scoop it up, tapping the screen as he stands.

"I can run down and email them to you," Bobby offers, but he's already stepping backward toward the door.

"I have them in a drive folder. I can share them with you from my phone," Callum says, as his fingers move with urgency, still avoiding eye contact.

Callum moves to stand next to me, a bead of sweat sitting on his brow. He angles his phone so I can see his screen, which by some miracle isn't cracked from the hard floor. When he taps to open the folder, Bobby stays silent in the background.

"Here they all are," Callum says, keeping his eyes firmly on his phone screen as he scrolls quickly through the images for me to see.

There are a lot of images, which means I need a closer look, so I hold out my hand.

He hands his phone over, and I scroll through the mountain of photos until one captures my eye. The princess has her hands on her bodyguard's chest, looking up at him with desire, their bodies pressed together, his hands resting firmly on her waist, with their lips almost touching.

"How quickly can you edit this?" I ask, looking up at Callum as my thumb hovers over the photo on the screen.

Callum turns to look at Bobby, his hand scratching the base of his neck, and I feel my blood start to boil.

"I don't——" Bobby starts.

My nostrils flare as I cut him off, anticipating his crap excuse. "You know what? Just go, edit it quickly, and send it over." Extending the phone out to Callum, he looks as though he's seen a ghost.

Bobby drops his chin to his chest, as Callum takes his phone, and they leave my office without another word. I sit in my office chair, rubbing my brow to ward off a headache and get back to the article, knowing the new image will make this better.

I give them ten minutes before I am down on their floor. It's already been too long. As I step out of the elevators, my body turns to stone. Bobby is at Shyla——the editor-in-chief, and my right-hand woman's desk, talking. *You've got to be fucking kidding me.*

I'm practically shaking with how angry I am.

"Bobby. What are you doing?" I sneer.

He stands abruptly and swivels around, face paling at the sight of me. He wasn't expecting me. *Good.*

"Uh. I needed to talk to Shyla about the article," he rushes out, taking another step away from Shyla's desk.

"About?" I ask. I don't pay him to talk or distract my other employees.

She's not involved in this article—I am. But I don't need him to clarify because I heard their conversation, *Who would want her? She won't find anyone better than me...* which was nothing about work. He thinks I'm fucking stupid, and it only adds to my growing rage.

Those words remind me of my past and why I feel so unworthy of the good things that come my way. Is this the way my ex, Connie, spoke about me behind my back? Was I some fucking joke to her?

Was she laughing with the guy she was fucking behind my back, saying I won't find any better?

"Her opinion on the image," Bobby says, pulling me out of my past and back to the here and now.

My temple throbs as the headache slowly turns to a migraine. For fuck's sake, I don't need her approval to change the image. I'm the fucking CEO. What I say goes.

"You need to do what I asked you to do," I say. Stepping so I'm standing so close to him, our shoes touch, and I breathe heavily into his face.

"I am, Mr. Lincoln," he replies, his mouth trembling, as he takes another step back to give himself more space.

Lies.

I curl my lips in disgust. "You're meant to be editing, not talking."

Opening his mouth to respond, his eyes reflect anger as he shakes his head. But before he can speak, a throat clears, drawing my attention to Callum.

"Here, Mr. Lincoln, it's done," he says, briefly meeting my gaze before turning to his computer screen and gesturing for me to come and take a look.

"At least someone listens to me," I grumble under my breath to Bobby, as I stride to Callum's desk.

"I was working. I just needed to talk to Shyla," Bobby adds, either trying to have the last word or to rile me up—I was unsure which he was going for. Either way, it nearly pushes me to the breaking point.

"She's busy managing other articles. We don't need her expertise for this Bobby." My voice is loud, and everyone is silent; you could hear a pin drop.

Shyla looks at me with remorseful eyes. It's not her fault Bobby can't keep his dick in his pants. I need to get rid of this asshat. I just need to figure out how without him claiming unfair dismissal.

I force myself to concentrate on the task at hand so I can calm the fuck down, leaning over to see Callum's work. As I take in the new image and what he's been able to accomplish, the tightness in my shoulders melts away.

I slap the desk with a sharp thud. "Yes. This is better. Email this to me immediately. This is going to print now."

"Yes, Mr. Lincoln," Callum replies with a satisfied smile.

I step away from Callum, walk toward the elevators, noting that Bobby is back at his desk, doing God knows what. But right now I don't care. I have a breaking story to get out.

In the elevator, I run through my issues with Bobby, wondering if I have enough to fire him. There's something in my gut that says I need to do it before something big happens. I always find him "talking" to different women in the office. None of the women have filed a complaint against him. Does this mean he's not bothering them? It's probably just me. But my gut has never been wrong.

The elevator doors open to my office floor. My space. At this hour, it will be beautiful watching the sunrise as this news breaks. I love uncovering the liars and cheaters of the world. Here is another example of it. This story is a two-sided scandal. Not only is the princess cheating with her bodyguard, but so is her soon-to-be husband, who is cheating on her with her cousin.

Most relationships are built on lies. This just validates my choice to never be in a relationship again.

My desk phone rings, and I answer it.

"Gabby?"

"Mr. Lincoln, Aria is on the line."

Glancing at my watch, surprised my commercial real estate agent is working at this hour, I take a steeling breath and respond, "Thanks. Put her through."

"Hello, Mr. Lincoln," Aria drawls, her sickly-sweet tone causing a muscle in my jaw to tick. "I wanted to give you an update on the property."

"Hmm," I grunt, surveying the small room that will soon be my old office. I don't know how my dad managed to work here for so long. It's cramped, barely fitting a desk and some storage. I'm planning to add an oval table for meetings and create a home-away-from-home vibe, complete with a bathroom, bookshelves, gym, and even a kitchen. But this small office will be Shyla's. She needs her own space to work without distractions, especially now that I'm relying on her more and giving her additional responsibilities, like overseeing and approving articles. I need more time to focus on operations, finances, and overall business development.

"It's ready for a tour. Can you meet me on Thursday?"

If it wasn't out of her job description, I'd send Gabby just to avoid Aria. But I can't, so I need to suck it up and hope she can stop batting her eyelashes and keep her hands to herself just this one time. I'm not interested in anything other than finding the right spot for my new office.

I close my eyes and sigh. "Sure."

"Great!" she exclaims, a spark of excitement in her voice. "This place is perfect."

Her high-pitched voice pierces my eardrums. "If that's all, I need to go. I have somewhere to be."

"Okay, no problem. I'll see you Thursday," she replies.

I hang up and return to my computer, wiping my hand over my face before quickly getting back to work.

Within ten minutes, Gabby enters with a warm smile and a coffee from my favorite coffee shop, City Brew. Carrying my cold brew to the sofa that faces the window, I sit, sipping my drink as I watch the sunrise until my phone rings again. And then it continues ringing long after the scandal leaks. The rest of my workday is busy until I walk out and get in my car and drive over to Oliver's.

He opens the door to his Manhattan townhouse with a grin.

He's a cocky bastard.

But I fucking love him.

Being the eldest of my brothers, I feel like I must look out for them. I stroll through his house, which is very different from mine. His counters are white marble, with dark wood cabinets and floors. Ancient cream rugs with faded patterns and rich textures add coziness to the space. The walls are covered with a collection of paintings, in a variety of colors and styles. He loves art, specifically floral paintings.

We head to his dark, exposed brick den, where his gray oval-shaped poker table has a wine cabinet backdrop. Poker nights are almost never at my house because of my odd hours. I'm not always able to make it. Even though I try hard to. It's my only outlet. Poker is purely for entertainment. The laughs, the competition, and the fun. It's the only time I feel like I get to truly be myself. Because it's with people I care about.

Entering the den, I'm hit with the scent of cigars. Our friends Richard and Lukas are smoking.

"Only four of us tonight," Oliver states when he sees me looking around the table.

"Should be easy to whip your ass, then," I gloat.

Oliver snorts. "You wish, big bro. Sit your ass down and let me show you."

"Boys, boys, boys. We all know who the true winner will be," Richard adds.

"Let's just start playing and then the rest can burn through their cash," Lukas says.

These are our friends from high school. Richard recently got married and is expecting a child, but Lukas has been single for a year.

"Where's Jeremy?" I ask Oliver, knowing Harvey would be working.

"Jeremy is out with Nova."

Nova is Jeremy's fiancée.

I nod and pick up my cards to begin. A butler sets a drink in front of me, and I quickly lift it to my lips, taking a sip as I unwind from the chaotic day. Generally, I avoid sharing personal things about my day because of my ex's betrayal. I don't want to be hurt again, so I keep my guard up. But Bobby's words and the whole cheating scandal are playing heavily on my mind.

"I have a question for you all," I say, taking another big sip of my drink and then add, "I have a photographer at work. He's fucking sleazy. I need to fire him."

Oliver's eyebrows cinch together as he scowls. "You can't get rid of someone just because you don't like them."

I blow out a breath and explain, "I know, but something tells me he's no good, and if I don't get rid of him soon, I'll regret it."

"I understand. But you can't fire him without a reason. Have any of your staff complained? Or is he overly nice, but you view it as flirting?" Richard argues. He's a successful real estate developer and one of the few people I trust who's not family.

I slam my palm on the table, my eyes on Richard's, the intensity of my frustration clear as I lean in, every word dripping with seriousness. "Nothing formal but, come on, he's not just being a flirt. He's harassing my employees. This could be a lawsuit on my hands."

"You just don't trust anyone," Oliver adds.

Everyone goes quiet. It's like my ex is an elephant in the room, and I know it's my fault because I won't talk about what happened with Connie. But I'm still not ready; I'm still processing the pain and trying to protect myself from further emotional damage.

The woman cheated on me with a co-worker, and I only found out the day of our wedding. To say I was gutted would be an understatement. The humiliation I felt telling everyone the wedding was off was overwhelming. It was the hardest time in my life. I gave her everything. All of me. I loved her with my entire soul. I feel like I have been carrying an albatross with me. An albatross I can't let go. I wish she'd have given me a reason. Maybe she didn't find me attractive, or she fell out of love with me, or I wasn't romantic enough or I couldn't make her happy. It could be any one of those things, but I'll never know. She never explained, and her deception and silence broke something inside me. A happiness replaced with darkness. I feel empty where love should be.

"Where's Harvey tonight, Lukas?" Oliver asks, winking at me when my eyes flick to his. He's got my back. Even though I never shared anything about the breakup, they stick up for me. I love my family. They are everything to me.

"He's in a meeting. With that businesswoman he's obsessed with." Lukas laughs.

Harvey is adamant he doesn't care about this woman at all, but he sure has given her a lot of his spare time.

"I fold," Richard calls out. Throwing in his hand, he lets the cards drop onto the table as he grabs a handful of peanuts to eat.

"Come on." Oliver tosses his cards too, losing his hand.

After today, I need to win. I'm confident I'm the best player at this table tonight. I stick to basics; they try fancy and high-stakes plays. Whereas I go for the obvious, and that is, not the trickiest play. And after an hour, I walk away with a win.

CHAPTER 3

CHELSEA

I STEP INTO MY apartment, tossing my purse onto the
counter without a second thought, and head straight for
the freezer. The stress of another painfully long day at the
recruiting agency makes me crave comfort food. I open
the freezer and grab a frozen pretzel, shoving it into the
microwave. The work at the agency is mind-numbing, and
although everyone is nice enough, the monotony drains
me. Bobby never supported my dream of owning a Pilates
studio, which is what I'm really passionate about, and why
I work casually as a Pilates instructor too. He used to beg
me to resign but, for some reason, I couldn't. When he'd
ask me how the talk with Colette——my boss——went,
I lied and said, "She wasn't in today, or she begged me
to help out a little longer." But he kept pushing because
being a Pilates instructor isn't the right job for a woman
in a relationship. It's just a silly "hobby" to him. He never
viewed it as a real job. If I had my way, I would work in
my own studio full-time. I've often wondered if I could

manage without this second job, but the risk feels too big. If Nova was still our roommate, I might have considered it, but with her moving into her fiancé Jeremy's place, Summer and I have to split the bills now, so it doesn't seem wise.

As I wait for the pretzel to heat up, my phone rings. I rummage through my bag and notice a stack of letters. On top is a note from Summer, saying Nova is coming over and we're having Chinese for dinner. The girls have been checking in on me daily, worried I might go back to Bobby. I keep assuring them that's not happening.

The phone rings again, and I see a missed call and a text from Bobby. I ignore it, grabbing my food, letters, and phone before settling on the sofa. There's no way I'm answering Bobby. He hasn't given up since I ended things, calling and texting constantly, thinking we can fix our relationship. But how can we fix something broken by his cheating? Even Summer overheard it. All those late nights at work now seem like lies, and I can't get past that. He never made me feel like a priority. Now he can sweat over what to do without me, because there's no way I'm letting him back into my life.

I take a bite of the pretzel and glance at the letters. The first is a bill, but the second is a birthday card, and I open it. I gasp at the sight of a large check sitting inside of it. What's this for? Grabbing my phone, I immediately call my mom.

"Hello?" my younger sister Anna answers. She lives with our parents in Connecticut while she's in college studying psychology.

"Hey, Anna. It's me."

She laughs. "I know your voice, Chelse."

I lean back, sinking into the sofa. "Yeah, habit, I guess. How's college?"

"Six more months, but who's counting?"

Her cheery voice lifts my spirits despite the heaviness of the day.

"It will be worth it." I sigh. She will get the job of her dreams while I come home every day miserable. It reminds me why I left Connecticut. I knew a Pilates studio would thrive in New York, so I headed off two years ago and never looked back. My parents gave me a loan to purchase my own studio, but after only a month in New York, I met Bobby. I haven't used the money yet. And now, they've given me more?

I didn't open the studio because Bobby didn't see it as a viable career for his future wife. I held out hope he'd understand how happy being an instructor makes me. But now, what was all that for? My stomach knots thinking about it, and I put the pretzel down, no longer hungry.

"Are you okay?" Anna asks. She's always had reservations about Bobby, psychoanalyzing him through her career lens.

I sigh heavily. "As much as I can be."

"This is a good thing, you'll see." Her optimism is refreshing. I hope time will help me feel the same.

"Is Mom there?" I ask.

"Yeah, she's just coming in from helping Dad in the garden. Hang on, I'll get her." She puts the phone down, and I hear her yell, "Mom, Chelsea is on the phone for you."

I smile for the first time today, ignoring the sharp twinge in my chest, imagining her calling out to Mom from the porch, making me miss home even more. Nothing compares to the peace I feel there. But Connecticut isn't my forever place. The last time I went home, I was six months into dating Bobby. Alone, as usual. There were so many red flags in our relationship, yet I ignored them, blinded by the idea of love.

"Hi, darling," Mom says, slightly out of breath as she answers the phone.

"Hey, Mom."

"I was going to call you soon." She's been calling every night to see how I'm doing, offering to drive out, but I insisted she didn't since I'd be working every day.

"I beat you to it."

"And how are you doing today?" she asks, her tone laced with concern.

"Well, alright," I say, not wanting to waste energy on Bobby. "I called to thank you for the birthday card, but you put a check in by mistake."

Her hearty laugh bubbles down the line. "It wasn't a mistake, darling. It's to encourage you to open the studio."

I touch the check, still in disbelief. "This is a lot of money."

I stare at the one hundred thousand dollars as if I am seeing an extra zero, but every time I glance down, it's there.

"It's from your grandparents. They wanted us to look out for you."

Clutching the phone, I swallow past the pain in the back of my throat. "You and Dad should enjoy it."

They could go on more holidays together, buy a different house, anything but give this to me.

"We do, but we don't need that much to be happy."

I pull the elastic from my ponytail, my hand raking through my hair as I try to ease the tension that has shifted from my throat to my head. "I don't know about a studio."

"It might be a good distraction. And darling, you hate the assistant job."

The sound of wind through the phone has me picturing her now sitting on the porch, in one of the chairs, looking out into their picturesque garden. It's my dad's pride and joy.

"I do hate it." Bobby found it and begged I apply, saying "his wife needed a stable job." He knew my weakness for marriage, and he fucking played on it. Whenever I considered leaving him, he'd make comments about how he'd looked at rings or how he'd dreamt of a rooftop wedding, all to keep me from walking away. He manipulated my desires and fears, using them to control and keep me in the relationship.

"Only you can turn your life around," she says softly.

Taking a deep breath, I close my eyes and say, "It's just a big risk."

"Do you need more money to survive until it's up and running? I'll send you more."

Tears prick at the back of my eyes, but I hold them back. "No, you've given me more than enough."

"Then what is it?"

It's funny how much my mother knows I'm holding back, even from miles away.

I sigh a heavy breath and reopen my eyes. "I'm scared to fail. I don't have a clue about how to run a business."

"You won't know if you don't try," she says.

I hold the check, staring at it again.

"This will give you a new focus," she adds, sensing I need more encouragement.

"And you think I can do it?" I whisper.

"Yes!" she shrieks. "You are a Macfarlane. It's in your blood."

"What if I can't get clients?"

"You will, but you can always sell it and come back home and figure out your next move."

I sit up straight, feeling my pulse rise with possibilities. "I have no idea where to start."

"First, quit that miserable job. Then, go look at some spaces."

I wish I could match her enthusiasm. "I don't know…"

"Do you want me to come out and look at a few places with you?"

"No, I need to do this on my own. But I'll definitely have you out here for the grand opening."

"We wouldn't miss it for the world."

And I know she means my dad and Anna too.

I bite the inside of my cheek. "Do you really think I can be a good boss?"

"Yes. And stop overthinking. This is your time to follow what you went to New York for."

"I think you're right." New determination fills me; it feels like a rush of adrenaline. I'm finally ready to fulfill my dream, only two years late.

"I know I'm right. I'm so excited for you. Send me lots of photos."

"Don't forget to organize Anna's surprise graduation dinner."

"Yes, I'm planning it this week. You'll be able to make it, right?"

"Of course, I wouldn't miss it for the world."

At least now I don't have to dread arguing with Bobby about him coming. We had yet to meet each other's families. It wasn't through lack of trying on my end.

Mom and I chat about our ideas for Anna's dinner, and when I get off the phone, I pick up my food and eat it cold. Then I start searching for potential studio places, excitement bubbling within me as I wait for Summer and Nova to get here to celebrate.

Chapter 4

Chelsea

"So how many viewings do you have?" Summer asks from beside me. Her and Nova came with me today to inspect some potential locations for my new pilates studio.

"Six, but they aren't far from each other," I tell them both, wondering if I should have elaborated before now.

"That's okay, we're excited to go on this adventure with you," Nova sing-songs.

I peer in the rearview mirror at her wearing a genuine smile as she looks out the window.

"Pull up anywhere here," Summer says pointing on the left, reading what I can see on the GPS.

I park the car and climb out with my heart beating wildly in my chest. We all stand on the sidewalk, gaping up at the beautifully aged New York building.

Mitchell——the agent showing the listing——will be joining us here soon.

"This is huge," Summer says, taking the words right out of my mouth.

The street is busy with people walking by and I'm having to get out of their way.

"Come over here and I'll call——" I start, but I'm cut off by his voice.

"Chelsea?" Mitchell calls out. He walks toward us, wearing a nice navy suit. He seems young for an agent.. .maybe early twenties? Stopping short in front of me, he smiles and holds out his hand. "I'm Mitchell. It's nice to meet you in person."

I slip my hand into his and shake it. "Hi, Mitchell. Nice to meet you." Pulling my hand out of his grip, I point beside me to the girls. "These are my friends, Summer and Nova."

"Nice to meet you, too," he says, stepping over to them and shaking their hands too. Then he returns his focus to me. "Are we ready to find you the perfect property?"

"Yes, please."

"Okay, good. So this building here..." he starts to say, pointing to the one we're standing in front of, "...is the first one. Follow me." With a nod to us, he walks to the entrance.

The girls are mouthing behind his back, emphasizing how hot he is. They're pretending to fan their faces, and I shake my head but roll my lips to contain a laugh. I hope they don't get caught. I'd be mortified if he saw them obsessing over him. He's nice enough, but I'm not here to date; I'm here to find a property. This is all about the new Chelsea.

He opens the door, and we walk inside as he explains about the history of the property. As we look around getting a tour, I snap photos and write some thoughts down in my notes app in my phone. Including things I like and dislike. Even ideas of how to transform the spot with more ideas the girls point out.

We leave that space after thirty-five minutes, and I don't give him clues as to whether I will go ahead with it or not. I've only seen one so far and after my conversation with my mom, I want to make sure I do this for me. I'm going to trust my instincts and get the right studio space. That means exploring all my options.

"The next one is right next door," Mitchell announces, striding to the entrance next door.

We follow along and explore the second space, doing the same things as the previous——taking photos and notes. I prefer the first one to this one, so with less questions, we are out after twenty minutes.

When we exit the building and stand on the sidewalk, the girls and I are ready to head to the next location.

"Let's grab a coffee after the next so we can debrief," he suggests, looking directly at me and sounding hopeful.

"Sure. I can't say no to a vanilla latte," I say with a tight smile. Caffeine sounds good right now. After only two, my head is beginning to pound, and I'm ready to sit down for a break; I suspect today is going to be a really long day.

He shows us through a third property before he takes us to a cute coffee shop, the perfect location for a pit stop to refuel.

We all order the same——vanilla lattes. Sitting down at a table together, he asks me what I thought about the first three. So I explain to him that, so far, the first one is more my style, with the fact it's more of an open concept. The second is too small, with too many rooms, and the third doesn't have enough natural light where the studio is. Only a portion of the room gets great light. A part of me worries I'm being too picky, but I refuse to settle. I've spent the last few years doing that, and now I'm determined to get exactly what I want.

I plan to hand in my resignation at the firm and finish up within two weeks, as per my contract. I try not to let my mind wander about how long I can last with just Pilates if it takes too long to find the right studio location. But I can't afford any mistakes. I can do this. I just need to trust myself and more so my gut. It won't steer me wrong.

Mitchell explains where the next location is, and I tell him I'll drive there because it's too long of a walk for Nova. She was in a car accident over a year ago, which resulted in her getting a fractured pelvis and internal bleeding. Since then, she hasn't been able to walk as much as she used to.

The next two are pretty close to each other, but they're in areas where I wouldn't feel safe running late-night classes.

My pulse pounds in my temple, and I'm starting to get nauseas. "I think we should break. I need to eat. I'm fading fast."

"Same." Summer sighs.

"Me too," Nova says.

"We could have lunch——" Mitchell starts.

I wince and swallow the lump that's formed at his insinuation. "If you don't mind, I'd like to grab lunch with my friends," I say, hoping he takes the hint.

His eyes widen and he clears his throat. "Sure thing. Let's meet at the next spot at two. Will that give you enough time?"

His response has me relieved. "That would be great, thanks."

He nods, a small smile on his face as he walks away.

"I think he has a soft spot for you." Summer elbows me as she slips beside me, pulling my attention to her.

My eyes flick to Nova, who is rolling her lips to hold back a laugh.

"No chance. I'm not interested in anything but my business."

"Summer is only playing. We know you're still hurting," Nova says.

It's all still raw, but it's not as bad as I thought it would be. I worry what that says about me. Shouldn't I still be crying over the breakup?

"Let's go have lunch," I say, ready to walk down the street to find something.

"My hip needs a rest. I'll wait over there," Nova says as she points to the nearby park bench.

"Of course. Summer, could you please help Nova, and I'll grab us all some food."

"I'll be fine on my own." Nova waves us off.

"No. You're not sitting at the park on your own," I say. "Summer, stay with Nova."

Summer winks at me and loops her arm with Nova's.

Nova is mouthing off at how we're being ridiculous. But as they walk off, I pause, watching as Nova limps slightly. I'll have to offer to drive her home after lunch. I'm grateful for her support and really appreciate the girls coming out today. But I'd hate to push Nova too far.

I walk over to a sandwich shop and enter. Inside, I move to the menu and can't help but recognize the voice at the counter ordering. Deep, yet raspy and soothing.

I can't believe my eyes when I see Evan, Nova's brother-in-law. My breath catches, horrified. *You've got to be kidding me.*

I've only met him briefly once; it was over a year ago now, at his parents' place, when Bobby canceled our date. Evan found me crying outside and asked if I was okay.

Instead of answering with words, I stepped forward and cried into his chest. After the initial shock, he wrapped his arms around me. I quickly realized what I was doing and got so embarrassed, rushing off before he could say a word.

Thankfully, I haven't had to face him since. *And I really don't want to now...*

I shrink behind the woman in front of me, which is silly, because I'm five-nine and she looks to be five feet. *I still hope he doesn't recognize me.*

As he stands with his back to me, I can't help but take in how impeccably dressed he is in a creaseless dark gray suit, crisp white shirt, tie, and shiny designer shoes, which makes me internally groan. He stands out, looking every bit the powerful man he is.

Why did he have to show up now, without Summer and Nova as a buffer?

I keep my chin down and gaze on my comfy activewear set, which I just realized are covered in stains.

Crap.

He'll keep walking because he's probably forgotten what I look like.

But when his shoes appear in front of me, I recognize him by his familiar, rich, spicy scent, making my nostrils flare as I take in his distinctive smell. I slowly straighten, but I freeze as I look up at him, seeing he's wearing a smug smirk.

Double crap.

I stare blankly at him for a few seconds as my face heats. He knows exactly what I was trying to do.

"Hello, Chelsea," he says in a gritty voice.

"Hi, Evan."

"No hug for me today?" he asks, teasing.

"Oh my God," I wince, cringing at the memory. "I still can't believe I did that. I'm never going to live it down, am I?"

"Absolutely not," he says with a grin. "But it's not every day I get to have a beautiful woman in my arms." His eyes double in size, locking me in place. The air leaves my lungs in a silent whoosh at his words.

"Definitely not beautiful today. You always catch me at my worst," I mumble, flustered, looking down at my trainers before meeting his piercing gaze.

"I'll try better next time."

I don't reply because the line is moving, and there's only the woman in front of me. I haven't even looked at the menu, too preoccupied with Evan. He's just so easy to talk to, and I don't want it to end yet, so I blurt out, "Did you order a sandwich?"

A playful smirk tugs at the corner of his mouth. "Well, that's usually what you do at a sandwich shop, right?"

"I know, I'm just trying to get your recommendation," I tease.

"Hmm, let me think," he says, leaning in slightly as if sharing a secret. "It's a sandwich shop...they offer sandwiches."

Laughing lightly, I roll my eyes at his deadpan delivery. "Seems popular," I counter, pretending to be unimpressed, but fully aware of the butterflies dancing in my stomach. "Is it always this busy?"

"Pretty much," he says, his tone softening as he holds my gaze a second longer than necessary.

Just then, they call out his order number. He hesitates, as if torn between grabbing his food and staying a little longer. I'm relieved, but only because I need a moment to gather myself.

"I better grab that," he says, but there's a lingering note in his voice, like he's not quite ready to leave.

His jaw clenches, and for a moment, I expect him to say something else, but he turns and strides to the counter. I watch him as he grabs the bag, and when he spins around, catching me checking him out, I quickly dart my eyes away. To my surprise, he returns.

When he's beside me again, I force myself to look at him, and my stomach somersaults and then grumbles loudly. I wrap my arms around myself, as if that's going to help shut it up.

"You better go order," he says. His eyebrows have joined in the middle, assessing me.

"I'm in line to do just that," I reply, just as my stomach rumbles loudly again. *Seriously?*

"You're really pale. Go sit over there, and I'll get you something," he insists, directing me to a chair. His eyes drop slowly over my body, settling on my legs before meeting my gaze. I'm a little lightheaded and really nauseous now, and I bet it's from my recent loss of appetite and sleep.

"I'm fine..." *I think...*

"You look like you're going to pass out," he argues.

Turning my hands so my palms are facing up, I inspect the color of them, but they don't look unusually pale. Still, I'm not about to argue with him or find a mirror to check. I don't care that much, it's just food. And my body clearly needs something to shut it up and stop screaming at me. Before I faint, I nod. "Okay. But I need enough for three."

He stares at me for a moment, and I get a sense he's about to ask me something else, but instead, he shakes his head. I find myself stunned, watching him move effortlessly to the counter before I turn and find a table in a quiet corner with a view of outside.

I smooth down my pants, trying to make them look better. It's pointless, because I'm sitting in stained clothes, with three-day-old oily hair tied in a bun on my head, and old, crusty makeup, which is so ungodly embarrassing next to his pristine suit. Usually, I'm not this self-conscious. I don't even know why I care what he thinks of me. I shouldn't…But I worry that my appearance screams, "I just broke up with my boyfriend," and I don't need his sympathy.

But for some dumb reason, I care what Mr. Evan Lincoln thinks of me.

I stare absentmindedly out the window when a soft bang snaps me out of my daydream, and I see Evan has returned with a tray full of food and drinks. The wrinkle in between his brows and the lines beside his eyes remind me that he is older than me. Maybe late thirties.

He takes a seat opposite me, filling the chair with his large frame.

"You must be hungry," I tease, trying to ignore the warm rush I feel when our knees touch from under the table.

"It's for three," he replies as he leans his elbows on the table.

I shift far back in my seat so there's no more physical contact between us. I stop and try to think of the last time a guy did something like this for me. I come up short. Yet here's this man, generously spending time and money on me.

"That's still a lot," I protest, looking at the amount to feed an army, not three girls.

He shrugs, unfazed. "Eat what you want."

"What will you do?" I ask when I notice he hasn't moved.

"Eat my sandwich," he replies simply.

Emotion clogs my throat, and I fight back a laugh. I clear my throat and pick up the bottle of Coke, taking a sip. The sweet sugary liquid soothes me, and I close my eyes, savoring the taste.

When I lower the bottle, I find Evan's gaze fixed on my face. I can't sit here like this any longer. The intensity of his look is too much.

"Can you start eating? I'm uncomfortable with you watching me," I say, hoping to break the tension.

He doesn't answer, but he sits up, dropping his elbow from the table and closing the distance between us.

Unwrapping his sandwich, he takes a bite while staring at me with a popped brow as if to say, *you happy now?*

I giggle at his sour expression.

"What?" he asks, leaning back, his eyes tightening at the corners.

"The fact that you were going to sit and wait for me to eat, when you're clearly hungry too is adorable."

Evan's powerful presence is intimidating. So when his flat expression softens——and I swear a flicker of amusement hits his face——it relaxes me. It makes him more approachable.

We return to silence, my stomach dancing now that I'm giving it some sugar, but I'm still not completely at ease. There's still a strange fire burning in my body. Distracting myself, I sip more of my drink. When I feel satisfied, I sink down into my chair, totally forgetting about his legs. But this time, instead of moving my knees, I leave them be. The connection between us feels less uncomfortable now.

I pick up the chicken pesto sandwich and take a bite. "This is amazing!" I mumble around a bite full of food.

He nods but doesn't speak.

"Now I see why there's a line," I babble, even when I should shut up because he's not replying.

I keep eating until I'm satisfied; Evan watches me between bites of his own food until his is all gone.

I stop eating to take another sip of Coke.

"Are you feeling better?" he asks.

"Much." I rub my stomach and begin to fold the rest up to have with the girls in the park.

He leans forward so his head is closer to mine, our eyes level, and my breath hitches when his mouth moves to my ear. I stay frozen, my pulse rising as his low voice says, "It's nice seeing you again. Next time I see you, make sure you're well fed."

When he pulls back, giving me a smug expression, I can't help but give him a smart response. "Yes, sir."

The fire that blazes in his eyes makes me swallow hard.

"I need to head to work. Where can I take you?" He's clearly changing the subject, which I'm glad about.

My lips twitch. "Right. CEO of The New York Press, right?"

"Yeah," he confirms, rising to his feet.

Resentment flares in my chest as I watch him straighten his expensive suit. How many nights had Bobby stayed late——missing dinner, missing me——just to impress this guy? The thought makes my stomach churn. It snaps something in me.

I stand. "I can walk back on my own. I need to take lunch to Summer and Nova."

He grabs the dirty tray, which looks ridiculous with his designer suit. But before I can protest, he speaks, "I'll walk you back. My brother will kill me otherwise." Then he turns and disposes of the trash before rejoining me.

That's right, Nova's fiancé.

"Whatever," I say, picking up their food and exiting the shop.

We walk side by side down the street, the thickness and silence between us overwhelming me. I can't wait to get back to Summer and Nova so I can catch my breath. Being around Evan confuses me; he gives me that hot-and-cold feeling.

When we close in on Nova and Summer, their lips twitch into a satisfied smile. "Hey," they greet us. "We were about to send a search party."

"Look who I bumped into at the sandwich shop," I say, gesturing to Evan, who's standing beside me.

He nods before speaking. "I'm heading back to work."

I turn toward Evan, giving him a genuine smile. "Thanks for lunch."

With another clipped nod, he strides away. I mindlessly watch him, and when he's out of my sight, I settle into the chair beside them and hand over their food.

Summer clears her throat. "Um, excuse me. Care to tell me how lunch went?"

I shrug and shift on the chair to face them. "It was alright. We barely spoke, to be honest."

Summer scrunches up her face, puzzled. "Really?"

"I'm sure he thinks I'm a blubbering mess," I reply, wondering why he made me so skittish?

Nova giggles. "It's okay, that's Evan."

My mind replays the moments our legs touched or when he said, "*next time I see you, make sure you're well fed.*" Those weren't awkward, but I keep that to myself. I don't need her in my ear about Evan. We have nothing in common. I'd occasionally see him at Nova and Jeremy's events, but that would be it. Our paths won't cross.

Evan remains an enigma, and I wonder why he's being so kind to me. It has to be for Jeremy's sake.

I shake my head and sink farther into the chair while the girls eat. We get back in the car and move to the next location, but the next few properties just aren't right. Either too small, too big, too expensive or have a weird layout that would cost too much to renovate.

"I have one more, but it isn't available to view yet," Mitchell informs us once I explain that I'm not really interested in any of them.

"Are you talking a month or longer?"

"Oh no." He shakes his head. "Within the next two weeks."

"That's okay. I'd like to view it before I make my decision."

"I'll call you when it's open and organize an inspection."

"Great," I say as we say goodbye and head to the car.

On the way home, we decided to have a girls' night with an array of snacks and fast food. Like a little treat for our long and tiring day. We pull up and, the moment we step inside, I feel like I've been on an all-night bender, completely wiped out.

After a quick shower, I slip into my favorite black sweats and join Nova and Summer in the living room. The moment I sink into the sofa, I tuck my legs under my butt and throw a blanket over them. Ready to watch a drama-filled show about selling expensive homes.

Summer gets a bottle of wine.

"Can't forget these." She holds the bottle of wine by the neck and the glasses in the other hand.

"I need a big glass tonight," I remark, accepting the wine with a grateful smile.

She offers me an apologetic smile. "You'll find the right place soon."

"I know." I sigh, opening the Pinot Grigio and pouring each of us a full glass. "Thanks for keeping me company, girls. Here's to friendship," I toast, smiling through my exhaustion.

"And to your new life that will be filled with love and passion," Summer adds.

I hum into my glass, taking a sip as my excitement for this new life adventure returns.

CHAPTER 5

CHELSEA

A week later

"CRAP," I MUTTER, SLAMMING my fists against the steering wheel. My car won't start, and I'm stranded on the side of the road. I suck in a breath, scanning the area for the latch I need in order to pop the hood, but I can't find it.

I can't afford to be late for full back-to-back Saturday classes. I'm covering for another instructor today. I live in a suburban area outside the city, so it's easier for me to drive to work, but days like today, I'm reminded why so many people use public transportation.

I get out of my car and circle it, searching for the problem, but I can't pinpoint it. Leaning against the side of my white Volkswagen Beetle, I take in the surroundings. The New York architecture stands out against the early morning light. The skyline of dawn leaves the prettiest glow, and I watch the activity surrounding me: delivery trucks, a few joggers, other people walking and talking while holding coffee cups. These moments make me love early mornings. Even at work, it's all a buzz of excitement. *If I can get there.*

It's 5:40 a.m., and my first class starts at 6:30. Once I look at my phone, I realize another five minutes have passed. I need to make a decision quickly.

I call Summer, but she doesn't answer. Nova is definitely out of the question because she can't drive. With no other options, I call AAA, and they inform me they won't be coming for another half hour. Missing one class is better than the entire day...

Leaning against my car, I wait impatiently for AAA to come. I realize I haven't called my boss to tell her my situation. I'm about to hit call, when a car pulls over, and I shuffle closer to the door. The passenger side opens, revealing a tall man with wavy brown hair. It's not until his piercing blue eyes meet mine that it registers who this man is——it's Evan.

He strides toward me dressed in a black suit; I'm assuming he's on his way to work. I run my hand over my ponytail, grateful that I'm not in my dirty sweats like last time he saw me. No, today, I'm in my favorite black leggings, baby blue crop, and a black long-sleeved jacket.

"Evan?" I say, stepping away from the car. A ribbon of hope twirls inside me.

His face is pinched tight, especially between his brows.

"Chelsea. I thought it was you," he responds with a blank expression, coming to stand beside me.

The waves of nausea in my belly make me try to lighten the mood. "Do you usually pull over for anyone who looks like me?"

Seeing a familiar face right now brings immense relief.

He rubs the back of his neck before tucking his hands into his pockets. "No."

"I'm only playing with you." The words die on my tongue when he doesn't laugh with me. His usual unreadable expression is firmly in place.

"What's wrong?" he asks, nudging toward my car.

I release a strangled breath. "My car won't start. It started fine this morning, but halfway to my job, it just died," I explain, knowing I'm already starting to babble.

It seems I do that a lot with him. Well, more than my normal amount.

"Did you call AAA?" he asks, keeping his eyes down on my car.

"Yeah, they said they'd be here in half an hour," I reply, lips pressed together to prevent further rambling.

A glint touches his eyes under the early morning light. "What time do you start work?"

"My first Pilates class starts at six-thirty."

He runs his hand along his jaw, which is noticeably smoother than the last time I saw him.

Nodding, he peers at his watch. Which I can't help but notice is silver with gold details embossed with the Rolex logo. "My driver can drop you at work, and he can come back for me. I'll deal with AAA for you."

I scoff. "Don't be ridiculous. I'll order a taxi after I've dealt with this."

"No, just take the ride."

I can't imagine this handsome man waiting by a white beetle to tell AAA it broke down.

No, just no.

"I don't want to be the reason you're late to work. Your job is important." I wave him off. Being a CEO has to be demanding. He has better things to do with his time. It's my problem. I can deal with it.

"So is yours," he counters.

I shake my head. He's just being nice; he isn't serious. "It's only Pilates. I'm not saving the world or anything."

"You instruct people to care for their health. Don't discredit yourself," he says sincerely.

I gaze stupidly at him, momentarily stunned. My lips part as I suck in slow, deep breaths. Why does he have to remind me that my job isn't just a hobby? Did the damn universe set this up? Bobby and his boss sure do have very different views on Pilates.

"Thanks, but I can't take your ride. I can cancel my first class. I was just about to call my boss."

He steps toward me so his face is closer to mine, his eyes hard, demanding. "No, take my car. I have nothing important due today," he urges.

My knees buckle at him being close again. "But you'll have to wait here." I point at the sidewalk.

"And?" he counters, his expression blank.

I press my lips together and force myself to look at the car and not at him.

"This doesn't seem like something you'd normally do," I murmur, wondering why he's doing this. What's in it for him?

"And how would you know?" he challenges in a low annoyed tone.

I'm judging him when I shouldn't; it's unfair to him. "True."

Each time I'm around Evan, I learn something new about him. Like a new layer is peeled back that surprises me every time. He also doesn't know that I'm not used to guys helping out. Bobby would occasionally lend a hand if he wasn't too busy, but even then, it was rare. I'm used to handling everything on my own, so the idea of someone actually stepping in to help feels foreign. My dad would, but he lives in Connecticut.

"Go," he commands.

Glancing at the time, I see it's already ten-past six. I need to leave if I'm going to make it to the class. I'll have to argue with him later.

"Alright, but Evan, thank you. I mean it." I hope he can see the sincerity and appreciation in my eyes; that I mean that from the bottom of my heart. I've had the shittiest start to the day and that selfless act means the world to me. I'll have to figure out a way to pay him back. "I owe you a drink!"

He rubs the back of his neck, and I notice a slight flush on his skin. But I don't have time to respond, I need to get going.

But just as I walk off, he calls out, "Wait up. Give me your keys."

I turn, rush back and hand over my keys. The brush of his fingers over my hand causes the hairs on my arm to stand up. His brows furrow, and I wonder, did he feel that rush too?

When I peer up from under my lashes, I find his lips thin and his face contorted. Shaking off the weird exchange, I turn and walk back.

Before I climb into the car, I pause, taking one last look at this man who just postponed his entire day to help me out. His stance remains unchanged—tall, dark, and powerful, with his hands tucked into his pockets. Intimidating, yet confident. A force to be reckoned with. I shake my head, clearing thoughts of Evan out of it, before sinking into the leather seat.

Evan must have texted the driver because he knew my name. After I climbed in, he asked for the address of the studio. I don't understand why Evan did it, but he did. He's been doing things, like hugging me back when I cried in his arms, caring for me when I was about to faint, walked me to my friends to make sure I was safe, and now this...I don't understand, and I don't have the time, headspace, or emotional energy to dwell on it. Right now, I just need to get to work.

Chapter 6

Chelsea

"Mom, I'm here," I say into the phone, raising my voice so she can hear me above the taxi honks and pedestrian noise.

Yellow cabs zip by, their horns blaring, while people weave through the crowded streets. A street vendor nearby sells hotdogs, the aroma mingling with the city. Across the street, a busy cafe has tables spilling onto the sidewalk. I stare at the tall glass building on Madison Avenue. The noise of the subway beneath my feet adds to the positives this location offers. Especially after my breakdown.

Evan was quick to get my car fixed because it just needed a new battery, and it was sitting at home after Summer picked me up. I couldn't thank him because I don't have his number, and I didn't want to call up Nova to get it. My body shudders, imagining the interrogation.

"I have a good feeling about this one."

I hope she's right. This is the property Mitchell mentioned to me a few weeks ago.

"We'll see, Mom," I reply, not wanting to get my hopes up.

"Alright, keep me updated," she replies.

Her voice feels like a giant hug. "Will do."

"I love you and good luck."

"I love you too, Mom. I'll call you later."

I hang up as nerves ripple through me. Taking a big inhale through my nose, I exhale heavily through my mouth to shake them off.

"Chelsea?" a deep male voice calls from my left.

I twist, turning my head to follow the familiar voice, and my lips part into a smile.

"Evan."

He closes the car door and joins me on the sidewalk. I take in the light gray suit and blue tie. His hair is freshly styled and not a curl out of place. It's almost two in the afternoon, and he's still looking this good. Unfair. I'm glad I chose to wear my new favorite activewear, including my navy flare pants and matching crop sweatshirt. But my traditional bangs are hidden beneath a baseball cap.

"How did you know it was me?" I tap my hat.

I swear the way his cheeks turn a slight shade of pink makes him seem younger. His eyes sweep over my body quickly before meeting my gaze. "I've seen you a few times now." He runs his hand over his clean-shaven jawline, as if I hadn't already noticed it.

Which reminds me of our last run-in.

"Thanks for getting my car fixed. It was a huge relief, and you pretty much saved the day."

"I'm glad I could help," he says simply. Something about it makes my stomach flutter.

"How much do I owe you?"

He shakes his head. "Nothing."

I roll my eyes. "You can't expect me to let you pay for it."

"Why? We're friends, right?"

"Yes, but..." I stutter out, totally caught off guard.

"But nothing. That's what friends do."

My mouth opens and closes, trying to think of something to say, and he just watches me with a wolfish grin.

"Thank you so much, Evan. I really appreciate you taking care of everything. It means a lot to me."

"I'm glad I could help."

His usual controlled stance seems a little softer today. More relaxed.

I drop the idea of trying to pay him back. We'll argue, and it will get me nowhere. Considering it's only a new battery and not a whole new car, it probably won't make a dent in his account.

"What are you doing here?" I ask with a smile. "Stalking me?"

"No, of course not," he rushes out in a quick, sharp voice, his eyes narrowing.

"I'm kidding, relax," I tease, loving how easy it is to rile him up.

He nods curtly before his eyes shift to the top of the building and then back to me. "Checking out a new office space," he answers.

My jaw slacks. I hope it's not the same as mine. I won't be able to outbid him.

"You?" he asks, his eyes drop briefly to my outfit.

It adds to my nerves, so I blurt, "I'm meeting a real-estate agent to check out a potential space for my own Pilates studio."

His brow lifts. "Which floor?"

"Second. You?"

Please don't be the same.

"The top," he murmurs.

Is he embarrassed to say that?

I don't care. If I could afford the top, I'd buy it. My budget is already generous enough, thanks to my parents. Without them, I wouldn't be looking on Madison Avenue at all.

"Chelsea?" Mitchell says.

Evan quickly crosses his arms in front of his chest and gives Mitchell a sullen look. Mitchell walks right up to us and stands beside me. He's wearing a cheesy smile and a pinstripe suit, his blond hair swept back.

My teeth tug on my bottom lip before letting it go so I can speak. "Hi."

"I got you a vanilla latte," Mitchell says.

He's charming and obviously desperate for a sale.

"Thanks." I smile and take the cup from his outstretched hand.

Evan makes a noise in his throat and drops his hands from his chest to his pockets. Does he actually think I could forget about him? Because nobody could. His tall, broad frame takes up my peripheral vision.

"Sorry, where are my manners? Evan, this is Mitchell. He's the agent showing me the second floor. Mitchell, this is Evan, he——"

Mitchell thrusts his hand out toward Evan, and I watch with fascination as Evan looks between Mitchell's face and his palm before eventually meeting Mitchell for a tight handshake. I don't miss the squeeze that Evan gives Mitchell before they separate. My eyebrows pull together. *What's that about?*

"A friend," I add quietly.

"Are you ready, Chelsea?" Mitchell asks, inclining his head toward the building.

My eyes flick to peer up at Evan, who's pressing his lips into a thin line. It's clear he doesn't want me to leave with Mitchell.

"Yea—"

"Can I have a second?" Evan asks, his eyes holding mine with a tight expression. It confuses me, but I peer at Mitchell with a sympathetic smile.

"Mitchell, could you give me a second to say goodbye to Evan?"

"Sure. I'll meet you in the lobby," Mitchell says, already walking inside the building.

I twist back to face Evan, who is wearing a visible flush on his cheeks. His eyes lock with mine, and I get lost in them for a second.

"Care if I tag along?" he asks.

It takes a second to pull myself out from staring into his eyes and take in his question.

My lips part slightly. "You want to come up?" I ask in a higher pitch than normal. "Don't you have a meeting with a realtor?"

Why would he want to see the second floor? I'm sure compared to the top, it won't be as nice.

"I'm early, so I can come with you."

He's so direct it makes me nervous. "If you want to. It'll be nice to have someone else's opinion."

He nods.

"Does this mean I can come to yours?" I ask with a slight smirk.

I'd love to see what his money could buy. I can imagine it's going to make me jealous. But a girl can dream. Maybe if I work hard enough...

"If you want."

"I do."

He looks at me, dips his chin, and leads me to the door with a hand on my back, before letting go to grab the door and hold it open for me.

I shake my head, trying to refocus my thoughts on why I'm here and not on the handsome man in a suit and tie who just had his hand on me.

Evan and I walk inside and join Mitchell. We enter the elevator, and the silence feels thick and heavy. I shift uncomfortably, the noise of the elevator the only sound breaking the stillness. Glancing at the floor numbers as they light up, I try to avoid eye contact, while the walls seem to close in, adding to the awkwardness.

The elevator doesn't take long, and it opens to a large empty space, with brightly painted white walls, and soft oak wooden floors.

My jaw is on the floor.

"Are you ready?" Mitchell says.

I open and close my mouth repeatedly as I take it in. My heart thumps inside my chest. This is gorgeous, and I can imagine all the Pilates beds set up in this area.

"What are you thinking?" Mitchell asks.

I look to Evan and watch his eyes scan the room, also taking in the space. I'd love to know what he's thinking.

My lips turn up as I answer from my heart. "It's exactly what I had in mind."

"White walls, tons of natural light," Mitchell rattles off. "All open space."

Evan comes closer, so I ask him in a whisper, "What do you think?"

He doesn't answer. Instead, he taps the back of my arm, inclines his head, and moves away from Mitchell. I follow, understanding he wants us to talk in private.

"What does your gut tell you?"

My brow furrows with confusion. Why does my gut have any say right now? And more importantly, why is he asking me that?

He must read my bewildered look because he whispers, "I'm serious. Every time I have a funny feeling in my gut, it's because something isn't right."

I stop and take his words seriously. My gut doesn't feel off.

"I'm happy with this place. Deep down, I think it's the right choice."

"And how much do they want for it?"

"$445,000."

He taps his finger on his lips, and it's weirdly distracting. They are thin and pink. And I'm still staring at them. Fantasizing about what they would feel like against mine when he turns to me.

"Good price. Good location. And if your gut isn't off, I say go for it."

I bring my gaze to his quickly, noticing the arch in his eyebrow, but I ignore the fact he caught me looking at his mouth and focus on the fact he's encouraging me to buy it.

My eyes light up as I bounce on the balls of my feet, beaming with happiness. "I can really see the set up."

"Tell me what you're thinking," he replies.

I walk to the entry. He follows quietly behind me.

"Here, I'd have the reception desk and merchandise. Then I would need a locker room, so I would need to get that built as soon as possible. Then, starting here and filling up the whole space, I'd have Pilate beds."

"How much does a Pilates class cost?"

I pause and twist to face him. "Why, are you going to attend?" I giggle, running my eyes over him. I force myself to stop imagining him on a bed.

"No."

I'm teasing. I know a man like him wouldn't be caught dead doing Pilates. Men built like him like to run and hit the weights. But it would be nice to be a fly on the wall and watch him workout.

I clear my throat and refocus on his question. "I'm thinking $40 a class, and I'd offer bundles. You know...if you attended a class, it would help me."

He doesn't answer, instead he just grunts his disapproval.

"I'd hope to have at least fifteen people in here."

"That would work."

Evan's phone rings. He steps away, and I move toward the floor-to-ceiling windows, looking over the streets and buildings as people go about their day and in their work suits. I used to wear office attire, but I'm so glad I don't have to go to that miserable job anymore. I'm lost in my thoughts, so I don't hear the footsteps that come up behind me. I think it's Evan, but when I hear Mitchell's voice, I close my eyes for a moment. Disappointment floods my senses.

What is wrong with me?

Mitchell begins talking numbers, and I take the contract to read over tonight with my parents over a video call.

"I need to go," Evan announces.

"We are done here right, Mitchell?" I ask.

"Just read and sign the contact. Then send it to me when it's all done," Mitchell says smiling with victory.

"I will, and thanks again."

I follow Evan out to the elevator. He hits the up button, and then starts madly typing away on his phone.

He finishes the moment we enter the elevator. Tension in the air swirls as we stand side by side. I'm watching the floor numbers move up and sip my latte. We're almost there when he tucks his phone away. "I'm unsure about this spot."

I turn my head, baffled by his declaration. "Why?"

The views and the big open floor space are to die for. I saw it online when I was looking to buy the second floor. If he doesn't want it, maybe...No, don't be ridiculous, I can't afford it.

"It seems too big just for me."

"This would be a place just for you?" I ask, sipping and enjoying the sweet, warm drink.

"Yeah."

The elevator stops, and the door opens. I walk out along the light brown tile concrete floors and stare out through the floor length windows, glancing at the view of the river. Wow, this is so much better than my spot on level two.

Turning to scan the rest of the space, I take in the brown timber cupboards, black lighting fixtures, and brown timber shelves. It's all dark, yet at the same time very inviting.

"What's your plan for the space, if you go ahead with it?" I ask.

He scratches his temple, and his eyes move around the empty floor. I expect him to clam up and give me only a few words, so the next breath of words shocks me.

"This will be my hideaway, so I want it filled with things that bring me comfort. Over there," he continues and points to a bare wall, "I'll have a bookshelf for all my favorite books. And over here..." He gestures to the corner by the window. "I'll set up some weights and a treadmill for working out."

"Definitely," I murmur, staring out the window again.

"Kitchen, bathroom, closet, and maybe a bed."

"What would you need all that for?" I ask, lowering my cup to remove my sweater and tie it around my neck, before picking my drink back up.

"My work hours are all over the place; it would be nice to have somewhere to crash between media blitzes."

"What are your normal hours?"

He makes a noise at the back of his throat. "My normal hours are no sleep or social life."

"Isn't that the life of a CEO?" I give him a playful wink and gently tap him on the arm, ignoring the flex of muscle when I do.

His eyes hold mine. There's softness there and a hint of humor hits his face.

"You seem ready to be one too."

"Born ready," I say, dropping my eyes away from his intense stare, suddenly shy under his inspection, as if he can see straight through me.

"What were you waiting for?"

The heaviness of his question sits in the bottom of my stomach. I don't feel like talking about Bobby. The last time I did, it brought me down. Today I don't want Bobby to steal my happiness.

"To be experienced at the basics first." My eyes flick back up and his turn dark.

"You'll make a good business owner."

How does he know I needed to hear that? And the fact it's from someone as successful as him means something.

We're staring at each other, and the energy shifts. I can't help but feel a strong, almost magnetic connection, but it's mixed with a touch of fear. I'm unsure if I want to explore this bond or if it's safer to keep my distance. The intensity of his gaze makes me question what could be between us, whether I'm ready for it.

My phone alarm rings, reminding me I have a class to teach in half an hour. *Saved by the alarm.*

"I gotta go teach."

He only nods. Dipping my chin, I walk out, still feeling remaining tension from being in his presence. I'm at the elevators, and when they open, a realtor exits. I step inside, and when I turn around, Evan has moved. He's standing by his office doors, his eyes are fixed on me as the realtor says, "Hi, Evan," in the most over-the-top voice, but he doesn't let go of my eyes until the elevator doors close.

Finally, sucking in a deep breath, I collapse against the elevator wall.

What was that?

CHAPTER 7

CHELSEA

AFTER WORK, I CARRY a bag of Bobby's belongings to his job. I don't want his crap at my place; it's a constant reminder of what a shit boyfriend he was.

I march into his office building and hit the tenth floor. My heart is in my throat, pounding with each step I take. Evan is the CEO here, which brings me some peace in this situation where I would usually feel unsettled. A part of me hopes I'll get to see him before I leave, even if just for a brief moment.

Now that I'm here, my palms are sweating, with fear Bobby's not here. I guess I can leave it on his desk and go. That would be even better because I wouldn't have to see or speak to him.

I already feel like a weight has been lifted off my chest since we broke up. The only childish thing I decided to do was put his stuff in a trash bag. I wasn't giving him a nice bag for his items or folding his clothes. His clothes and toothbrush aren't my problem anymore.

It felt good to not care for once.

The elevator doors open, and I step out onto floor ten. Soft chatter and light keyboard tapping filling the air remind me of the job I recently quit. The job I got to please this cheating bastard. My back straightens as my eyes scan the open-plan room——its sleek, modern design, with glass partitions, and minimalist decor. They land on familiar dark locks. I move closer, weaving through the maze of cubicles, but as I approach, I catch sight of a platinum blonde beneath him. Her mouth is tipped up in a coy smile, her eyes batting up at him flirtatiously. He's got his hands on either side of her chair, caging her in, and his mouth is inches away from hers. Their bodies almost touching. I suddenly have no idea where to look or what to do. A wave of dizziness washes over me, and I clutch the nearest desk for support, but my hand knocks into a flowerpot. It topples over, smashing into the ground with a loud crash. The sound echoes through the office, drawing every eye to me.

"Chelsea?" Bobby's voice rises, and he takes a sudden step back.

"Yeah. Ah. Sorry."

Why am I apologizing?

I shake my head to push away any sudden regret of coming here, reminding myself he isn't my problem anymore, and I'm here to give him his things.

"What are you doing here?" he asks, narrowing his eyes as his brow furrows.

I straighten my spine and walk closer. His female friend's eyes are wide, her mouth is parted. I'd be shocked if I were her too.

"I'm returning your stuff."

Maybe I should've dumped it at his place, but a small part of me wanted to confront him at the place he pretended to be all the time...

See the woman on the other end of the phone.

"You could have left it downstairs with reception," he snaps, crossing his arms. The way he's looking at me with annoyance grates on my nerves.

"No one is at the desk," I argue, raising my voice.

"Because they leave work on time." Evan's deep voice comes from behind me, sending a tingle down my spine. He's here.

My eyes close momentarily before I quickly spin around, and my breath catches at the sight of him. All dark and broody. His eyes zero in on Bobby, his lips curling.

"I'm almost done, Mr. Lincoln," Bobby answers quickly and softly.

He's definitely scared of Evan.

"I'm leaving now," the blonde says as she grabs her bag and stands up. She's moving past Bobby, avoiding eye contact and rushing past me toward the elevator. I offer her a sympathetic smile, recognizing her voice from the phone.

She is welcome to have Bobby; I hold no grudge against her. He might treat her better than he did me. I doubt that...

"Goodnight, Shyla," Evan says, his tone clipped as she rushes out of the room.

It sounds like Evan expects people to leave on time. Then why was Bobby always working and too busy to see me? Was he with her every night? I'm shaking, I can't help it. Why did I put up with him for so long? Hope. I was holding on to hope of a future that matched my dreams.

Bobby stays silent.

My hand is numb, and I realize it's because I'm still holding the trash bag. I step forward, and it hits me. This is the first time Bobby's not in control of me, and God, that feels amazing.

I lower the bag to the desk with a soft thud, aware that Evan is watching. But for some reason, I'm not embarrassed. Evan's support for my studio makes me feel like he has my back in here, even if he hasn't said those words himself.

"Here," I say, shaking my hand to bring it back to life before crossing my arms over my chest.

"I don't want them," Bobby replies with an icy glare.

"Neither do I," I argue.

"Just put the bag in the bin and go. I need to finish my work so I can go home," Bobby says, and I snap.

"Home? You never tried to make it home." I uncross my arms. "Clearly, you weren't working. You were too busy with Shyla and God knows who else every night..."

He curls his lips and snarls, "You are so out of line."

I slap my hand on my thighs as an exasperated sigh leaves me. "Are you kidding me right now?"

Evan clears his throat, the sound sharp and authoritative. "Do we have a problem here?" His piercing eyes scan us.

"No. Chelsea was just leaving," Bobby replies, his hard glare shifting to Evan, a challenge in his eyes.

Evan steps closer to position himself beside me. "You need to keep your personal life away from here." His voice is low and gruff, vibrating with barely contained anger. It makes all the hair on my body stand up.

"I do," Bobby spits, pointing a finger at me. "She shouldn't have come here."

"I'm not talking about Chelsea." Evan's eyes flick to where Shyla sat earlier, before shifting back to Bobby. "I'm talking about your personal life. It's affecting my business. I need it to stop. Got it?"

"Yes," Bobby says through gritted teeth, his jaw tight, supressed with anger.

"This goes for everyone else here." Evan's voice carries a clear warning to the entire floor.

I gasp. Shit. I thought it was just us three...

Murmurs ripple through the office as employees exchange glances. Bobby nods quickly, mumbling a barely audible yes.

"Good. Now Chelsea, let's go." His strong hand finds my lower back, and I almost buckle from the warmth of his touch.

I spin around to face Evan. His jaw is tight, a muscle in his face ticks, and his blue eyes are a richer shade.

With only a few words and a simple touch, I already feel like Evan is looking out for me more than Bobby ever did. I don't bother saying bye to Bobby, because he just lied to my face when he had the opportunity to come clean. I walk off with my head held high, leaving Evan, who stays still with his eyes on me.

I don't stop until I reach the elevator, where I release a heavy breath and hit the down button. The door opens a few moments later, and I step in. I don't see Evan or Bobby following me. I lean against the elevator wall as the doors begin to close, and just as they are, a hand reaches in and stops it. The doors reopen and reveal Evan, making my breath catch.

Pushing away from the wall, I stand up as straight as possible. I don't want Evan feeling sorry for me, so I need to appear in control. Breaking up with Bobby was the best thing that could have happened and what unfolded today was proof of that. This was the closure I needed.

I'm just exhausted by the weight of the emotions Bobby brings out of me, and the unexpected connection I feel with Evan.

He turns around, and the doors close, leaving us alone and a new set of nerves taking over. It's silent in the elevator as I watch each floor light up, and when we reach the lobby, he finally speaks. "I feel like I need a drink. Will you grab one with me?"

CHAPTER 8

EVAN

HER HEAD TWISTS TO face me, eyes widened slightly. "Now?"

"Yeah, unless you're busy?"

Now, I wish I had kept my mouth shut, but the moment I saw Bobby, her face dropped. Seeing it reminds me of how I felt discovering my fiancée fucking another man. Devastation.

I knew Bobby was dating, but I had no idea he was with Chelsea. If I had, I would've told her he was cheating on her and to break things off. No one deserves to feel like that. Bobby told her the same lies my ex told me. *Working late.*

What a cop out. What's worse is she gave Bobby a way to come clean after she caught him almost kissing Shyla. Karma will get him, just like it did my ex. Knowing the guy Connie cheated on me with and left her for someone else was the best revenge.

"I'm not busy..."

"But?"

"I'm surprised, that's all."

"Why?" I ask. We've hung out before so it shouldn't be a big deal.

"I thought you'd have somewhere to be."

Does she think I'm with someone?

We exit and stroll through the lobby. I text my driver to take us to a bar I know has private spots. I'd like to talk to her more, and I don't want a lot of people around. There's something about Chelsea that reminds me of myself. A strength in her ability to keep moving forward and stand her ground when the odds are against her. I find it incredibly compelling and attractive. And it's frustrating because I haven't been with anyone since my ex, and that was eight years ago. I'm unable to move on from the betrayal.

"Where are we going?" Her sweet voice pulls me away from my phone.

"A bar nearby. It felt like the right private spot."

"Are you just pitying me?" she asks, almost hesitantly.

"How could you think that?" I ask, my voice steady and sincere. "I want to be here with you."

"It will be nice to have a chance to get to know you better."

I doubt that...

I was always the solemn, brooding one. In big groups, you'll forget I'm there. It's not that I don't care. I do, I'm just more comfortable inside myself. I find comfort in my own thoughts and feelings. It helps me handle situations with a calm, centered approach, but it's also safer. *A place I can't be hurt.*

"If I can get to know you..."

She offers me a small smile.

We arrive twenty minutes later, and she pauses before turning and grabbing my suited arm with a gentle squeeze.

"This is around the corner from the studio space."

I nod.

"This could be trouble," she murmurs.

I want to reply, but my brain isn't working properly, her hand is still on me, and I swear the temperature has increased. There's a spark between us. I thought it was just a one-off, but the same thing is happening again.

I'm definitely losing it. I remain silent, as my brain tries to work out what my body is doing. She giggles before shaking her head and removing her hand from me. I want to catch her hand to continue holding her just to see if this weird heart-thumping, overheating feeling will fade. Surely, over time it will, and then I'll go back to...back to what?

We arrive at a set of steps that leads down to a dark wooden door. It's an underground bar. Reaching for the handle, I open it for her.

Her eyes flick from me to the door. I see the wheels turning in her head. Instead of speaking, she surprises me by walking past me, her tall frame brushing my chest. My nostrils flare as I follow her inside. I'll take a guess that no guy has opened any fucking doors for her.

I try to let that wash over me as we make our way inside. I follow behind, watching as she takes in the bar for the very first time. It's unlike most bars, not dingy or sticky. They have the best cocktails and vibe. If anywhere can get me to relax, it's here.

The server spots me and ushers us to the corner, where the burgundy lounges are surrounded by curtains. The tealight candle in the middle of the table adds to the mood.

Chelsea takes a seat, and I sit beside her. The server hands us each a menu, but I know what I want.

He says he will come back in a few moments to take our order.

"I feel out of place," she whispers, her brown eyes inspecting the place before looking down at her sneakers.

I tilt my head to the side, not understanding.

She runs her hand over her training outfit. "I'm not wearing the right outfit for a place like this. Maybe we should go somewhere else?"

My eyes have traced the outline of her delicious curves——enhanced by the figure-hugging material that fits her like a glove——more than just a few times today.

Each time I catch myself, I remind myself she just broke up with Bobby.

"No. There's nothing wrong with what you're wearing."

Her teeth graze her bottom lip, and I watch with fascination. I bring my gaze up to her eyes, noticing they're heated.

"Thanks, but you're in a suit."

It's silent, but her eyes scan the area around us as she settles into the chair.

"I don't care what you wear with me."

Her gaze radiates affection, and silence descends upon us once again. But our eyes stay on each other's. My mouth suddenly dries from the intensity passing between us.

Like she's snapping out of a daze, she shifts her attention. "This place is cool."

"It is."

"And this menu, I'm going to have trouble deciding what I want."

"I have a few suggestions."

Her lips tip up in a smile. She's incredibly sexy when she gives you one of her genuine smiles.

"Sure."

I nod and point on her menu at the few that are gin or tequila based. "Women usually want this."

"I'm not like other women," she replies with a teasing smirk.

I lean closer, my voice barely a whisper. "No, you're not." The electricity between us thickens, a spark of something unspoken hanging in the air.

Her throat works as she swallows. "What are you order-ing?"

"Whiskey's business."

Her eyes drop to find the name.

"Mmm, cinnamon is my favorite. I think I'll get that too."

My eyebrows pull together. "Are you sure?"

"Yeah, what's wrong with it?"

"Nothing," I want to say, *you order vanilla lattes, are you sure you don't want a sweet drink?* But instead, I say, "Order whatever you want."

Her tongue runs along the base of her full bottom lip, and my mind wanders to what she would taste like with whiskey on her tongue.

I drop my head to the menu and rub my forehead, trying to control my racing heart.

What's happening to me?

My brain seems to be on a loop of thoughts about the way she smells, what she would taste like, what she would feel like beneath my hands.

Thankfully, she decides to ask a question.

"Can we order something to eat? I'm a little hungry."

I nod. "They don't have much for a menu, but we can go somewhere later."

Her eyes widen as she drops the menu to the table with a thud, fixing me with a sharp gaze. "Later?" she repeats, her tone laced with surprise and curiosity.

I drop my gaze to the menu, focusing intently on the words to avoid the conversation. "They have olives, cheese, and bread." My fingers fidget with the edge of the menu.

I wasn't insinuating anything other than if she needed to eat, I'd take her to get food. I don't know why she acted like I asked her to jump on a plane to Paris.

The server comes back, and we order our food and drinks. I'm supposed to be looking for reasons to find her unattractive because she just broke up with someone else, but I can't find a single flaw.

"Sorry about the scene I caused with Bobby."

"I would've told you about him…if I had known he was *the* boyfriend. I mean, your ex-boyfriend."

Saying those words feel like swallowing poison. *The boyfriend.*

She dips her chin and laughs. "The older you get, the more lessons you learn."

"You almost sound…grateful?" I tilt my head to the side, fascinated.

The relief that follows once something toxic ends is a feeling I know all too well.

"I let myself slowly morph into the woman he wanted," she says. "I used to be fun."

I don't know what she was like before. But the few times I've seen her, she seemed fun to me. Well, more fun than me…

"I've seen you laugh," I murmur, and it's probably not the right thing to say, so I add. "I meant...you seem to be happy now."

Fuck, that sounds so stuck up. Like of course she'd be having a great time with me.

"I feel at ease around you. Like I'm safe... That's probably weird, sorry." The tip of her nose flushes the cutest shade of pink.

"Don't be sorry. It's actually, um, nice to hear that. I'm normally too intimidating for anyone other than my family to be around."

She snorts. "I can see how people might think you're intimidating."

"Really?"

She opens her mouth to say something else, but the server comes with our drinks and walks away. Picking up her drink, she holds it out, waiting to clink glasses. I can't remember the last time I had fun just being out and about with someone.

I follow and pick up my glass and clink. "To a good night."

Nodding, I bring the glass to my lips and welcome the burn down my throat. I watch her over the rim of my glass, expecting her to wince or splutter the drink, but she does neither. Her dark eyes hold mine and we sip while holding gazes. It makes a tingle spread over my skin. Lowering the glass, I clear my throat.

"What do you think?"

She licks her lips, and it's so distracting. I can see her lipstick is coming off, and the natural shade of pink is peeking through on her lips. "It's delicious."

Swallowing hard, I shift uncomfortably in my seat, reminding myself that I'm not looking for a relationship. Trust doesn't come easily to me, and I'm not ready to open my heart.

"What were we saying before the drinks came?" she asks as she settles back into the reddish-brown velvet chair.

"You said people think I'm intimidating."

She glances away uneasily.

"Is that how you feel about me?"

That has her eyes moving to meet mine. I don't miss how wide they are.

"Yeah, but mine's a little different," she mumbles.

"Start then with why others do."

The server quietly lowers our snacks down and walks away. I grab a piece of cheese and chew as I watch her do the same.

When she swallows, her eyes flicking up. "I think your quietness can make them unsure about how you feel, so it feels like a threat. People have a hard time reading you."

"Which is probably why I have a problem with people not giving me their opinions or disagreeing with me. Unless it's Bobby."

She giggles at that. Adorably.

I take an olive and pop it into my mouth. "And why are you intimidated by me?"

Her eyes remain fixed on mine, but when her hand trembles to pick up her drink, I smile inside at her nervousness. I'm curious if she'll be honest or hold back her thoughts.

"You're successful, strong, intelligent, wise, and confident," she replies, the flush on her nose spreading to her cheeks.

A slow smile breaks on my face.

"I'm so embarrassed. You probably think I'm envious of you. I promise I'm not. I just admire you." She picks up her drink and takes a decent sip.

"Would it make you feel better if I told you that you intimidate me?"

"No way." She shakes her head in total disbelief.

"I'm serious. The way you stood up to Bobby, your femininity, your health, your uniqueness, and your hobbies."

She beams as I trail off the list. I know how damaging to your self-esteem getting cheated on can be. I could barely look at myself in the mirror some days. I wish I had someone there to remind me that I was enough.

"You're honest, and I can't tell you how unnerving that is to me."

"Why?" she breathes, and I feel my own lungs burning with words I'm unsure if I want to speak.

I pick up my drink and take a sip before lowering it and cradling it between my fingers on the table. "I have a past too."

"We all have one. You know mine."

I nod. That's the problem, hers is too similar to mine. The only difference is she wasn't engaged to be married to Bobby.

My teeth grind together. Why does that thought anger me?

"Yes, and mine isn't so different."

I can't believe this is seriously leaving my mouth right now. I blame the way her firm dark eyes bore into mine, and I can't help but blurt everything to her.

I want to help her heal.

But how can I tell her how to heal if I'm still not quite there yet? And it's been almost eight fucking years.

When I'm around Chelsea, I act differently, and it's something I can't ignore. The honesty in my admission catches me off guard because I haven't felt this way in a long time...if ever. It leaves me feeling conflicted. On one hand, she challenges me to open up, but on the other, I worry that it could mean I'm losing control. What makes Chelsea special is how unafraid she is to be herself; it makes me want to push past my fears and see where this connection could lead. So, I take a deep breath and share my humiliating past.

"My fiancée cheated on me, and I found out the day we were getting married."

She heaves an audible breath, and her eyes widen at the same time her hand flies up to cover her open mouth.

"I had naked photos sent to me as I was getting into my suit."

CHAPTER 9

EVAN

REACHING ACROSS THE TABLE, she lays her hand on top of mine. "I am so sorry."

I nod, remove my hand, pick up my drink, and take a sip.

The alcohol warms me, but whether it's the alcohol or just Chelsea's presence, I can't quite tell, though I find myself relaxing more than I thought. I'm shocked I confided something only my brothers know to her. I usually keep that part of my past to myself, as it's too humiliating to speak about. I don't want anyone feeling sorry for me, but that's not what's happening here. Chelsea's reaction isn't pity; she's genuinely shocked.

I fall silent, not wanting to delve deeper into that topic. There's nothing more to say. We separated, and I haven't seen or spoken to her since.

"Let's not talk about it tonight," Chelsea suggests, grabbing a piece of bread and taking a bite.

I'm glad she doesn't push for more. I appreciate how she respects my need for space; she has no idea how much that simple little gesture affects me. I feel like I've known her all my life...We share the same values, want for complete honesty, and the way we appreciate genuine communication.

Chelsea looks beautiful under the dim lights, as she reclines in her chair. I shift my gaze to the bread, contemplating what to say next.

What do I really want to know?

"Are you close with your family?" I ask, grabbing a piece of bread and chewing it slowly. Her face lights up.

I ease back, relieved we left the ex conversation behind.

"I'm extremely close with my family. They are everything to me."

I nod, my heart pounding. Another commonality we share.

"My parents actually gave me the money for the studio."

"Where are they?"

"They don't live here. I left my hometown in Connecticut to come to New York two years ago. I knew there were more opportunities for me as a Pilates instructor here."

I nod once more, agreeing. The wellness scene here is thriving, so her studio has great potential to be successful.

"Why did you wait this long to start a studio?"

She seems intelligent and capable enough to have already purchased and be in business already.

Her eyes shift away before meeting mine again. "Bobby didn't see it as a career; he thought Pilates was just a hobby."

I shift in my seat, giving her my full attention. I can sense the hurt in her words, and it pisses me off that he'd diminish her passion that way. "I met Bobby shortly after arriving in New York," she says quietly.

"Do you have brothers and sisters?" I ask. I wonder if her friends and family knew what kind of man he was.

"Yeah," she chuckles. "Anna. She's younger, studying psychology. She also hated Bobby."

"Weren't your parents bothered by him?" I ask incredulously.

"My parents are incredibly kind; they just wanted me to be happy. I actually wish Bobby had met them."

"He never met them?" I grunt, gripping the arm of the chair.

She shakes her head. "No."

"How long were you two together?"

"Two years."

I glare at her and grit my teeth so hard, my jaw aches.

She sighs, though there's strain in it. "And all he did was leave me hurt."

"You mean humiliated," I correct gently.

She nods, her eyes dropping.

I want to hurt him too. My fingers curl into a ball on my lap. The other one settles on the back of the chair.

"And your family?" she asks, her eyes lift to mine again.

I'm the quiet Lincoln child who always had his head absorbed in a fiction book under an oak tree while my rowdy brothers played together in the backyard.

"I'm close with mine too. I'm the eldest of three brothers, and I inherited the business from my father, but I suppose you already know that."

She nods, her teeth catching her lip. "Does your dad involve himself with the business?"

I shake my head. "No, I grew up working with him. I've expanded it since taking over. If anything, my father is proud of what I've done with it." I sigh before adding, "But that's because I've sacrificed everything."

"So that's why you mentioned being intimidated by my social skills," she teases.

"Exactly. I've given everything to The New York Press. I love it, but I'm almost forty, and all I have is money and a successful business."

Holy fuck. She does it again, effortlessly drawing out information. The way she listens, the genuine curiosity in her eyes—it makes it impossible to keep my guard up.

I wipe my face with my hand. "What is it about you?"

Her eyebrows pull together. "What?"

"You make me spill my secrets. I sound so fucking depressing."

"It sounds like you haven't trusted anyone enough to speak about these things," she observes, and her soft expression warms me from the inside out.

"And I can trust you?"

"Yes."

I stare deeply at her, half expecting my body to scream at me that she's lying. But it doesn't. I still feel oddly warm and a strong attraction to her.

Can I trust her?

We order another round of drinks from the server before she speaks again. "I envy your ability to stand up for things you believe in."

"I wish I had stood up for myself more when it happened to me."

I see the acknowledgement in her eyes. Eyes that say, *me too*.

"Have you been with anyone else?" she asks, taking a sip of her drink.

I hesitate. Am I about to admit my dry spell? Fuck it. "No."

"Why?" she probes, watching me over her drink.

I stay silent for a moment.

"I don't trust easily. But it's more than that...I don't want to lead anyone on."

"Maybe falling in love with someone would help rebuild your trust," she suggests.

I pick up my drink and drain the glass. This conversation is so hard for me. I keep my eyes down, lost in thought. "Maybe."

She takes another sip, and I order us another round.

I'm not ready to end the conversation. It feels good letting it all out.

"I fell out of love with my ex the moment I found out. The thought of touching her made me sick."

"How do you do that?" she wonders out loud, swaying slightly.

I frown.

"How do you fall out of love?" I repeat, realizing she wants to do the same with Bobby. Who can blame her? She deserves a great guy who values her, who wants her happy and doesn't hold her back.

"Hatred does that to you." I chuckle bitterly as I rub the back of my neck. When was the last time I did that?

"I need to hate him more," she mutters, her eyes glassy from all the alcohol she's consumed.

It's Bobby. I'm sure he hasn't finished fucking up.

But I don't want to see her get hurt again.

"These drinks are going down too easily," she tells the server as he lowers another two on our table.

"You chose the most popular drink. Do you want more food?" the server asks.

Chelsea glances at me, as if to see what I want to do.

I'm not ready to go home. "Yes, bring more."

Chelsea's face lights up with a big smile. "You're not sick of me yet?"

"No," I reply, picking up my drink and wondering why that is. I haven't spent this much time talking to a woman in years. Definitely not like this. Alcohol, food, good conversation—I'm surprised I'm enjoying it this much.

I haven't even felt the slightest urge to check my phone. Sitting here with Chelsea makes me forget I have a job.

"I'm going to use the bathroom," she says.

"I'll be right here," I reassure her.

She gives me a smile that forces my heart into overdrive, and I watch her slip out of our area and wander through the place. I can't stop myself from letting my gaze linger on her, and I can't help the way they stop on her luscious, firm ass. She has a great figure, no doubt from all the Pilates.

Even after she disappears into the bathroom, I can't stop staring. It's only when the server comes to clean up and refill our drinks that I snap out of it. I give him a generous tip.

Chelsea rejoins me not long after the server leaves, but I immediately notice something is wrong. Her glow is gone.

"Are you okay?" I ask.

She plops down with a huff. "You noticed."

I nod. "Yeah."

She gestures toward the bar where Bobby and Shyla are standing. I hadn't even noticed them walk in; I was too focused on the stunning woman in front of me. I wish I'd seen them first and told them to leave, just to keep her safe.

"He never took me out anywhere. Actually, this is my first time in a bar with a guy since I met him," she says, her voice shaking from the nerves.

She's angry. "I wish he could feel as humiliated as I feel."

I slowly take a final sip of my drink, an idea forming. "What if I told you we can do that?"

"I doubt it. He doesn't care about anything but his job."

She grabs her hair, sweeping it to the side. I try not to stare at the slope of her delicate neck. Licking my lips, I shift my focus to her eyes.

I mull over that information once more, and I barely believe the sentence that comes out of my mouth.

"I can help you. He should know what he lost. He deserves to see you happy, looking good, and that you've moved on."

Her getting revenge on him will also work in my favor. He'll want to quit working for my company and, well, honestly, I'm trying to live vicariously through Chelsea. I was cheated on too, and seeing her get even feels like my own form of justice.

She sits up eagerly as her dull eyes come to life. "How?"

CHAPTER 10

CHELSEA

WITHOUT ANOTHER WORD, HE leans in and presses his lips to mine. His kiss is rough and commanding. After the initial shock, I lean into the kiss, enjoying its warmth.

I hadn't realized how nice it would feel to have a guy initiate a kiss. Not just any guy, but one I've found myself recently attracted to.

I'm drunk, so when he pulls back to ask, "Do you want to be my fake girlfriend?"

I blink rapidly, my brain slow from all the alcohol and the drugging kiss. A giggle slips out of me as I reply, "Why not."

I have nothing else to lose. With our new friendship, it's kind of fun, especially if I get to kiss him without any strings.

Summer said to have fun...So that's what I'm going to do.

What's even better, is the fact I know Bobby was watching us. He's no longer touching the woman. No, his eyes are fixed on me.

"Do you have plans Friday?" Evan asks, pulling my attention back to his face.

"No."

"You do now."

My eyebrows draw together in confusion. "Where are we going?"

"I'm throwing a party to celebrate a breaking news article. I want to reward my staff for their hard work."

I smile at that. "Let's have some fun."

The smash of glass draws my attention toward the bar, where Bobby is storming away to the bathroom. My phone chimes, and I read the text with my pulse skyrocketing.

> **Bobby**: *You're such a fucking slut.*

Staring at his icy words, I retreat into myself. Memories of my relationship with Bobby flash before my eyes. I didn't realize that even in a relationship with him, I still felt isolated. He was there, but when someone doesn't give you affection or care about you in the way you deserve, you might as well be alone.

Part of me wants to disappear right now because he makes me believe I am a slut, that I'm not supposed to be here. Flirting and kissing a guy so soon. He makes me believe I still owe him respect and loyalty. But when I look at Evan, I am reminded I don't.

I can't remember the last time I've been this vulnerable or laughed with a man. Tonight, with Evan, I've truly enjoyed myself.

Feeling buzzed from the alcohol, I grab some more bread and cheese, trying to distract myself from my negative thoughts.

Should I have been more sexual?

Should I have given him more space?

Was I not funny enough, pretty enough, interesting enough?

Evan sighs, staring at my face as he considers his next words carefully. "You know I've been in your shoes before. You don't have to hide your hurt and anger with me."

I close my eyes, appreciating his words. He didn't have to share his past with me, but he did, and I appreciate it. It makes our friendship feel more genuine.

The corner of my mouth tips up. "Thank you."

Having already paid, he stands and offers me a hand. "Let's go."

I walk with a trembling chin, trying not to let anyone see how bumping into Bobby has affected me. My eyes stay focused on the exit, and I hold my breath, hoping Bobby doesn't spot us leaving.

I make it to the door, but a hand reached out to grab it before I can.

Evan...

He pushes the door wide open and holds it out for me.

Outside, I welcome the light traffic, the night sky, and the fresh breeze that cools my skin from all the drinks.

I walk cautiously and stop midway along the sidewalk, where I think Bobby won't see us. I'm not ready for a confrontation tonight. Not after his text.

Evan's in his late thirties, so I suppose he's more mature compared to someone in their late twenties, like Bobby. So I decide to blame Evan's age for him being such a gentleman all night long.

"I won't lie, showing up on your arm will piss Bobby off," I say.

Evan hisses as his fingers still. "He won't step a foot out of line with me there."

I roll my eyes and shove his chest playfully. "You can't babysit me all night."

From trying to push his weight around, my feet wobble, and before I drunkenly fall over, his hands catch me by the arms. He holds me firmly until I straighten. "It's not called babysitting when you're my date. I won't leave your side."

"What if I need to go to the bathroom?" I tease.

He narrows his eyes at me. "I'll watch over you."

I shake my head at his silly suggestion. "I don't expect you to be with me the whole night."

"Why?" He frowns, and I miss the way I could see clearly into his bright blue eyes.

"You're the CEO, you'll need to mingle."

"I don't need to do anything I don't want to do." Standing face-to-face with him as he challenges me makes me drop my gaze and shuffle my feet from side to side.

"You don't want to stand with me all night."

His hand grabs my chin and brings my gaze back to his.

"What if I want to?"

I'm breathing heavier now, the alcohol hitting me harder. "You couldn't possibly."

"I do."

My head spins. "Thank you for tonight. I had a really good time. Minus you randomly drunk kissing me to piss off Bobby."

He tips his head back and laughs harder. "You'll forget this happened tomorrow. But it plays well into our temporary relationship."

I giggle until I hiccup. "I know. I'm a little drunk. But you know we have to look like a real couple."

His eyebrow rises as he laughs again. "A little? And yes, unless you change your mind."

I go to shake my head but immediately stop when spots form in front of my eyes. "No changing my mind. He's going down. But..." I hiccup again. "How will it work?"

"We pretend to be a real couple, but with no real feelings, until Bobby quits and leaves the city."

"You know couples hang out, hold hands, and kiss."

I never thought I'd be faking a relationship, but if this works, Bobby will see me doing just fine without him. I just hope I don't end up feeling something for my new boyfriend.

"I'm well aware, and I promise to be a good showman. He'll be convinced we're the real thing."

And if I get to kiss him again, I don't mind at all. "I like your plan."

He waves at a car. "My driver will take you home."

"What will you do?"

"Don't worry about me."

"But——"

"Chelsea..." He looks at me with a fixed stare again, his fingers caressing, as his mouth moves closer, and I feel his breath tickle my lips. "I'll be fine, but I need your number," he asks in a deep raspy voice.

I'm shaking all over, the anticipation and alcohol too much. I give him my number and then stand there, biting my lip, waiting and hoping he will tell me what he's thinking. Or better, what he's feeling. But he doesn't lean in and close the distance, he just stands there, leaving me with a mix of longing and uncertainty. Each second stretches, my thoughts spiraling with doubt and desire. Is he hesitating, or am I reading too much into this moment?

CHAPTER 11

CHELSEA

SINCE FINISHING UP AT the recruitment agency, I've picked up extra shifts at the studio while I wait for the opening of my own. Tonight, I'm preparing for the last class of the day, setting up beds, Pilates balls, and rings. I've been working here casually for the last two years. I met the manager as a client because I would come every day when I first moved to New York. Taking care of my health always kept me grounded and stopped me from running to Connecticut out of fear of being alone. The energy of this studio allowed me to call this place home. It's more dimly lit, with dark flooring, but it's fantastic to work at regardless. Now, everything is ready to go. I open the door and grab my list of names. They're all regulars.

I adjust the mic on my head and test it out. The music playlist is set. This class is advanced, which means everyone joining is familiar with Pilates. The clients start pouring in, and I chat with a few, asking how their day was. One of the clients is a co-worker of mine. We do this a lot. Train as a client to try out moves we could use in our own classes or just to get a good workout in, because after a full day of work, the last thing I feel like doing is my own class. I find that I don't push myself as much.

I am about ready to begin, when Evan walks in, catching my attention, and all the air in the room gets sucked out. My eyes blink rapidly, as if I'm imagining things. I know I asked him to come, but I never in a million years thought he'd turn up. But he did. Standing in the doorway, he's wearing workout clothes, along with a tight expression.

His muscular arms are on full display, the contours of his biceps rippling slightly under the studio lights. The black tank top clings to his torso, highlighting the defined lines of his chest and the faint outline of his abs. His training shorts hang just above the knee, loose enough for movement but fitted enough to reveal the muscles in his legs.

He's so hot it makes me want to melt into a puddle.

He's here.

He's really here.

Does he realize how much this means to me? There's no way Bobby would be caught dead here. And that's when I realize, this is an advanced class. Shit. I'll definitely have to modify his workout.

Evan's jaw is set, brows drawn together, lips pressed firmly into a thin line, and his eyes—usually bright blue—are now intense, focused. The other students in the class have noticed him too, their conversations dropped to murmurs as they sneak glances in his direction.

His presence is commanding, the kind that has my body moving toward him, ignoring the buzz between us. He's paused in the doorway, seeming like he's ready to turn around and walk right out of here. His uneasiness is so different to the powerful and controlled Evan I've witnessed.

Standing directly in front of him, I move the mic away from my mouth. "Hi. I'm glad you came."

"I wanted to support my girlfriend," he murmurs.

I smile as a blush creeps onto my skin. "Come on in, I'll take care of you."

His eyes drop over my body, and I know he hasn't seen me in anything like this before. A sky-blue set of short shorts and a matching crop top. Yeah, there's nothing left to the imagination today. And because he's in my space, I don't feel self-conscious about it. The way he's looking at me, I would say he's not mad about my outfit either.

I point over to one of the few free beds. "Come over to this one."

He drops his head and strides over to the bed, holding his wallet and drink bottle.

I go to the desk to grab him a towel and hand it to him. He frowns.

"Trust me, you'll need it." I thrust it toward him.

He takes the towel with a pinched expression and looks around the bed.

"Take a seat. I'll start with a warm-up," I whisper to him before moving the microphone back to my mouth and speaking into it. "Alright, class, please begin with a warm-up spring, extend your legs, and push the carriage out."

I adjust Evan's springs and get him to lie down. Seeing him on this carriage (Pilates bed) has my mind going places it shouldn't go. All I can think about is straddling him. Naked.

What is wrong with me? I can't remember the last time I felt this bothered over a guy. I've never had this problem with a client before. Shaking off those thoughts, I move to the other side of the room, helping other clients correct their form or push themselves.

After a few minutes of warm-up, I get their legs in the tabletop position and do some crunches with hands in straps.

Then, I wander back to Evan, his strong arms contracting during this exercise, and God the trickle of sweat glistening on his forehead nearly kills me. The fact he's trying makes my heart swell.

I tell the class to do the side plank with rotation. Then I step over to Evan and tell him to just try a normal plank, but he follows the others in the class effortlessly. For someone who has never done Pilates before, he's doing amazing.

I know he will be in pain this week. Part of me wishes I was brave enough to offer him a private cool down.

We reach the end of class, and before I know it, I am on the last exercise.

I choose an exercise to test him.

"Alright, everyone, it's time to feel the burn. Let's go for those lean back bicep curls you love," I call out, watching the class intently. Of course, he follows the advanced clients, refusing to give up.

As I pass by, I can't help but notice the way his veins bulge on his arm, adding to my already flustered state. "Feeling strong today?" I tease, trying to keep my voice steady while adjusting the twisted strap. My hand brushes against his warm skin, sending a spark of electricity through me.

He grins, not missing a beat. "Always. Are you trying to make me quit?"

"Just making sure you're getting your money's worth," I reply with a smirk, then move to the next person.

He chuckles. "Well, you're doing a great job. I'll need a nap after this."

Glancing back at him, I raise an eyebrow. "A nap, huh?" My gaze slowly drops to those arms again and my tongue skims my bottom lip. "You look strong."

"Strong, not Superman," he retorts, a playful glint in his eye.

I laugh and shake my head. "Keep those curls going. You've got this."

"Evil," he mumbles but continues on.

It's time to cool down, and I drag it out a little longer than usual. I'm running over time, but I don't care about the pay. I just want to soak in this moment for a few more minutes.

After the class ends, Evie helps me by starting to clean the beds. She looks at me and then at Evan. I bet she has a million questions running through her mind, which means she will definitely find a way to get me alone to quench her curiosity.

I say goodbye to my clients, and I can see Evie is still cleaning. She's waving at me behind Evan's back. He's wiping his face with the towel.

I mouth a thank you to her.

Evan twists his water bottle and drinks half of it in one go.

"You know I was trying to give you easier options."

With a quirked eyebrow, he screws the lid back on his bottle. "I was trying to fit in."

I laugh. "You don't have to."

His blue eyes narrow in on me. "But I want to."

"Why?" I ask in a soft voice.

I'm confused why a guy like Evan, who seems like he doesn't care about other people's opinions, would feel the need to fit in.

"I didn't want to let my girlfriend down," he says matter-of-factly.

I'm taken aback by the ease in which he shared that out loud.

"You didn't have to, but don't complain to me when you're in pain."

"I'll be fine."

His cocky confidence has me grinning widely. "You say that now."

Inside, I feel light and free, like my old bubbly self is coming back. For the first time in over a year, I can be myself without having to fit into someone else's expectations.

He looks at his phone. "My brother's calling, I better go."

"Jeremy?" I ask.

"No, Oliver."

I swallow. "Well, thanks again for coming."

An expression has settled on his face that I can't understand. "Thanks for having me last minute. You're a great teacher."

I snort, but it's combined with a laugh. "It's only Pilates. I'm not a CEO of a media company."

"Two things. One, I was given the company, and two, you're going to be a CEO soon, right? And I bet you could run Lincoln Media for me if I ever let you."

My lips twist to the side. "That was three."

The corner of his mouth quirks, making me giggle.

"I don't want to hear you compare yourself to anyone. You stand out in the sea, *Shell*."

He reaches out and strokes my cheek, leaning in to peck me briefly before turning and leaving. I stand there dumbstruck. Bobby never used a nickname on me—no "Chelse," "baby," "babe," ...nothing. Yet Evan just gave me a nickname no one else has ever used before, *Shell*.

I don't get long to think about what that means because a whistle sounds loudly behind me.

I spin around to face an amused Evie. You'd never guess she's in her mid-thirties with long black hair that is currently tied up in a messy pony, her bluish green top and matching color shorts complimenting her skin tone.

No point in denying I'm into him. Because I'd be lying. I'm more attracted now, if that is even possible.

This fake dating isn't going to end well.

"He's fine, Chelsea."

"I know." I bite the corner of my lip.

"How did you meet him?" She wiggles her eyebrows at me.

"His brother is dating my friend, and um, he's also Bobby's CEO."

She whistles again. "Bobby must be pissed."

"Yep, and it's about to get really interesting."

"Why's that?"

I blow out a breath. "Friday night, I'm going with Evan to their work party as his date."

"Oh, to be a fly on that wall."

I giggle. "Right. I'm nervous. I've only ever been with Bobby. I don't even know how to react near a man like Evan. Bonus points for pissing off Bobby though."

She rolls her eyes. "But he deserves it."

He does.

"Don't overthink it. You're not replacing his shampoo with hair removal cream... Relax."

Her words pull me back to the here and now.

"Have you done that before?"

She tries to stop a full-blown smile, but she fails. "Maybe."

"Brutal."

We laugh, which helps relieve the tension I had building from Evan being in my class tonight.

I clean up the rest of the studio and we discuss my new place.

"When do you get the keys?" Evie asks.

"Not until next month." The purchase contract set a later date to allow the previous owner time to make repairs, and it gives me time to secure a building permit for the changes I want to make, like installing the lockers.

Her mouth turns downward. "I'll miss you."

"Are you going to take the Friday class I offered?" I know that Evie doesn't have enough shifts here, and I would love to offer her a day at my studio. I've discussed it with the boss already. I just need Evie to accept it.

"You have just over three weeks to decide." I don't want to be too pushy, but I need to get contracts and insurance all set up for each instructor.

"Can you show me the studio?"

I grin with new hope. "Sure. Maybe it will help persuade you."

She giggles. "Maybe."

After showing her some pictures, we leave the studio, locking up behind us, and then we walk a few miles to mine. As we pass a restaurant, my steps falter. A familiar face catches my eye through the window, and I stop in my tracks, my breath hitching.

Bobby.

"What are you doing?" Evie asks when she realizes I stopped walking.

My eyes are glued to Bobby because he's not with Shyla; instead, he's with a stunning red-haired woman. Another woman. I know that because as they sit opposite each other, they both lean in, smiling. Their hands on top of the white linen table, their fingers entangled as they chat.

What happened to Shyla?

And once again, he's out and about. Not working late into the night here either.

Does this mean he's cheating on Shyla, or is he just hooking up with a bunch of different girls?

"Who's that?"

"Bobby."

She has only heard about him because he only met my roommates or co-workers from recruiting. He never wanted to meet anyone from my Pilates job.

"Oh fuck. Your ex."

I giggle at her reaction, but it's strained. He's not only moved on, but he's on a date at the same bar we first met.

I don't bother explaining the situation with Shyla. It would be a waste of my breath. Bobby will get to see me exactly how I am seeing him now. My stomach flutters from both nerves and excitement. This vision in front of me confirms how much he deserves it. I've never been the revenge type, but he's a douchebag who deserves to feel the way he makes women feel.

CHAPTER 12

CHELSEA

> **Evan:** Are you free for coffee?

> **Me:** Sounds great. I can meet you in forty minutes. Where are you thinking?

> **Evan:** Cafe Brew?

> **Me:** Done. See you soon.

I enter the cafe through the glass door and peer around, searching for Evan. The scent of freshly ground coffee beans surrounds me. The space is warm compared to the cool breeze outside. I spot his tall figure on the right, the sunlight catching his hard profile. His eyes are focused on me. As I approach, he rises to greet me. "Hi."

"Hey, this is a cool spot," I say, shrugging off my coat and hanging it on the back of my chair before sitting down.

Our chairs are close together, and I wonder if he arranged them that way on purpose.

Don't be ridiculous...

"It's the best place for coffee in this part of Manhattan," he says, his tone casual as he settles back into his seat.

"What do you usually get?" I ask, glancing at the menu board above the counter, which lists a range of specialty brews.

"An iced brew."

I scrunch up my face. "I'll get a vanilla latte."

"I'll order it and be right back," he says, slipping out of his seat and moving to join the line. I admire his outfit to-day—a blue suit with a white shirt and a pink tie. He looks good. I'm still watching him as he reaches the counter and orders. The barista gives him a bright smile, but when he turns back and notices me staring, his expression softens and a slight smile tugs at the corners of his mouth. My stomach flips in response.

He knows me well...that's why he's smiling. There's no other reason.

He returns with our drinks, handing me my latte before sitting down again, our chairs practically touching. I grab the drink but the warmth from the cup onto my hand tells me it's too hot to take my first sip.

"So what's the plan of attack?" I ask.

"For you to relax and pretend like we're dating."

I snort. "You make it sound easy. No one we know is here."

"I thought we could capture this moment on socials."

My eyebrows lift. "Oh yeah?"

I pull up my phone ready to take a picture of our drink.

"No," he says. I stop and tilt my head, frowning.

"What's wrong?"

He grabs my waist, pulling me closer until I can feel the warmth of his body and hear his breathing. The flutters in my stomach are hard to ignore, but I push them aside to play along, wrapping one arm around his neck and holding out my phone with the other.

I'm about to snap the photo when he nuzzles his face into the curve of my neck, and I can't help but smile as I capture the moment. When I lower my phone, he lifts his head, and I finally breathe again.

"How'd we do?" I ask, but a figure stands in front of our table.

"Callum," Evan says.

"I thought you two looked great, but I can take the shot for you?" Callum offers.

"He is a professional photographer at my work..." Evan says with a smirk.

My mouth drops open in a mock offense. "Are you saying it's a bad photo?"

I glance at the picture again, and it's hot. We look like a real couple.

"No, it's great. But post it, and I'll get one for my socials," Evan suggests.

I hit post on the picture, adding a heart emoji and the caption *cafe dates with this one*...before lowering my phone to the table. Evan hands his phone to Callum, his arm sliding around my waist again. I'm almost in his lap, and though I want to move, I can't...not with Callum watching us. We're supposed to look like a real couple, after all.

We smile for a picture, and I think that's it, we can finally drink our coffees, and I'll be able to relax again. But Callum isn't done. "One more. The lighting is really good here," he says, adjusting the phone angle.

I start smiling again, but Evan has other ideas. "Chelsea."

I turn, and he leans in closer, his voice dropping to a low growl. "Come here."

His lips meet mine, and I freeze for a split second before I respond, my lips moving with his in a kiss that feels surprisingly sweet for one so unexpected. When we finally pull apart, my lips tingle and I'm left a little breathless.

"That's a good one," Callum says, handing Evan's phone back and pulling me out of my thoughts. I lean toward Evan to see the screen, and his other hand slides up the side of my body in a soothing motion. I'm not sure if he realizes he's doing it, but I know it's to show Callum that we're a couple. We both stare at the photo. This shot is both hot and convincingly real.

"You two look great together. Cute couple," Callum remarks, and his genuine smile makes my stomach twist with guilt.

"Thanks," I murmur, smiling back at him.

Evan starts adding the picture to his socials, captioning it *with my girl* and a pink heart emoji. When he posts it, I feel a strange tingling sensation spread through me.

"I need to head back. I was just grabbing a coffee on my break. See you later."

"Bye," Evan and I say in unison.

As Callum walks off, Evan's phone begins to chime repeatedly with notifications. "How do I turn this off?" he mutters, tapping the screen.

"I'll help."

I take it and quickly adjust the settings before returning the phone to him.

The next sound to leave his phone is a call. He doesn't pick it up, but he reads a message.

"I'm sorry. I need to go. I have a stock meeting to get to. I'll walk you back," Evan says, standing up.

"Actually, I'd like to stay a bit longer." I want to add *to cool down and clear my head*, but I keep that to myself.

"Did you want another drink or something to eat?" he asks, concerned.

"No, thanks," I reply with a smile to ease his worry.

My phone rings, and it's my Pilates boss calling.

"I'll let you go. I'll talk to you later." He leans down to kiss my cheek, making me dizzy with surprise.

"Bye," I breathe, letting the call ring out.

"You better call her back." He winks, turning and exiting the shop and leaving me reeling from that kiss. And he's such a good kisser. I wouldn't have minded another one on the lips. Fake dating him is turning out to be a lot easier than I thought.

Chapter 13

Evan

"Here is the write-up you asked for, Mr. Lincoln," Shyla says. I turn away from the monitor to face her.

"The one about the new Lincoln Gallery?"

She nods. "Yeah, your brother Oliver answered all my questions."

She obviously didn't expect him to be so forthcoming. I bet she thought he was like me. None of my brothers are, though. I'm most similar to Harvey, because of his cool demeanor.

Thinking about it, Harvey has that same calculated calmness I do, but there's a warmth to it that I lack. He's the kind of guy who can win people over with just a smile; he's effortlessly charming. The others? Each unique in their own way. While I keep my cards close to my chest, they wear their hearts on their sleeves.

"Can I have a look?" I hold out my hand, ready to take the paper.

"Oh. Sorry." She steps closer to my desk and hands it over.

I read the interview, and I'm damn impressed. She's been with us for six months after I poached her from our competition for double the salary.

"Take a seat," I command, pointing to the chair opposite my large wooden desk.

"You're not happy, Mr. Lincoln?" She sits down, and her fingers interlace on her lap.

Her back is ramrod straight, and her professionalism makes me wonder why she'd let a weasel like Bobby distract her.

Fucking Bobby...

I close my eyes and suck in a cleansing breath. What is it about him that had two intelligent women fall for him?

"This isn't about the interview. This"—I hold the paper up—"is fantastic. You've been a wonderful addition to the team."

Her shoulders drop, her posture not so stiff anymore.

"Thank you. I'm really enjoying working here."

I don't like having long conversations, but this one is important.

"Is anyone making you uncomfortable?" I ask, ignoring the way a muscle beats in my jaw, thinking about Bobby.

She shakes her head. "No."

"Is there anything you'd like to tell me? Obviously, this conversation is strictly confidential."

Her eyebrows knit together. "No. But is there something you want me to be aware of?"

I lower the paper to my desk to give myself a moment to collect my thoughts. "I just wanted to affirm that you can always bring any issues within the office to me."

Relief floods her face, and she smiles kindly at me. "Thank you, Mr. Lincoln. It's nice to work for someone who cares about their staff."

I nod. Some would say I care too much. But I'd rather be on the floor and hands-on, than a pencil pusher. "Here, take this and publish it on the allocated date."

Standing promptly, she takes the paper from my hands and turns to leave.

When I'm alone, I spin back to face my computer so I can continue working, but I can't concentrate. My mind is back on Chelsea.

Why would Bobby cheat on her?

I come up empty before I'm shaking my head at myself. I can't believe I went to a Pilates class of hers.

It's because I remember after my breakup, things were rough. I spent days wondering when and how it all went wrong. I threw myself into work, trying to drown out the pain. My family was my lifeline during that time. I remember Jeremy being the first to come over; he didn't say much, just sat with me, sharing a drink in silence. His way of letting me know he was there for me, no questions asked.

Next was my brother Harvey. He'd drag me out of bed on the weekends to run with him. I was never in the mood, but he wouldn't leave my house unless I did it. I must admit the fresh air and exertion did help me sleep better.

Oliver was there with my parents and Gram; they were the practical thinkers, sharing their optimism and offering emotional support. They helped me pack and move houses. I could have stayed and paid her off, but I wanted to escape the memories we shared in that place. They would talk to me about which items needed to be divided, and Gram made sure I was eating properly.

All of them reassured me I could get through it and didn't allow me to drown in self-pity. They pulled me through the darkest of days. Now, I'm doing the same for Chelsea, as well as Nova and Summer. I know her family isn't able to help her.

I grab my phone that's sitting on my desk and see an alert for a new message. She replied to a text I sent her earlier. I'm fighting this attraction I feel for her because I don't want a relationship, but fuck, I can't stay away.

> **Me:** You're right. Today, the pain is intense. I can barely move.

> **Chelsea:** I warned you; 48 hours after is the worst. Take a magnesium bath, go for a walk and stretch.

Me: I don't like baths.

Chelsea: Buy the magnesium tablets or the topical spray.

I don't get a chance to reply before I get another text.

Chelsea: Or you could come in for another class. (Smiley face emoji)

Me: You're kidding, right. How would another class help?

The damn thought makes my muscles quiver.

Chelsea: It helps your muscles recover quicker.

Me: I'd rather stick pins in my eyes.

Chelsea: You're so dramatic.

Me: You're crazy for thinking that's a form of exercise. It's more like a form of torture.

Chelsea: *Alright, if you change your mind before Friday, let me know.*

A knock sounds at my office door, so I lower the phone to my desk. "Come in."

The door swings open and reveals my brother Oliver.

"Hey. Big E."

"Hi." I grumble at his nickname for me. Gram calls me E and he calls me Big E.

Striding in, he closes the door. "I finished my interview with Shyla."

"I just read her write-up about you." I stand up and walk over to make a drink.

"Is it good?" He follows me over to the bar cart.

"Yeah, you'll like it."

I hold up a glass, and Oliver nods.

"Will it help drum up business for opening night?"

I pour two glasses of bourbon into tumblers. "Yeah, she'll create a buzz with this article."

"I need all the art to be sold at auction."

"Your mug on the front page will surely bring in extra eyes."

He beams at me before his brow furrows. "I haven't gotten my photo taken yet."

I hand a glass of bourbon to him. "Why?"

He takes the drink from me and sips the amber liquid before answering. "They're busy at the moment."

I can't understand. This article needs to be finished ASAP. I don't like work strung along; I expect it to be done quickly and efficiently.

Walking back to my desk, I lower my glass with a thud. "Wait a second." I pick up my phone and call Bobby.

He doesn't answer, so I hang up. Irritation prickles my skin.

My desk phone rings, and my personal assistant Gabby informs me Bobby is on the line.

"Hi, Mr. Lincoln," he says when I answer.

"In thirty minutes, I expect someone to take a photo of Oliver Lincoln for his upcoming news article."

"Yes, sir, we just—"

I close my eyes and try not to let my personal feelings about Bobby become too apparent, reminding myself I'm at work. But I can't keep all my irritation out of my words.

"I don't want to hear it. Finish what needs to be done, and he'll be there soon." I hang up after he mumbles his agreement.

"Look at you being all fancy and shit." Oliver snickers, sinking into the chair.

I narrow my eyes at him. "Shut up."

"Make me."

Oliver is more of the goofy, relaxed one. He's the second youngest of the four Lincoln brothers, and he knows how to flirt his way into anything.

"Tell me, what do you need help with for opening night?" I ask.

"Nothing, everything is ready to go. I just need to convince an artist to come."

I frown. "That shouldn't be too hard."

"She won't answer my calls, emails, nothing."

"Hmm, do you need any help?"

"Do you think she'll listen to you? Owner of The New York Press?" He laughs, but before I can ask what's funny, he expands. "I think the problem is she doesn't want to be identified."

"But you said you have a few pieces of hers?"

He dips his head as he straightens across from me. "Yes. Her lines and paintings are something I've never seen before."

"How do you know they're by a *she*?"

"There's a flower in the corner of the picture where the signature should be. No dude is going to do that."

I run my hand over my jaw thinking. "Hmm. You never know."

"Yeah. Either way, I want them at my opening night. I've emailed the person every week."

"What if you keep turning up to the studio?" I offer as I let the bourbon warm me up and calm my Bobby irritation down. Which then easily shifts to thoughts of Chelsea. And how drinking reminds me of what her lips looked like sipping on her glass while drinking my favorite drink.

I must have zoned out because I have to get Oliver to repeat what he said.

"Will I see you at Gram's for dinner tonight?" he replies with a curious look.

I straighten in my chair, refocusing on him. "Yes, and are you coming to poker on Thursday at Jeremy's?"

He drains his glass. "Yeah, but I've practically seen you every day."

My lips roll together as I return my gaze to my computer screen. "Yeah, it's way too fucking much." Jutting my chin toward my office door, I tell him, "Get out of here and get your mugshot taken."

He flashes me a cocky wink. "Sounds like you're bitter, brother."

I sigh, eyeing him over my screen as I answer. "Wouldn't you be bitter if you were almost fucking forty?" *With nothing but a job to make you happy?* I want to add.

He purses his lips in an expression of discomfort. "Now that you say it, that sounds depressing."

I lean back in my chair, crossing my arms over my chest, holding his gaze. "Right? You're a baby at thirty-five."

His lips twitch as he runs his hand through his hair. "Fuck, it doesn't feel like it."

"Being a CEO is never easy, but it's worth it. I promise," I announce as he stands and offers me his hand. I shake it, and he leaves.

I walk over to the window, taking in the city views. Yeah, this is definitely worth it. I have a wonderful family, great friends, and a fulfilling job. Then why am I not happy?

CHAPTER 14

CHELSEA

"DO YOU THINK THIS is the one?" I ask Summer, who is lounging on my bed with her head propped up on her hand.

I stare at her through the full-length mirror, running my hands along the black silk that envelops my body like a second skin. The dress hugs every curve perfectly, the fabric cool and smooth against my flushed complexion.

"Yes, it'll have Evan drooling, for sure," she assures, her eyes sparkling with approval.

"Do you think the neckline is too low?" I question further as my fingers trace the edge of the delicate straps.

"No way. It would be too simple without the diamond strap neckline," she responds confidently. "The diamonds sparkle when they catch the light. It's perfect."

It's brand new; I bought it with Nova and Summer. I trust them, but I'm second-guessing my choice. This event and dress are so out of my comfort zone. I'm used to casual events, not black tie.

"I don't have anything else to wear anyway, and I don't have time to go and get something. I still need to finish my makeup."

Summer sits up on the bed.

I spin around and step barefoot toward my bathroom. "What's it for anyway?" Summer asks.

I put foundation on my face. "He wants to reward his staff for all their hard work." Once I'm finished with that step, I add my concealer next.

"Now that's a freaking boss!" she sing-songs.

An airy laugh bubbles out of me as I pat my undereyes gently with the makeup sponge. "Yeah. I'm taking notes for my studio."

"I'm sure you are going to come up with your own creative ways to make your staff happy."

I hum as I concentrate on my eyeliner next, taking my time due to my shaky hands.

She lifts herself up from my bed, turning to leave my bedroom. "Well, I'll go downstairs if you don't need me anymore."

I turn and blurt, "Wait, help me pick my shoes."

She spins around to face me again, trekking back. "Finish your makeup, and I'll wait for you."

I finish with mascara, bronzer, blush, and my mauve lipstick. It doesn't take long because I wear the same look every day. It's only the eyeliner that is more dramatic tonight.

"Alright, so…" I walk barefoot to my closet and pull out the two stilettos. One black and one silver.

I slip one of each on, then hold up the bottom of my dress and show her.

"The black," she says, pointing without thinking.

"That's what I was thinking too. Thanks," I reply, then slip them on and grab my purse as we head downstairs, awaiting the knock.

Five minutes later, the heavy knock comes, and Summer's eyes flick to mine. She's wearing a smirk and it doesn't help calm my nerves.

They've met before, and I know she thinks he's hot. She wants me to hook up with him, and I wouldn't say I haven't thought about it. But I just broke up with Bobby, and my work life is in disarray. I need to sort myself out and establish a routine first.

She takes a seat on the sofa, peering over it as I open the door. He looks incredible in a black tux and bow tie, his hair swept back with his natural wave tamed. But it's not what has me melting on the spot. It's the smile he's wearing. He barely smiles. So I can only assume that smile is for me. "You look handsome," I blurt out.

His gaze seductively caresses my body as if his hands are on me. When he brings his eyes back up, he announces, "And you look beautiful."

He pushes a bouquet toward me. My mouth opens as I try to get words out. Taking them from his hands, I welcome the warm brush of his touch. I stare at the mix of white roses, white orchids, and a few others. It's stunning. The subtle fragrance hits the air, and it's all tied together with delicate lace.

"Thank you. These are so unexpected," I manage to say after a beat, my voice wobbling slightly.

"When a man picks a woman up for a date, he brings her flowers."

I feel dizzy, not from his words, but from the light they shine on what I've been missing all this time. I've never received flowers from anyone, yet Evan is pretending to date me and brings the biggest bunch I have ever seen. This doesn't feel very fake to me...

His eyes search mine, as if trying to read my thoughts. "Is everything okay?" he asks, concern creeping into his voice.

Suddenly, the bouquet feels heavy. "Yes, everything's fine. It just...no guy has given me flowers before."

His eyebrows knit together, and he takes a step closer, the space between us sparking electricity. "Well, you deserve it," he says. "You deserve so much more."

The sincerity in his words makes my heart skip a beat, and I clutch the flowers tighter, trying to steady myself. The room closes in around us, the air thick and I open my mouth to respond, but the words catch in my throat.

He reaches out and gently lifts my chin so our eyes meet. "You okay?" he asks again, his voice softer now.

I nod slowly, unable to look away from his intense gaze. "Yeah," I breathe, my voice barely audible. "I think I am now."

"Good." Dropping his hand from my chin, I swallow a whimper at the loss.

"Let me put these in water. Come in," I say, opening the door and letting him pass. But he stops at the entry and peers down at me before leaning in and kissing my cheek. His lips are soft, but there's a slight scratch on his face from where he's shaved. I'm weak at the knees when his cologne hits me. It's so good. I want to douse myself in it.

He pulls back, keeping his head close, his piercing eyes focused on me. I wet my lips, feeling the anticipation building.

Summer clears her throat, breaking our eye contact. Stealing our attention.

I close my eyes and curse in my head. Roommates are fun until moments like this, but as much as my body wants him, I can't let my body take over my mind.

He straightens and peers over to the living room.

"Summer is here," I announce in a shaky voice.

He goes silent as his gaze becomes distant. Running his hand through his hair, he pulls away from me. I hope he hasn't withdrawn into himself again.

I close the door when he strides over to her. He says hello and shakes her hand. Her smile widens as her eyes have that awestruck look that only Evan can give when he's fully focused on you. Like you're the most important person in the room. It's compelling and intoxicating.

"Are you ready?" I ask, flicking my gaze from an amused Summer to his bright blues.

"Yeah." He walks toward me and holds out his arm.

"Have fun, you two," Summer says in an amused tone.

"Nice seeing you again, Summer," Evan replies.

I wave at Summer, who winks at me. Shaking my head at her, I walk to the door.

Outside, the air sends a chill down my spine. We approach the car, and his hand on the handle pauses.

"Did you want to go back and grab a jacket?" he asks.

I shake my head. "No. I'd hate to be late."

He stares at me with an unreadable expression before shaking his head.

My stomach drops. "What?" I ask.

"I'm not used to a woman being on time."

I open my mouth to speak, but he cuts me off.

"I don't mean women I date, but you know," he rambles in a fluster, and it makes the corner of my lip twitch. He's cute when he's rattled.

"I get it."

We climb into the car and buckle up as the car begins to move.

It's strange having a driver. I'd never had this experience before I met Evan. I stare out the window, watching the city buildings pass by.

"I like your hair," he suddenly says. I turn my head to face him. My hand automatically comes up to touch it. It's not a new hairstyle, but I guess he usually sees me with my hair up.

"Thanks." Another thing I can't believe he noticed. I guess the shock in my face tells him as much.

"I notice everything," he answers my silent question.

I feel my cheeks tingle with heat. I want to change the subject to something safer.

"How are you feeling? You never came to another class."

"You were serious," he says, eyes bulging with disbelief.

A soft giggle leaves me as I answer lightly, "Yes. I'm serious, it helps."

"I could barely move for days," he murmurs, as if he's still bewildered from the experience.

I sit up, loving the fact that another person has said Pilates is hard. It's way harder than it looks. I couldn't get Bobby to one, so Evan attending a class means something. It proves to me that Evan is willing to take interest in things that are important to me.

The car stops. We unbuckle and get ready to climb out. Evan is already opening my door and holding out his hand.

He's so attentive, and I love it, but now he's raising the bar so my standards for men are way higher.

My hand slips into his, and our touch causes my heart to race. His hand is large, warm, and rough. I let go as soon as I'm out of the car and standing. Our connection is too much right now. I need to concentrate on being a good guest for him. I spot the entrance to the exclusive event space, which is in an historic building in Manhattan. My temperature rises with anticipation, the grandness of the venue adding to the gravity of the night ahead.

Glancing at my *date*, I take a deep breath. This fake dating arrangement seemed like a simple plan at first, but now, standing at the entrance, it feels like so much more. As if I spoke the words out loud, he asks, "Are you ready for this?"

I turn my face toward him, with a reassuring smile.

"Yeah," I reply through a shaky exhale. "Just remember, we're supposed to act like we're crazy about each other."

He chuckles, encouraging me to link my arm through his. So I do, and touching him again is making my insides flip. There's this old-school gentleman in Evan that hits me hard in the chest. "I think I can manage that. Let's go have some fun."

"Okay," I splutter out.

We walk closer to the doors of the grand entrance, and before we walk through, he leans in closer, his lips to the shell of my ear, his warm breath against my ear. "Relax. We've got this."

For a moment, the Manhattan noise is all drowned out, and all I can hear is my heartbeat in my ear and feel his breath on my skin.

I nod, hoping he doesn't notice the slight tremor in my hand. "Right. Just a night pretending."

His hold on my arm tightens slightly, a comforting gesture that sends a shiver down my spine. "Exactly. And who knows, it might even be fun."

His heated gaze grips mine, and for a second, I don't want to go in, wanting to stay alone with him. But he encourages me along.

We step through the doors, and the interior makes my heart race even faster. Chandeliers glimmer above, highlighting sleek modern furniture, and elegant floral arrangements drape from the ceiling. We walk through until we join the crowd inside. Soft Jazz music is playing in the background of the ambient lit room.

I look straight ahead, plastering on a smile, expecting people to be watching us walk in, but it seems every group is too invested in their own conversations. I sigh in relief. Most are dressed in stylish evening gowns and designer suits, holding glasses of alcohol in their hands, while wearing easy smiles. I wasn't expecting this. People seem to be genuinely happy. No one is happy at a work function. Well, not unless you're drunk.

"Let's go to the bar." He's not asking, he's telling me, and I love that because I'd kill for some alcohol just to take the edge off.

A server passes with a tray of delectable hors d'oeuvres, and I grab one as Evan walks me over to the bar's edge so we can be away from prying eyes. A few have noticed him, but he's shaken his head at them. A silent *leave me the fuck alone*, and I have to give it to him, they are following his instructions.

He orders us both drinks, without ever having to ask me what I want.

"I don't expect you to stand by my side the whole night, you know," I say with a crooked grin while we wait for our drinks.

He turns to face me, staring at me for a long moment. I feel naked under his intense stare. When he speaks, I release the breath I was holding.

"I'm not."

I clear my throat before I answer, needing to sound stronger than I feel. I wouldn't mind a second to have a drink and pull myself together. "You can talk to your colleagues, and I can wait here." I point to the spot I'm standing in.

His hand slips to the small spot on my back. "I'd rather hang out with you," he says, like it's the most natural thing in the world, effectively blurring the line of what's real and what's fake.

CHAPTER 15

CHELSEA

I LOOK BACK AT Evan and smile. "Don't blame me if you're bored."

The bartender makes the drink in front of us. He moves around the bar effortlessly in a crisp dress shirt and sleek, fitted vest, while smiling at the few patrons waiting down the bar for a drink.

As soon as he places the drink on top of the wooden bar, I recognize what it is from the other night. *Whiskey business...*

"That should help you." He gazes at me as if he's trying to read me.

"I'm not nervous," I insist.

"You're with me. We're both going to be just fine."

He understands how insecure I am about Bobby's betrayal. Evan knows this feeling all too well.

I stare at him in awe.

The intensity of our stare is intoxicating.

A colleague of Evans interrupts, and as Evan starts a polite conversation, I scan the room. I still feel sick over the fact I'm here to get revenge on Bobby. Why the fuck do I still care? What difference is it going to make? Why is it so important for me to cause him the same pain he caused me?

Just as I think that I spot Shyla with her blonde hair in beach waves and a stunning navy floor-length dress. I can only see her from the side, but I know what she looks like because it's engraved in my mind.

A walking reminder I look nothing like that.

Between the blonde and the redhead, if Bobby has a type, I obviously wasn't it.

I watch Shyla laugh and smile. She's beautiful. I realize I don't feel angry anymore. Even as I stare and watch Bobby slide up beside her and touch her lower back in a *she's mine* type of way. It's not her fault he's sleazy. How about the other night? Did she know he was having dinner with another woman? I suspect not. And knowing how heartbroken I've been, I can only assume she will be too when she figures out the truth.

"Chelsea," Evans says, louder than usual.

I shake my head. "Sorry. I was distracted."

His jaw ticks. "I see."

"It's fine. I knew I'd be forced to confront them. That was the whole point of me coming with you as a date tonight."

He steps closer to me, invading all my senses. My heart beats harder inside my chest.

"It upsets you."

I can't lie to him. "It makes me feel stupid," I say on a breath.

He lowers his head toward mine, and I close my eyes.

"I'll make sure you never feel stupid again."

"Ho–"

He steps closer and drops his mouth onto my lips, then down to my neck, where he peppers soft kisses along the side of it. The heat of his lips sends a shudder down my spine, and my heart races. Is this really happening? My mind spins, trying to catch up with this sudden touch. Once I get over the initial shock, I sink into it. My head tips to the side, giving him more access, and letting the feeling of his lips take over. His hand grabs my hip, pulling me closer, and he growls against my throat, the sound vibrating through me and igniting a fire between my thighs.

Needing to touch him, I reach my hands to his head, threading my fingers through his hair and encouraging him. I'm astonished at how natural this feels, how right. This is supposed to be fake, a performance for everyone else, but nothing about this moment feels staged.

The touch of his warm lips, the tickle of his breath on my skin, it's intoxicating. My body reacts to him in ways I never expected, heat pooling in my core and a dizzying rush of desire. I'm getting lost in the moment, each kiss making me crave more. So when he pulls away, I'm breathless and confused. A sense of loss washes over me, and I want him to continue. It seems he does too. His blue eyes are now dark storms as he stares at me hungrily, his chest rising and falling rapidly.

What's happening to me? This was all supposed to be an arrangement, but every kiss and touch blur the lines more and more. I can't deny the chemistry between us; it's magnetic, and it scares me as much as it excites me.

"So..." He releases his hand from my hip and steps back. It causes my hand to drop.

I take a centering breath, trying to calm the radiating heat on my skin and concentrate on what we were talking about. His gaze moves to the other side of the room.

I follow his line of sight and notice Bobby glaring at us. "Bobby is stupid. He let you go." With a grunt, he takes a big sip from his glass.

Gripping my glass tighter, I shake my head, disgusted with myself. "I can't believe I was in a relationship with him."

"What makes you say that?" He turns back to face me.

But it's my turn to look away. "Because if he can cheat and move on that fast, I never mattered to him."

"At least you weren't engaged to him."

"But I wanted to be," I admit, hoping it makes him feel better about his own past mistake.

"Then it's a good thing you found out before it happened."

I sigh heavily before finishing my drink.

"Let's dance." He cocks his head toward the dance floor.

The energy of the room is more relaxed as the night unfolds; people sway to the beat of the music, holding their drinks under the flickering neon lights. There's a group of people in one corner of the dance floor who are cheering on a guy as he shows off some freestyle moves. In another section, a couple dances alone. The DJ is perched higher than the crowd, illuminated under the lights, the atmosphere in the room is captivating and my hips move on their own. I love what's currently playing. "Do you know how to dance?"

"Yes."

I eye him critically with a smirk.

"My gram taught me."

I smile. "Well, at least one of us had lessons."

I'm not a great dancer, but I have fun trying. As if he can read my apprehension, he says, "I can teach you."

I bring the glass to my lips and tip the rest of the drink down my throat.

He copies and then holds out his arm. Linking my arm through his, we walk to the dance floor.

The music changes to "Photograph" by Ed Sheeran.

We join the small crowd in the middle, and I turn to face him. Our chests collide. My hand goes to his shoulders, and his hands settle on my lower back. We sway to the beat. He moves one of his hands to peel my hand off his shoulder, causing me to frown in confusion. What's he doing?

"Have you ever spun before?"

"No." I smile, knowing I've always wanted a guy to do that with me.

"Follow my lead."

"Just don't drop me."

He gives me a wolfish grin. "I'd never let you down."

My eyes ping-pong between his as my throat constricts. He gently pushes me out, and I spin, laughing when he catches me easily.

His touch, our connection, it's all effortless.

"That was fun."

"Again?"

"Again," I say with a giddy grin.

He does it again before we return to our easy side swaying. Our bodies flush together. Hearts beating as one.

The song ends and another one begins, neither of us wants it to end, so we don't stop dancing and laughing through multiple songs.

"I had no idea you'd be this good. You're full of surprises, Mr. Lincoln."

His gaze makes another shiver run down my spine. His nearness, his touch, his body heat is all too much. The song changes to a slower melody, but neither one of us makes a move to leave. Instead, he pushes on my lower back, pulling me closer to him. His breath hitting my temple stirs intense desire that makes it difficult for me to think clearly.

Evan dances as easy as breathing and I don't want him to stop touching me. So I keep my mouth shut. We continue to dance, no words spoken between us, but our eyes stay on each other as our bodies sway in tune to the beat.

We finally stop once the song ends. Evan's fingers draw circles on my lower back, and I get lost in his blue eyes.

He clears his throat. "I need to make a speech now."

Stepping back, I wave my hand in a go motion. "Go. I'll be here." I point over to the spot near the bar, planning to order another drink, suddenly needing one to cool down.

"No. You're coming."

I frown. "Why?"

"I want you there."

His answer makes my head spin and all that comes out is a measly, "Okay."

He grabs my hand and walks me through the crowded dance floor until we're at the front of the room. I don't miss the looks or the whispering going on around us. Not that I can blame them. It's Evan. They'll want to know everything about me. He's in media, for God's sake.

Stopping, he moves in front of me. His eyes bore into mine, holding my attention as if I could look anywhere but at him.

"I won't be long."

As he turns to go to the stage, I watch his every step. The room silences when he taps the mic.

"Thanks for coming tonight. You all know I'm a man of few words, so this speech will be short and sweet. Each of you are what makes this company amazing. Thank you for all your hard work and the teamwork you demonstrate every day. Enjoy tonight, this is all about you."

I'm smiling from ear to ear. The crowd erupts, and as I take a look around the room. I'm not the only one who is mesmerised by him.

He walks off the stage and strides over to me.

"That was great," I say.

He takes a deep breath. "Thank you. I'm fortunate to have such an incredible team and I'm glad we could honor them tonight."

The music is turned up, and the lights are dimmed.

"Ready for another drink?"

I take it we aren't dancing again.

"Evan, you've been babysitting me all night. I can be alone for a few. You should socialize with your employees."

I feel bad; we're at his work function and he hasn't spoken to more than a couple of people.

"No. I hate socializing."

"But you've been doing that with me all night." I laugh.

"It's different with you."

I don't argue; instead, I welcome his attention. His honesty makes me let go and stop second-guessing his need to be beside me.

"Let's grab a drink. I want to show you some pictures of the studio."

He holds out his arm. I link mine through, even if I'm bummed because I wanted to hold his hand.

We arrive at the bar and wait only a few minutes before getting our drinks.

"Come over here," he says, and we move away from the bar to a seating area.

The tables are arranged so each table has two seats and are at a distance that allows for private conversation, instead of smashed together like most events. I appreciate the break from the crowd.

I sink into the chair, crossing my legs and settling the glass on top of my thigh.

"So, my studio is getting thirty beds. I have ordered the balls, weights and rings, but I want supplements to sell," I say as I show him photos on my phone. As I scroll, it lands on pictures of potential supplement brands.

"Mmm," he murmurs as he drinks.

"I don't know which one to sell. There's so many on the market."

He lowers his glass. "Have you tried any?"

"A few."

"My advice would be for you to never sell a product you can't vouch for."

"My clients might have different needs."

"I have a friend who might be able to help. He's in the pharmaceutical area."

"You have a lot of friends."

He nods and cradles his glass in both hands.

I uncross my legs as I answer. "I'd love help."

His gaze drops to my legs and then slowly tracks back up to my face. "What else are you doing for the studio?"

"I have towels being embroidered to sell, and my signage is being made out of acrylic."

"What colors?"

I'm so distracted by the intensity of his stare, I forget momentarily what we were talking about. "Of what?"

"Both."

I shuffle in the seat, trying to refocus. "I like the neutral tones, so a mix of brown, nude, and taupe."

His eyebrows lift. "The sign?"

"No, sorry, those are for the towels, booty bands, and mats. As for the sign, I'm thinking it should be brown."

"I love how excited you look when you are talking about this."

With a mischievous grin, I tease, "You'll have to take a class there when it opens. Practice makes perfect."

He sinks farther into the chair, leaning to one side with a tilt of his head. "Not happening. I've had my lifetime quota of Pilates."

I giggle. "I know, I'm just teasing. I appreciate you coming to check it out, though. You're the first to come to one of my classes."

"You're fucking kidding me, right?" The rasp in his voice has my belly flipping.

My teeth scrapes along my bottom lip. "No, everyone was too busy."

"Bullshit. No one can be that busy to support their girlfriend." He shakes his head.

"I obviously wasn't a priority," I mumble, unable to hide how small I felt in the relationship. Evan knows exactly what I went through.

"Remind me why you stayed with him so long?"

"He made me believe I wasn't good enough. So that only made me want to prove that I was and that we were great together."

He shakes his head, but his lips turn up. "Promise me you won't believe that again."

I lower my voice. "I promise."

"Good," he says with a crooked grin, his eyes darkening before surprising me by leaning in and kissing my temple.

It feels like the air has shifted between us. I take a sip of alcohol to wet my throat.

He shifts forward on the chair. "Are you ready to leave?"

My pulse picks up pace. "It only started two hours ago and you're the host."

He shrugs and says nonchalantly, "They'll have more fun without me."

"How do you know?"

"I hear all the stories from Gabby."

He adjusts the strap on my dress, sending a tingle down my arm.

"Of course," I breathe.

His tongue skims his bottom lip. "Come on, I'll take you somewhere else."

I twist and glance around the room, but Bobby is nowhere in sight. Not that it matters. I haven't seen him since the start of the night, and the thought of him now feels insignificant. The plan for revenge, the idea of fake dating...it all seems stupid now. The only thing that truly matters tonight is the connection between us. The rest of the world, including Bobby, has faded into the distance.

I lower my glass to the table as Evan stands.

"Let's go." I stand, and he takes my hand in his as we slip out the exit. The cool air is refreshing and instantly wakes me up.

Evan's thumb moves along my hand in a soft pattern. The electricity bouncing between us has been growing all night. Now we're alone. Which means I'm about to test my restraint.

Just before I get a chance to speak, Evan yanks my hand, causing me to spin.

His hand lands on my hip, gripping me tightly. I let out a shuddery breath when his other hand breaks from our hold and slides deep into my hair. "I love your hair."

A slow, easy smile stretches on my face. "Thanks."

He laughs. "You're not used to compliments. I should know."

I frown. "What do you mean?"

His hand skims my face, and I tremble at the touch. "I never received one fucking compliment. But with you..."

"What about me?" I push, pleading to know what he's thinking. We share the same insecurities. Never feeling good enough. Always giving and never receiving.

"You should be told how beautiful you are."

My bottom lip wobbles. "I never heard those words," I admit, my voice barely a whisper.

"I know," he says, his blue eyes locking onto mine with an intensity that makes my heart skip a beat. "And you should've. You fucking deserve to know how incredible you are. Not just beautiful, but smart too."

I'm trembling inside at words I've longed to hear. Is he saying this because he means it, or is this part of the arrangement? I can't help but hold a flicker of hope that this is genuine. But then, why now, when he always kept his distance emotionally?

As if no one else is around, he steps closer, and I follow. We're both breathing hard, and I know he wants to kiss me just as I want to kiss him. My eyes roam his face, taking in every inch of it. There's conflict in his eyes before it's gone and replaced with darkness. As if reading his thoughts, my hands dive into his hair, and he brings his mouth an inch from mine.

"What the fuck is going on?" Bobby's words slice through the air, like a bucket of ice water is poured on us.

With my breath caught in my throat, Bobby closes in on me.

"Step away," Evan cuts in, his tone icy. The command makes my skin prickle with worry, a wave of unease taking over any happiness and desire from just moments ago.

CHAPTER 16

EVAN

I'VE GONE FROM ALMOST kissing Chelsea to her ex wanting to punch me square in the face.

Bobby's hands are curled into fists by his sides.

I'm not a fighter. Even if I've thought about punching him myself, I'd never act on it.

"Why does who I'm with matter to you?" Chelsea says.

Bobby doesn't answer her because he's too busy glaring at me. He finally moves his eyes to her, but instead of looking at her gorgeous face, his gaze drops straight down to her chest. Her exposed cleavage is enticing, but watching him looking at it sends blood rushing to my brain. If I don't calm down, I might get physical for the first time in my life.

"He's my boss," Bobby says, finally bringing his eyes to hers.

So that's the issue. Not the fact he let a good woman go—of course not.

"So?" she replies.

His eye twitches at her.

"Watch how you talk to me," he spits.

The rise and tone of his voice sends the hairs on the back of my neck rising. "No, Bobby, you're the one who needs to think about how you're talking to her."

He's irritated but bites his tongue. He knows he needs to be careful right now or he'll lose his job. I'm past the point of caring. I won't have abusive people working for me.

HR will need to figure it out.

"Why him?" Bobby asks Chelsea.

"It wasn't planned, if that's what you're asking," she says, keeping her voice steady and strong, even though I can tell she's nervous.

"How do I know that? You're going for someone twelve years older," he sneers, his voice dripping with venom. "Are you that desperate, or just looking for a sugar daddy?"

"Don't be pathetic, Bobby. I get it, you're hurt, but let me be real clear, I'm not her sugar daddy. Grow up and stop making excuses."

"You're seeing other women, so why do you care about me?" Chelsea asks.

"I don't."

Bullshit.

"Unless you want me to let Shyla know about your dinner date with the redhead the other day," she says, crossing her arms over her chest.

My lips turn up at that. I'm proud of her. She's not giving in to him.

I want to kiss her again, get her out of my system because I don't want attachments. She's the first person I've connected with in a long time so it's natural for me to want more.

"She's a friend."

"You seem to have a lot of them," Chelsea mumbles.

"I'm not wasting my breath repeating myself to someone who clearly thinks I'm a cheater."

"You are! But I've had enough. Get the fuck out of here and leave us be," I command, unable to listen to any more of his lies.

His face is tight, and I expect some pushback, but to my surprise, he flicks his gaze from mine to Chelsea's before storming back inside.

And fuck, his stomping reminds me of a toddler.

Once he's completely gone from our sight, her eyes come back to mine. A hint of shame settles on her face. "I'm sorry," she murmurs, dropping her crossed arms.

"What are you sorry for?" My fingers brush her arm, which earns me a small smile.

"Bringing this much drama to your work function. I didn't think he'd care this much." Her chin dips again.

My fingers touch her jaw, and she looks up. "That's not your fault."

"It is."

Regret fills her, and I hate that I forced her into getting revenge because of my own past.

"It's mine, actually."

I drop my hand and rub the back of my neck, self-disgust filling me.

She shakes her head. "No, it's not."

"I thought of this revenge idea. This isn't something you'd naturally do. You're kind, and I'm bitter."

She comes closer, and she leans her hands on my chest. My heart beats faster as she stares up at me with her brown eyes.

"No, you helped me realize he was hurting me. I agreed to the revenge and, to be honest, I wouldn't take it back."

"You wouldn't?"

Biting her lip, she shakes her head. "No, I enjoyed hanging out with you. It's the first time I've felt something real."

She means butterflies, and I understand because I have that same feeling with her.

"I like being with you too," I say quietly.

Her face brightens as her eyes grow wide.

I don't want to end tonight here on this note, but we don't want to return to the party.

"Did you want to go do something?"

I want to spend some more time with her before she goes home.

"Can we go back to my studio and order takeout?" she asks.

"Sounds perfect."

I turn, and we walk side by side to the car. I want to hold her hand, but I don't know if she wants to. All my reasons for not wanting a relationship fade away. Because I want her in a way I've never wanted anyone else. There's never been a time I wanted to hold hands, yet with her, I do.

Inside, she makes me feel young again. Light, fun, and as if we're in high school. When Chelsea cares about something or someone, she gives it her all. What would it be like to be on the receiving end of that attention?

It wouldn't be lonely——she sees me, touches me, she could heal me.

Before her, all I was, was a hollow version of myself, and now, I don't think that's true. Since she entered my life, I'm more trusting. From the way she wears her heart on her sleeve, no hidden agendas, and more importantly, no fucking lies. She makes me want to try for the first time in my life.

As I'm in my head, debating what to do, she links her arm through mine.

I tilt my head, and she peeks up at me at the same time. We continue walking, but her face is tight with discomfort. I can't help but wonder if those high heels are killing her feet.

I squat down and say, "Jump on my back. I'll carry you."

She falters, eyes wide. "You're going to give me a piggy-back ride."

"Yeah, why not?"

"That's what a real boyfriend would do," she teases.

I grin. "Exactly. Come on."

She hesitates for just a moment before climbing on, linking her arms around my neck and resting her body against my back. Her warmth seeps into me as I straighten up, and I can feel her relaxing slightly. I walk slowly, feeling her hot breath on my neck, and we continue this way until we arrive at our building. Once I stop, she slides down, I try to ignore that I know she's not wearing a bra and that I could feel her erect nipples as she slipped down my back.

Her hands shake as she opens the door to her studio. Inside, she turns on the lights, which sets an elegant dim glow over the entire room.

Shrugging off my jacket, I sit down on the floor. She tracks my movements with her eyes, and when our gazes meet, she quickly shifts her focus to her phone, clearly aware that I caught her checking me out.

I sit back and watch, her eyebrows pulled together as she's deep in thought. She lifts her head as she sits down opposite me. "Do you eat Thai?"

"I'll eat anything," I answer, leaning back on my elbows, my eyes focused on her.

She orders our food, and while we wait, she shows me Pilates sitting boxes that she needs to order.

"What do you do with those?"

She grins and shifts into a seated position, hands behind her, chest pushed up, knees tucked. Her body looks amazing in that tight dress. I shift to get comfortable and try not to imagine her naked in those positions, but I can't help it. *All the things I could do to her...*

"I'm not flexible enough for that," I rasp, failing miserably to hide my thoughts.

She rolls her eyes. "Which is code for 'I'm scared I'll pull something.'"

My mouth twitches with how spot-on she is.

Her phone chimes, which means the food's here.

"I'll be back," she says, reaching for her purse.

"No. I've got it." I stand and head outside, grab the food, and come back up. As I enter, I take a moment to admire how delicate she looks tonight, lost in thought as she gazes out the windows.

She catches my eye, and it causes the corner of my lips to lift.

"Are you feeling better now?" I ask, sitting back down on the floor. I need to know how she really feels. Bobby said some fucked-up shit to her.

She nods and walks over to join me on the floor. "I'm happy you're here."

I can read between the lines. I'm taking her mind off things. "You know I understand what you're feeling. You don't need to be a martyr."

"I know, but I don't want a pity party." She sighs as if she can relax again.

I remember when I was in her shoes. "But if you had left..."

"I'd be replaying his words. Feeling worse than I do right now."

"He doesn't deserve any space in your pretty head."

Her eyebrows squish together. "What do you mean?"

"We need to replace the shitty memories with new ones."

She squirms at the intensity of my words.

"I would love that." She smiles shyly. "But I'm sure you don't have time."

My stomach hardens at her insinuation that I'm always working.

"I always make time for those I care about."

"But your job is important," she murmurs, lost in thought, I bet unable to fathom someone making time for their family when Bobby made no time for her.

I lean over, grab her chin with my hands, hold her face still, and swipe my thumb across her rosy lips. Her warm breath on my fingers, soft skin, and wild eyes leave me imagining what she'd look like surrendering to me.

Her breath hitches as my hand stays on her chin for a moment longer. "So are my Sunday dinners with my family or poker nights with my brothers. I make time for the people I love," I say in a strained voice, dropping my hand.

My chest rises and falls as anger burns inside me. I'm still trying to wrap my head around why Bobby didn't treat her like the intelligent woman she is. Now she thinks she's stupid, when he was the one in the wrong. I have wanted revenge on my ex, but not in the same way I do when it comes to Bobby. The desire to destroy another person is like acid and so unlike me. The desire to protect Chelsea is taking over. She deserves to be treated like a princess, and I suddenly want to be the knight in shining armor.

I shut down my wayward thoughts about hurting Bobby and be fully present with Chelsea. She deserves my full attention.

"We should've ordered dessert." She sighs as we begin opening the containers of food.

It surprises me she isn't a calorie-counting or no-carb kind of woman like my mom. "You eat dessert?"

"Yeah, I've got a massive sweet tooth."

"So you're not going to be the mom who bakes sugar-free stuff?"

She laughs. "No way. Some of my best memories are of me and my sister helping my mom in the kitchen. I want that for my kids too."

"Same here. My gram was the baker in our family."

"Your mom didn't bake?"

I laugh at the memories of the countless times my mom tried to bake, but her cakes, pies, or lemon bars would end up burnt or dry. "God, no. She's hopeless at cooking."

"At least you have your gram."

"Yeah, but being the oldest of four boys, I was expected to look after my brothers."

"I'm sure growing up with three brothers was—"

"As crazy as you're imagining." I finish her train of thought. Remembering one summer afternoon, I was reading my book when I heard their fit of giggles. I caught them hiding Gramps' false teeth in the cookie jar while he napped in the chair.

"But I bet you're protective of them."

"I'd say I'm the negotiator. Which helped me in business."

"Did you always want to take over your dad's company?"

I shrug. "It just happened."

"How?"

I sip my drink and explain. "He was my role model. I followed him around, so naturally after high school I studied journalism and business management. Then when Gram got older, my dad wanted to be with her more, so he retired and asked me to take over."

"Did you ever think about turning it down?"

"Never. I love what I do, but I think a big part was because I watched him my whole life. I was hands-on, always asking questions, and I was fascinated by it."

She's smiling as if my story is the most interesting thing in the world. I haven't felt like a woman was interested in my story——ever. My family, my money, yes, but never me. It unravels me from deep inside.

We finish eating and I realize it's getting late, and we both have work tomorrow.

"We should go."

She nods, rubbing her eyes and yawning.

I stand and hold out my hand, which she takes and rises. Our touching feels natural now.

"Can I visit your office between classes next week?" she asks, her voice pulling me back to the present.

I twist my body to face her. "I thought you were working?"

"I am, but during my lunch break?"

Her teeth nibble the corner of her lip. Again, she distracts me without trying.

I clear my throat, enjoying her initiative to catch up again. "Sure. I'll check my calendar." I pull out my phone and look at the schedule for next week. "Will one on Tuesday work?"

She scrunches up her face. "My afternoon class starts then."

I nod and look back down to the meeting, and I know I can move it by an hour. "How about twelve?"

"Don't move things around for me."

"I'm not," I lie, swiftly sending an email to Gabby to reschedule the meeting.

"Are you ready to go?" I step closer instinctively, unable to simply say goodbye.

Her hands grip my neck, holding me close and begging for me to kiss her. Her touch triggers a wave of doubt and memories of past betrayal.

But despite the alarms ringing in my mind about trusting people, I'm unable to resist her allure. What is it about her that I can't shake?

She's honest every time I've asked her a question; even the difficult ones she answers straight away with complete transparency. And compared to my ex who used to avoid my questions, or if I think about it, avoided me altogether.

Why was I so fucking stupid not to realize she was sleeping with another man. I didn't see the guarding of her phone, the sudden changes in her work schedule...and the worst was the defensiveness when I asked a simple question like where she was going that night. She'd turn it around on me and make me feel bad for asking. When all I did was care.

I trusted her too easily because I'd known her all my life. We were friends. And now, looking back, it was only ever friendship. I wasn't in love with her. I was in love with the idea of love. When I compare my ex-fiancée to the way I feel about Chelsea, it's like fire and water. Two different elements. Chelsea lights me up from within. I'm attracted to her mentally and physically. I can't get enough of her. We laugh and have fun together. With my ex, she never laughed with me or kissed me like she truly wanted me. My thoughts about Chelsea are so different. I don't think about just being her friend or fake boyfriend—no, it's more than that, which scares the fuck out of me. I see a future with Chelsea, but my emotional walls, built over eight years, seem too strong. It's going to take some more time before I'm ready to take that risk again. These thoughts cause me to keep my head on straight. I clear my throat. "I'll take you home."

She bites her lip and nods, and I can sense the disappointment in her, so this time instead of her slipping her arm in mine, I grab her hand and entwine our fingers.

I turn my head and catch her pouty lips in a soft smile when her hand squeezes mine. My heart aches as we stand facing each other at her studio door, neither of us ready to let go.

We lock up and my driver takes us to her place, where I walk her to the doorstep.

"Thanks for tonight. I had so much fun," she says, her cheeks flushed.

I stare down at her, my lips tugging up as I realize she's nervous. "Same. I never have fun with people like this."

"Work parties will never be the same for you."

"Never." Pulling on her hand, I bring her body close to mine, and as I'm about to give her a goodnight kiss, the TV turns on. Summer must be waiting for her.

I close my eyes briefly as disappointment she's not alone floods me.

She whispers with a tremor in her voice, "I better get inside."

I close my eyes, pressing my lips to her forehead, before I suck in a deep breath and reluctantly pull away from her. "I'll see you soon."

"Goodnight." She disconnects her hand from mine, and I watch her open the door and give me a wave before she clicks the door shut. I leave knowing I'll see her in eighty-four hours, but it doesn't seem soon enough.

CHAPTER 17

EVAN

I WALK INTO THE lobby on Monday morning, closing my eyes and sucking in a deep breath, trying to calm the tic in my neck at the strong masculine odor. Reopening my eyes, I spin around and face Bobby. "Are you here to apologize?"

"Well, yes, that, and something else."

"Let's start with the event. You were out of line."

"I know. I'm sorry."

My eyes narrow at his unfazed expression. Bobby seems too comfortable and agreeable. Uneasiness washes over me, making my skin prickle.

"I shouldn't have had so much to drink."

He didn't seem that affected by alcohol. "Next time, limit yourself if you can't be trusted. Otherwise, you'll have to find another company to work for."

"Yes, sir."

"What else did you want?"

He steps forward, clutching papers. "I've got this article I wanted your opinion on."

One thing he knows I can't do is turn down work. But I need to remember my boundaries and why I hired Shyla.

"You know you're supposed to go to Shyla for help, right?"

"Yes, but she's in a meeting and this is urgent."

All the staff know if they ask for my opinion, I'm happy to share the knowledge and experience that was passed down from my dad. But very soon, I won't be around as much. That's why Shyla is running the day-to-day operations.

"Follow me into my office." I turn and head to the elevator.

I don't speak. Bobby chooses to talk my ear off about his adventurous weekend.

He probably thinks if he opens up, I will too. Only, I won't. I'll remain tight-lipped. Chelsea isn't up for discussion.

We arrive at my office. I take my chair, and he takes the one opposite to me.

He hands over his papers, and I lay them out, my elbows on my desk as I read.

The picture is surprisingly good. When I am done reading, I glance up.

He's got a smug look on his face that I want to wipe off him.

Not wanting to add to his over-inflated ego, I say, "It's good. But I'd move the picture to the right. Other than that, go for it."

I hand back the papers and twist to my computer, ready to begin packing it up.

I'm moving the last few pieces to my new office. I can't wait to have no interruptions.

Out of the corner of my eye, I see Bobby still sitting there shifting awkwardly. "Is there something else?"

"I want to let you know that I've taken your advice and started leaving on time."

"You should've been doing that all along."

I want to add, *you shouldn't have treated Chelsea the way you did. You shouldn't have cheated on her.*

But this is not a conversation I want to have with him.

When he leaves, I recline back in my chair to take a breath before sending Chelsea a text to say hi and that I'm thinking about her.

It's a strange feeling to want to talk to her all the time and see what she's up to.

I still can't shake Bobby and his ultra nice attitude today. It was bizarre. But I don't have time to think about it. I'm meeting up with my brothers after work today to watch the NFL game at a midtown sports bar.

∞

When I get inside the loud and dimly lit bar, I stride through groups of fans wearing jerseys, all cheering or talking to other patrons, and make my way toward the back, where all the wooden tables and chairs are. I spot Harvey first, and then, after a quick scan, I spot the rest of the group sitting together. I give my brothers and friend, Richard, a nod before taking the empty chair.

"What took you so long?" Oliver asks.

"I was stuck at work."

I'm elbowed by Harvey. "You're turning into a workaholic like Jeremy."

I blow out my cheeks. "No fucking chance."

"You haven't missed much," Richard says.

I look at the TV and see the scores for the Chicago Eels, the NFL team we follow. The score is six to zero. Eels are up. I have a good view of a large TV screen from where I'm sitting.

The guys clutch glasses of beer.

"I'm heading to the bar."

It's my way of asking if anyone wants a drink.

"Can you grab me a fresh beer?" Richard says.

I nod.

"Order food while you're there," Harvey adds.

I stand and walk to the bar, ordering drinks for Richard and me. They have a wide selection of beer, wine, and spirits. I pick a bourbon and wings with a side of fries.

Carrying the drinks back over, I settle into the chair and start listening to their work chatter.

The smell of wings, burgers, and fries waft through the air, mingling perfectly with the smell of beer from pitchers being passed around. Lively banter, cheers, and groans add to the excitement of the game. The office is where I have to focus on running a business. It's all serious and quiet. But here, I can chill out, loosen my tie, and enjoy the company of my brothers and friends.

The service is fast, and all our meals are out within minutes of me sitting down. A different selection of burgers, fries, wings and other finger foods.

I enjoy the sweet and salty taste of my wings, dipping them into blue cheese.

"Shit!" Harvey spits.

My hand pauses mid-way to my mouth. I look over to him to see he is grimacing and sliding down in his chair. His eyes are focused all the way across at the crowded bar. Where a group of people are drinking, talking and watching TV.

No one looks familiar to me.

"Hide me," Harvey whisper-shouts.

I lower my wings and wipe my hands on the napkin.

Is he fucking serious?

Hide him where?

He slides himself under the table. I frown wide-eyed at him.

"I'm serious," he seethes.

I bend down to look at him.

"What the fuck are you doing?" I ask.

"My thoughts exactly," Oliver adds.

"Jemima's over there," Harvey announces.

I sit back up and look around.

"Who?"

"The owner of Recaredo Events."

Harvey is in a suit under a bar's table, hiding from a woman. I burst out laughing.

Everyone's heads whip around to me. I know, I know. I never laugh, but I've never seen anything more ridiculous in my life.

When I calm myself down, I ask him, "What does she look like?"

"Long brown hair, bright eyes, and curves for days," he rattles off, and I roll my eyes at how infatuated he is.

"What's she wearing?" I ask when I see multiple women with that description.

"A navy jacket and skirt."

Found her. She's at the bar with a blonde woman, leaning on the bar sipping Mojitos.

"Tell me when she leaves," he whispers.

"Hate to break it to you, but it doesn't look like she's leaving any time soon."

"She just got here and ordered a drink," Richard adds.

"Fucking hell," he says.

We all chuckle and shake our heads.

We've never seen him act this way. His usually cocky demeanor is nowhere to be found.

"Is there another way out of here?" he asks.

Peering around, I look toward the outside area, but he'd have to pass her to leave the bar or to head out back.

"No."

"You can't hide under the table until she leaves," Oliver says.

"I will."

He lifts and peers over at the bar before ducking back under, at the same time hitting his head on the wood.

"Fuck!"

I chuckle again, my eyes becoming misty. I haven't ever laughed this much with my brothers.

Movement has my eyes flicking up.

"Oh shit," I say.

"She's coming over," Richard adds.

"Harvey, is that you?" The woman looks to be in her early forties. She crouches down and Harvey grabs my leg.

I roll my lips together, preventing another foreign laugh.

My brothers and friends are already laughing hysterically.

I guess she got her answer.

"Why are you under the table?"

"You know why," he says.

She tips her head back and cackles. She finds this whole thing just as funny as we all do.

I pop a few fries in my mouth.

He finally pulls himself out. His face pinched tight as he scowls at her. He's a lot taller than her, but she stands proud and eyes him down.

They are standing opposite one another, in an epic staring battle. While we all sit here watching them like it's a TV show.

"Your——" she starts.

Harvey finally speaks quickly, cutting her off. "Let's not talk about it here."

"Why?" she counters, crossing her arms.

He sighs heavily, as if annoyed by this conversation. "This is not the place, nor the time."

Her eyebrow quirks as she looks at the table, clearly unbothered by the audience. "I'll talk to you about this tomorrow." Spinning on her heel, she struts away. He watches her like a lost puppy until she returns to the bar with her friend.

I watch Harvey's face, hard lines form, but there's a softness in his eyes as he looks at her. He doesn't look away until Richard speaks.

"She's feisty. I like her."

Harvey rubs the back of his neck as he takes his seat again. "I don't want to talk about it."

I just shake my head and go back to eating.

My wings and fries are cold now but still just as tasty.

The table resumes chatting and watching the TV screen.

I don't miss the way he peers over in her direction.

She doesn't turn around once to look back at him.

I can tell he wants her. But I also know my brothers are as stubborn as I am.

He's not interested in love right now; he's the playboy of us. But Jemima is different. She's older, feisty, and smart. The opposite type to his usual hookups.

We settle in for the next hour, watching the Eels win.

Before I call it a night, I text Chelsea again. She tells me she has one class left at her old studio.

I decide to surprise her by swinging by and saying hi.

Saying goodbye to everyone, I leave the bar after ordering takeout wings and brownies.

From the bar to the studio, it only takes me fifteen minutes. I wait outside the studio in the corridor, and from my position, I can see her through the glass doors, but she hasn't noticed me yet.

The door opens, and clients leave, smiling at me as they pass.

I clench my jaw when I spot a guy chatting her up. He's physically close. Too close. She laughs. His hand is on her shoulder, and my body tightens. The image of my ex in bed with a co-worker invades my senses. It feels like it's on replay in front of my eyes. Is it happening all over again?

I shake my head. No. Chelsea's different. She's not the same. We aren't together. We have an arrangement.

Then why does this single image before me rattle me and leave me doubting what we share?

He finally leaves, passing me with a nod. I don't move an inch. I don't want to gesture to him.

When the studio is empty, I slip inside.

"Hey," she says with a bright smile, walking over to me.

I hand over the box with wings. It's dented where I dug my finger in when I watched her with the guy. She's completely unaware of the turmoil running through me that I felt from witnessing the guy touching her.

Her lit-up face makes me push it out of my mind. I try to think of all the sweet words she's said to me.

She takes the container, and I pull her closer, my hand drifting to her lower back. I'm unable to stop myself from touching her.

"What's this?" she asks, her voice tinged with suspicion.

"Wings."

"Thanks. Where are they from?" she asks and pulls back, making me drop my hand.

"A midtown bar. I was there with my brothers. Figured you wouldn't have eaten yet."

She opens the box, shimmying a little when she sees what's inside.

"Buffalo wings and brownies. You spoil me."

"Hey, I know how to treat a lady," I say with a wink.

"So you're not that rusty, then?"

I wince and grab my middle as if she hurt me.

She laughs, closing the lid and peering back at me. "Did you want to come in while I finish cleaning up?"

"I can't. I have an early work call, and you need to clean up and get home."

"Oh, sure. Thanks for the food," she says hesitantly, like she's picking up on the *off vibe* I'm giving.

I don't want it to be a big deal so I speak before she can. "I'll see you tomorrow?"

"You will."

I smile and kiss her cheek, inhaling her sweet scent. "Don't stay up too late, wing queen."

"Only if you promise not to dream about wings all night," she teases back.

"Deal. But I can't promise I won't dream about you," I say with a grin.

She blushes, and I wish I could erase my thoughts right now. I want to stay longer, but I just need a moment to get the past out of my head.

The next day, I'm barking at everyone because I'm running late to meet Chelsea. *I hope she hasn't left.*

The car pulls up to my building, and I don't see her.

I get out and walk to the doors. I've already found her number and brought the phone to my ear.

I pull it away instantly and hang up. She's here. And she's wearing another activewear set. Navy blue shorts and a matching crop top. It's fucking distracting. No wonder I'm extra cranky today. Well, with everyone else...

"Hi." She smiles.

"Your hair is different."

Her hand glides along the top of her head. "Yeah, I pinned my bangs back."

Her bangs are still there. I like her bangs.

Standing here, I realize I missed her and those beautiful eyes. The ones that short circuit my brain. And it hasn't even been a day since I've last seen her.

"I like your suit."

A deep chuckle vibrates from my chest.

"I always wear suits."

"My favorite was the one you wore at the work party," she says, a flush rising from her chest to her cheeks.

I nod in recollection of that night. It was the first time I held her in my arms as we danced. It's been a long time since I embraced a woman. The desire to hug her right now burns within me.

Last night, I had my hands and lips on her. So why can't I do it again today? I'm acting like a fucking teenage boy talking to his first girlfriend.

That's how she makes me feel. Youthful, fun, and wanted.

"You ready?" she says, snapping me out of my thoughts.

She claps her hand together and smiles. "Yes. I can't wait."

She's so bubbly and vibrant. It can't be because of me, because no woman's mood has lifted from my presence; if anything, it has always done the opposite, as if I annoyed them. I push away my wayward thoughts and concentrate on why she's here.

We walk to the elevator, and I expect the comfortable silence, but she clearly has other ideas.

"You said you had an interior designer help you."

"I chose the pieces and colors. But I had help getting it here and setting it up."

She hums, twirling a piece of hair from her pony with her fingers. "I think I'll need that."

"I could give you her number. She'll look after you. Just mention my name."

She gives me a playful wink. "The connections."

I give her a subtle smirk back.

The doors open on the top floor, and we exit the elevator.

I let her go first so I can watch her take it all in. Her eyes scan the room with a slightly open mouth.

"You have a full kitchen," she gushes, running her hands along the commercial grade appliances. "Wow, this stovetop is incredible."

I'm blown away too. I have everything I asked for in this office.

She ambles along the floors, and I follow beside her. The way I gaze upon the completed work with her adds an extra layer of excitement to the experience. Her energy today is magnetic.

We look in the kitchen, full bathroom, meeting rooms, and spare desks. One is for my PA—Gabby—if she needs to work from here and not at the other office.

"Look at the view," she mumbles, walking to the window to the side of my desk.

"It's beautiful from here."

I lean against my desk, watching her stare at the city skyline.

To me, *she* is the view. The most beautiful view.

I stay silent as she scans the city. My gaze dips over her body. No matter how many times I've seen it, it's never enough. Worse since I've held her.

I bring my gaze back to her face, taking in her delicate nose, parted pouty lips, and lashes that show off her soft brown eyes. Her tied-up hair allows me to get a good look at her slender neck. Heat surges through me as I imagine my mouth on her throat again. Over that beating pulse, I can see in her neck...

She turns around and pinches her lips together as she wanders over to me.

Sitting beside me, she runs her hand over the wood. "This is a big desk."

I move so my hip leans against the desk.

"Custom-made."

"Is it sturdy?" she asks with a smirk.

I drop my eyes over her exquisite body again. "Let's test it out."

Her hand reaches out to grab my tie, an eyebrow raised in curiosity.

She tugs hard on it, encouraging me closer.

She's bold today.

I don't hesitate, grabbing her by her waist, lifting her effortlessly so she sits on my desk. I study her face as I part her legs and step between her thighs. Holding on to my navy tie in one hand, she leans back on the other. Her rich scent fills my nose. It draws me in. And I do what I've been wanting to do since I saw her today. My mouth advances to her neck, and I lay a kiss there, where her pulse thumps under my lips. The fast and hard rhythm matches my own.

I proceed to kiss her neck slowly. She pants as I continue peppering her with warm kisses until I reach the base of her neck. When I pull back, I find her eyes heavy with lust.

Her rosy mouth begs to be kissed.

Fuck it. I'll have her this one time. I lean forward and encourage her to lie back...

"Hey. Oh, shoot." Oliver walks in just as I'm about to spread her out on my desk.

I jump away and my heel connects with the chair. Double fuck.

The pain shooting in my Achilles reminds me how annoying brothers can be. But it's not his fault I left the door unlocked.

"I'll come back later," Oliver says, turning his head.

Oliver is always busy, so if he's here, he probably needs something. I can't turn away a brother.

"Oliver. Wait," I shout, stepping back to help Chelsea sit up. I adjust my tie as she slips off the desk to stand. Her cheeks are flushed, and she looks out the window, avoiding eye contact with me. A soft sigh leaves my mouth. I almost had her.

He stops at the doorway and turns around with some hesitation.

I nod in a 'it's fine, come back' way.

Oliver's shoulders drop. Yeah, he needs to talk to me about something.

"I-I've got to get back to my class anyway," Chelsea says.

"I can walk y——" I offer without thinking. I hate the thought of her walking alone.

"No. Stay. I'm fine," she cuts me off with a wave of her hand.

I glance at my watch. Shit, she's right. Even though I want to, I can't. I have a video meeting too, but Oliver will fill the final ten minutes.

Staring at her in an 'are you sure?' kind of way, she laughs, shaking her head before she lifts a gentle hand to my cheek.

"I'll talk to you soon."

She pulls away, and my jaw tics from her touch on my face.

"Nice to see you again, Oliver," she says as she walks her way to the elevator, and it's not until the sounds of the doors closing does Oliver bring his gaze to me and walk farther in.

His eyebrows rise. "Looks like I interrupted something..."

"I don't wanna talk about it," I murmur, looking down and fixing the papers that we moved on my desk. "I have ten minutes, and then I have a meeting to get to."

He smirks. "I'll make this quick, then."

I sit in my office chair and try not to linger my gaze to where Chelsea was reclining with her thighs apart. I was so close to finally kissing her again.

"I've got this gallery I want to buy, but the owner is old school and thinks I'm a young guy who plays the field and only pretends to be interested in art."

"And?" I encourage, wanting him to get to the point as quickly as possible.

"I'm thinking of asking Karley to pretend to be my wife until I get the gallery."

I exhale. "You mean your best friend's sister?"

"She's smart, pretty, and she knows a lot about art."

I snort. "She hates your guts."

He shrugs. "I'm willing to pay her."

Is he kidding? "She'll slap you if you say that."

"You think?"

"You're an idiot sometimes. Just be honest with her and tell her the truth."

I bet she gives him a hard time. But I keep that piece of information to myself.

His eyebrows pull together. "And she'll just do it?"

"Yes, but I bet she makes you pay for it in return."

He sighs heavily. "This gallery is important to me."

"Why?"

"It's the biggest one in New York. It will finally get my name taken seriously."

I frown. "And it isn't already? We're the Lincolns."

"Not in Art." He sits up, a discouraged look on his face.

"I'm the CEO of The New York Press."

He shakes his head. "I'm not talking about newspapers. I'm talking about the art world. Auctions are huge there."

"Well, I guess you better sweet talk that enemy of yours," I say with a pause. "And maybe her brother."

He winces. "He won't allow me to fake marry her."

"Maybe you have your answer, then."

"I have no other options and I'm running out of time."

"I'm not worried about him."

Oliver tilts his head, not understanding my insinuation about me being worried about her. But I now have no more time. He has to leave. "Good luck and try not to hurt her again."

"It was one time."

I touch my temple. "Women remember everything."

"You think?"

I roll my eyes at how young he really is sometimes. "I know. Now let's get out of here. I have a meeting. Make sure you keep me updated."

He leaves, and I take a second to breathe from that heated moment with Chelsea. She put herself out there, and, *fuck*, I wanted to finish what she started on my desk. I'm still trying to control my racing heart and cool down before this meeting.

CHAPTER 18

CHELSEA

I ADJUST THE STRAP on my tank top, feeling the warmth of the day mixed with a hint of freshness that comes in May. I am currently trying to convince Colby, a dear friend, to join my new team. I'd like to make sure all my employees are also my friends. My previous boss, Colette, did that, and it worked well. The team members were more willing to help in times of need and they also worked harder.

We reach the building's entrance where I show him how to gain access. Once inside, I pause by the elevator doors.

"What hours are you interested in?" I ask, my hand hovering over the elevator button.

I'd like to have a mix of male and female trainers. Who can offer a variety of intensity and styles. Offering diverse trainers and classes will differentiate my studio to others.

"I'd prefer a minimum of three hours, so three classes when I'm on the roster."

I nod, considering his preference. "I can do that."

"What are you offering for weekends?"

"I'd prefer to roster people who want them."

"That would be great. I'd prefer to keep my weekends free to visit my partner, but I'm willing to cover for others when needed," Colby replies with a smile.

His affectionate look is contagious. It's that look that fuel's my desire for love, weddings, and parenthood.

"Long distance?"

He nods.

That sounds challenging. I'm not sure I could handle a long-distance relationship.

"I'll schedule you Monday through Friday," I decide, pressing the elevator button. Noting it's on the top floor, I wonder for a second if Evan's up there. What's he doing?

I shake off my daydream. I'm unfocused because it's been less than twenty-four hours since I last saw him. And I miss his voice, his spicy scent, and his heated touch that makes my knees weak.

When the doors open, I step inside on instinct.

"What floor?" Colby asks, when I haven't pressed a button.

I'm pulled back into work mode. "Sorry," I say, reaching forward to press the second floor.

Just as the doors begin to close, a hand reaches out.

A smooth, deep voice penetrates the air, causing my knees to buckle. "There you are, Shell baby."

Evan.

I turn to see him enter the elevator, dressed sharply in his crisp black suit. As I bite the corner of my lip, I watch his eyes narrow at Colby, not looking at me yet. His focus on the twenty-something-year-old man standing beside me is intense. A man I have zero attraction to. But Evan can't read my mind. He won't know why Colby is actually here and going upstairs with me. Colby visibly shrinks under Evan's intense scrutiny.

To put both men out of their misery, I speak. "This is Colby——"

Evan moves beside me, his hand snaking across my lower back and pulling my body into his. His muscles are coiled tight. But his strong hand and affectionate touch is welcomed. I don't think I will ever get sick of it. When you've needed and craved it for so long and to finally have it makes it hard to push away. Despite the unprofessionalism of the situation, I struggle to fight the craving I have for him.

I'd normally play along or get mad at his possessiveness, but I'm aware of his past. Evan needs reassurance; his lack of trust still weighs heavily on him, and it breaks my heart that he went through that.

"This is Colby. He's looking at the studio because he's a new trainer I've hired. We met during our Pilates course."

Evan nods, drawing in a breath through his nose but keeping his eyes narrowed on Colby. "Nice to meet you. I'm Evan Lincoln."

Colby reaches out and shakes Evan's hand, his shoulders dropping away from his ears. He doesn't seem to be intimidated by Evan anymore. Instead, his eyes shine with awe.

"Evan from The New York Press, right?"

Evan gives him a curt nod, still not entirely comfortable with Colby. "That's me."

Colby beams. "Nice to meet you."

"My office is in this building too," Evan adds, like he needs Colby to know that piece of information. It's Evan's way of subtly warning Colby that he's keeping an eye on him. Or both of us? I shake off the idea; Evan shouldn't distrust me because I've given him no reason to. "Have you seen the studio?" Evan asks.

"Not yet," Colby says.

"I was getting to that," I interject, tilting my head to gaze up at Evan and giving him a silent warning.

Evan dips his head to bring his face close to mine. His hot, minty breath tickles my face. "Did you want to have that meeting we never finished after you're done showing Colby around?" He's staring at me through his dark lashes with a mischievous glint in his eyes. I know what he's insinuating, and a new ache stirs within me.

I should say no...

I let out a shaky breath. "I'm working."

He quirks an eyebrow. "Afterwards?"

I ignore the flip of my stomach and give him a playful wink. "Maybe."

The meeting with Colby is over. He took his contract to read over at home after I gave him a tour of the studio. He loved the place, and even offered to teach mat Pilates and yoga if it was something I wanted to offer. I would love that, so we talked about the layout and how many clients we could fit in a room for yoga.

I made a note to order more mats and any other accessories, like blocks that Colby suggested.

He was a great help, and we came up with some good ideas. He also recommended another trainer who would be a great fit. I tell him to share my number and have the person contact me. I have more interviews scheduled this week, but the more options, the better. I need additional staff for casual shifts.

Before I know it, half an hour has passed. I walk Colby downstairs, and as I wait by the elevator, I remember the way Evan grabbed me and called me *Shell* baby. I find myself grinning, strangely loving his possessiveness. I never thought I'd be into it, but with Evan, it feels right. Maybe it was because in my last relationship I was so out of control. With Evan, I willingly surrender the control because I trust him wholeheartedly to not hurt me. It's both refreshing and sexy.

As I step into the elevator, my phone chimes. I pull it out, expecting it to be a delivery update, but it's Bobby. I ignore it because I have zero interest in talking to him.

Another ping has me exhaling heavily. It's the delivery of towels and signage, but my jaw hits the floor when it says it's been delivered and signed for.

I rub my forehead, wondering where it is. There's been nothing left outside the studio door except a bouquet of roses, but I need my delivery for the opening, so I go back to the ground floor, and nothing is there either. When I go back up and pick up the roses, I notice the thorns are still intact and arranged perfectly. Putting them in the corner, I read the note. "Thinking of you, always."

I don't know who sent them, but I'm sure I'll figure out which family or friend sent them. My concern right now is finding my delivery.

I call the company, who puts me on hold. When I'm finally off hold and talk to someone, they tell me it was delivered to another studio, which I haven't heard of, but I tell them that's not where it was supposed to go. They can see that it's their error for not checking identification, and tell me they will try to fix it urgently.

My heart is in my throat. I need these on time. I don't want any problems with my studio opening.

A knock at the door interrupts my thoughts. I move on autopilot to open the door. Evan is standing there with a concerned expression. I completely forgot about meeting him. Time got away from me.

I force a smile on my face. "I'm sorry. I got held up with work."

His gaze shifts behind me.

I step aside to let him in.

"Working on?" he asks.

I glance around the room, but my mind races too slowly to think of a convincing lie.

"Something's wrong."

I wave off his concern. "Nothing is wrong." I walk toward my laptop, and power it on, avoiding his penetrating gaze. I can feel it burning a hole through my head.

Leaning forward, he grabs my chin and locks his accessing eyes with mine. "No, something's up." He gestures toward the chairs.

I exhale deeply, and my cheeks puff out with force. Knowing I won't win this argument, I lower my head, breaking his hold, and take a seat.

He settles opposite me. "Tell me what happened," Evan insists, dragging my chair closer to him.

I lace my fingers, keeping my gaze fixed on him.

"My delivery was mixed up and they sent my sign and towels to another studio in another state," I explain, but I must look like a mess because his nostrils flare, and my heart pounds rapidly in response.

"It might be faster to order new ones, or I can get someone to pick them up from the manufacturer. Do you want my helicopter?"

"No, they are making the job urgent. It should be here in time," I assure him. I can't believe he'd even offer to use his helicopter. Before I can thank him for that, though, his eyes flick to the roses.

"Who are they from?" And that rules out him buying them.

"I don't know."

"Bobby?" he asks, and then clenches his jaw.

"No. He never bought me flowers, and definitely never nice roses from a florist," I reply without hesitation, gripping his hands, hoping he believes me. His gaze holds mine, the connection between us so strong it's palpable.

"It could be Nova. She loves roses," I say.

He nods. "True. Do you have anything else you need to do here?"

I shake my head. "Not right now."

"Do you want to come back to my place?"

As much as I want him sexually, I'm exhausted. There's been so many changes recently that I just want to curl up on my sofa.

"I don't know…"

"Not for that. To relax. I'll make you a drink."

"Okay, one drink."

He gives me a wolfish grin before withdrawing one of his hands to grab his phone, quickly typing before putting it away. "Let's go."

Rising, he pulls me up with him, our bodies facing each other. We share a moment, simply staring at each other, until his phone rings. The electricity bounces between us but the notification snaps him into action.

He grabs my bag and begins to pack it. "Did you want to bring your laptop?"

I lift an eyebrow. "Do you want me to work?"

"No, definitely not."

"Then no, it can stay here. I can work tomorrow."

He loops my bag over his shoulder. "Ready."

As we take the elevator down, his hand stays on the middle of my back, then moves along to hold my hip. It's a soft, subtle touch that melts me inside. Arriving at the car, he opens my door. I can't deny the giddiness warming my chest at such a simple gesture. I'm loving every moment of his attention. When you've never had this before, it feels incredible. This attention could be addictive.

I slip into the back seat and realize I'm heading to his house. I wonder what it's like. I bet it's spacious, clean, masculine, organized.

"Good evening, sir," the driver greets Evan.

He dips his head. "My place."

Inside the car, the air is combustible. I sink into the leather, and my body suddenly grows heavy.

He leans over, his face close to mine, and my breath hitches. *What's he doing?* My gaze drops down to his lips before locking eyes with him again, heart racing. His lips curl into a smirk as if he can read my thoughts.

"Your seat belt," he murmurs, his voice low and his eyes dark and hooded. His breath brushes against my skin, sending a jolt of heat through me.

I blink, trying to steady myself. "Right," I manage to say, snapping out of my daze.

"What were you thinking about?" he asks.

His head is still close to mine. If I lean forward, our lips would touch. I resist the temptation, as thrilling as it may be.

"Your house. I wondered what it looked like inside."

"And what are you picturing?" he asks, his presence both suffocating and hypnotic.

I think about his office and rattle off the words that come to mind. "Grand, masculine, simple."

He moves his head close to my ear, the heat of his breath warm against my skin. I swallow, feeling a shiver run down my spine.

"You'll see soon enough...nothing about me is simple."

My lips part, and I'm getting ready to respond, but he moves away, reaching for the seat belt to buckle me in. As his fingers brush my body, the touch sends shock waves through me, and as he pulls his body away from mine, I shudder from the sudden cold, longing for his closeness again. He sits back and settles beside me.

I shift my gaze to the window, lost in the pretty city lights in the sky and the buildings, trying to distract myself from being in close quarters with Evan, unable to touch him. Fingers brush against my thigh, and I startle, turning to meet his pinning gaze.

My head drops to find his large hand resting on my thigh. I've never had this before——a step into foreign territory. My body is igniting into an inferno. He's not moving, but his fingers do, trailing higher up my leg. I suck in a new breath, close my lips quickly together, and concentrate on breathing. I'm not going to come in this car. He hasn't even touched me yet, but I'm already feeling jittery.

Luckily, the drive is quick, and when the car stops beside a Central Park tower, my eyes bulge.

Let's talk about being right. It's exactly what I was thinking——simple and manly.

When his hand disconnects from my thigh, I whimper.

Suddenly needing air, I move quickly, unbuckling my seat belt and opening the door, but he's faster. He pulls the door the rest of the way open and helps me get out. "It's my job to get the door," he says, his eyes telling me how serious he is.

I climb out, and the crisp night air hits me, instantly waking me up. Ignoring the chattering of my teeth, I step out and take in his sleek, modern material residence. Floor-to-ceiling glass windows wrap around the structure, giving the best panoramic views of the city. It makes me eager to get inside his place.

"I'm sorry..." The words start to fall from my lips.

"Don't be sorry. It's been a long time since I——" His eyes flick to his door, then he closes it and walks me through the house. But I want to know what he was going to say.

"Since you what?"

"Since I've looked after a woman." His voice is soft and unsure, which is surprising for him. He clears his throat and changes the subject. "Let's go." Tugging my hand, he leads me inside. I wave to the driver, who gives me a small smile.

Inside the elevator, he presses the penthouse button.

"You're on the top floor," I whisper.

"I own the entire building."

Tilting my head, my mouth parts as I blink rapidly at him. The differences in our lives hit me. The money and power he has never bothered me before, but now I'm wondering if I'm enough to keep up with his world.

"No one else lives here?"

He squeezes my hand. "No."

I turn to face the doors as they open, and we step out and enter his lavish penthouse.

CHAPTER 19

CHELSEA

STEPPING INTO HIS HOME, I take it all in. Wow. It's exactly what I imagined——grand, beautiful, my dream home. I could imagine watching all my crappy shows on that sofa.

"Is it what you pictured?" he asks.

"Better. My dream is to buy a place of my own."

"What would it look like?"

"Wooden floors, a big open kitchen, and a comfortable sofa."

"So, exactly like this?" He points to the room with a chuckle.

I laugh and look around at the simple modern house with big furniture, but it's lacking vases, photos, decorative plates, figurines, or collectibles. I want more of a lived-in feel; this feels a little too clean and staged.

"You don't have family photos around," I say, scanning the furniture and walls for one.

"No, I don't."

"Why?"

He shrugs. "I haven't gotten around to it."

I gasp, shaking my head at his confession. "You need to add some of your personality in here."

"I bet your house is full of knick-knacks."

"This may surprise you, but I'm not a hoarder. Just normal stuff, like photos on the TV console, beside my bed, and on the walls."

"I have a handmade poker table."

I snort. "That's not the same."

"My mom has a lot of keepsakes around the house."

"What about a drawing or painting from school?" I ask, remembering my parents sticking mine and my sister's all over their fridge, and my bedroom wall was covered with posters of my favorite bands.

He shakes his head. "I guess she threw them out."

I suck in a sharp breath. "Brutal."

"I guess now that I think about it. But at the time, it didn't bother me."

"I want my kids to be surrounded by pictures and art-work."

He scrunches up his face. "Why?"

"To make them feel special."

He strides to my dream kitchen and peels off his gray suit jacket, slinging it over the stool. I can't help but notice how well-fitted the white shirt is, showing off his strong shoulders and tapered waist. He pulls at his tie, and the way he tugs at it makes my mouth suddenly dry. I try to clear my throat as I walk to the marble island counter.

"Do you want a drink?"

I nod. "Please."

He pulls his tie free and tosses it on the stool with his jacket before moving around his kitchen effortlessly. I haven't moved, too transfixed by him. A man in a suit in the kitchen makes me all hot and bothered.

While he makes the drink, I look over the marble floors, to the custom chandelier in the living room that casts a beautiful warm glow throughout the place.

"Do the other floors look like this?"

"No. Some are more modern than others."

"Did you want to see them?" he asks, passing me my glass.

I take a sip, enjoying the smooth burn. "One day. But can I get a tour here?"

He inclines his head, and I follow him, wandering to the dining room that could host the most elegant of dinner parties. It has the same sophisticated high ceilings, artwork, designer furniture, that I'd seen in the entry, kitchen, and living spaces.

We stop inside the master. His room. My eyes go immediately to his bed. The creams, white and soft browns keep it modern yet cozy. No words are spoken. I can only hear the fast beat of my heart in my ears as I see his private space. It's a sanctuary of comfort and indulgence. My feet automatically move to the floor-to-ceiling window framing the most breathtaking view of the city. I've never seen it from a place like this. Imagine going to sleep and waking up to it. But would the view be this or him? I sneak a peek of Evan from the corner of my eye, noticing he's watching me.

He walks me to the bathroom that resembles a spa, with a deep-seated tub and a large shower.

"Incredible," I say, turning my head back to face him.

He sips his amber liquid, his eyes a sea of torment, dark and hungry. But before I can speak, he says, "Let me show you the terrace. The view's even better out there."

We step out, and it's an outdoor oasis. An infinity-edge pool, surrounded by lush trees and flowers in full bloom, adds subtle color to the area. But the green and white flowers stand out the most. Elegant and so romantic.

I soak up the city lit up in the night sky.

Sipping my drink, I welcome how my muscles have loosened from the stress I had earlier today. I appreciate the scenery and the simplicity of being here with Evan. He doesn't know it, but he soothes me. I don't know if it's the same for him.

"You ready to watch a movie on the sofa?"

My lips curl into an easy smile. "Definitely."

We stroll back the same way and pass spare bedrooms and bathrooms. It's much larger than I had expected.

"I'll order us some food."

My stomach growls. I hadn't realized the time. It's six o'clock. "Sounds good."

I take off my shoes, lower my glass to the coffee table, and sit on his luxurious cream sofa, letting out a groan. "It feels like I'm on a cloud."

Lowering his glass next to mine, he comes to join me on the sofa. I expect him to sit near but not close. So my mouth opens wide when he sits beside me, so our thighs are touching.

He turns on the TV, and the speakers surround us, giving us a cinema experience. At least it provides me with a distraction.

"What should we watch?" he asks as he scrolls through the options, and a movie catches my eye. "*The Hangover*?"

He sets it up. "How about Chick-fil-A?"

After the initial shock that he——a billionaire——is offering me Chick-fil-A, I reply, "Good choice."

"What's your order?"

"A chicken sandwich."

"Did you want to share waffle fries?"

"Only if you order some Chick-fil-A sauce."

He grins, but it's the soft expression that has me leaning back into the sofa, with a tingle growing on my cheeks.

"It'll be a while because of traffic. Let's start the movie while we wait."

"You don't need to work?"

I could watch the movie by myself.

"No, it's a classic. I'm watching it with you."

I can't stop the way the smile stretches across my mouth.

The movie begins, and a content sigh leaves my mouth. My legs curl up on the sofa, and I lie back. He grabs a throw and covers my legs with it.

"Thanks," I whisper, smiling up at him.

He settles back into the couch, and his arm drapes over my body, pulling me close. My head rests on his chest. It's strong, hot, and the beat of his heart is calming. His spicy scent is familiar, and when he tickles my back in soothing circles, my eyelids grow heavy. I fight against them, wanting to enjoy the moment, and dinner will be here soon. But I can't fight it. I surrender and fall asleep.

I gasp for air from a nightmare, sitting up in the darkness of the night. I blink awake and take in my surroundings. Where am I?

My vision settles on Evan's body sitting in the chair, clutching a drink. He's still in his clothes from earlier. I'm in his bed.

But he's on the chair?

I rub my eyes, thinking I'm still asleep.

"What happened?" His voice is gravelly and definitely real.

I peer down and see I'm still in the same clothes. He must have carried me here.

"Just a silly nightmare."

One where I'm alone without my business, husband, and kids. I'm old, sad, and very single.

"Must have been bad to wake you."

"Life problems."

That I really want to forget...

His dark eyes stay on me as he dips his head. He gets up, turning away, and my heart lurches.

"Wait."

He pauses midway to his bedroom door.

I scramble off the bed and stand in front of him. Grabbing his glass, I take a big sip of the bourbon, enjoying the warmth it brings.

I ask him a question that I've wanted to know but haven't been brave enough to ask.

"Has it been eight years since...everything?" I ask, suddenly shy.

He scratches his cheek. "Is this what your nightmare was about?"

"No. I'm just curious..."

His eyes narrow, and he exhales. "Yes. Doesn't mean I haven't gotten off in eight years. But no, I haven't been with a woman since her. You wouldn't understand since you've been with someone."

"Well...shit...this is pretty embarrassing," I mumble, taking another sip of his drink.

He's staring blankly at me, waiting for me to answer. He likes the truth, and he's about to get it. It's quite embarrassing for me, but if he's willing to tell me he hasn't been with a woman in years, I can tell him about my situation.

"The truth is, Bobby hasn't gotten me off for a long time. He tried. Well, most of the time," I continue with a wince, "it was easier to pretend."

He takes the glass from my hands, tipping back the rest of the drink. I've probably disappointed him because he doesn't appreciate liars. But I loved Bobby, even with all his flaws. In the end, I tried to avoid sex at all costs. I'm not proud of myself. I just did it on my own afterwards.

He moves to lower the glass on the table where a half bottle of bourbon sits.

I beg one last time. "I need you to help me forget about it."

He twists back to me. "I can't," he says with a pinched expression and runs his hand over his face. He's fighting himself.

"Why?" I ask softly.

As his eyes pin me in place, my breath catches in my lungs, and he steps toward me. "One touch would never be enough."

My eyebrows pinch together. "What do you mean?"

"Once I touch you, I could never let you go."

His eyes sweep slowly over my body, soaking me in. He likes what he sees. I work hard for it, so it's nice having my body be enjoyed by someone other than me. I know he's attracted to me just as much as I am attracted to him. The whole fake dating was just a drunk decision because the attraction was always there. Nothing between us has been fake.

"Then don't," I breathe out.

A dark rumble leaves his chest. "You don't know what you're asking for."

"Yes, I do. I want you."

He squeezes his eyes shut before they meet mine and the deep pools staring back at me are conflicted.

"Shell," he warns.

"Make me forget," I'm close to begging now.

"Last chance," he says through a tight jaw.

"Please." My heart thuds powerfully in anticipation.

His eyes glow with a savage inner fire as he stands in front of me. "Fine, but there's been something I wanted to do since the first moment I watched you drink whiskey."

I tilt my head with a pitched brow. "You d——"

He swallows the rest of my words when his mouth meets mine. Our lips move with ferociousness. His tongue glides along my lips, and I part them instantly. I whimper when our bodies touch and his tongue twirls with mine. He's no longer a temptation; his real, strong body against me feels amazing. His lips move against mine in a perfect rhythm, so delicate. I had never guessed he would be delicate, yet at the same time take control. My lips follow his movement with perfect synchronicity.

He pulls back slowly, seductively, commanding. It offers so much promise of what tonight could bring. As his eyes collide with mine, they're dark and feral. "The taste of bourbon in your mouth makes me wanna drown you in it, then lick it from your body."

The words cause goosebumps to scatter across my skin, the promise tempting. I can picture it in my mind. God, I want that too.

I raise my eyebrow and play along. "Only if I can do it too."

He shakes his head as he grips mine with both of his hands and kisses me again. A deep, guttural growl leaves his throat on contact. One of his hands on my hip and the other on the back of my jaw keeps me in place. The thumb sliding along my jaw sends tingles down my spine and pools of heat between my legs.

As his hands slip from my head down over my neck, I shiver from the touch of his thumb against my throat. My skin remembers his fingers, and I expect him to stop there, but he doesn't. His hand slips down along the side of me, and I inhale sharply when he skims the side of my breasts.

My skin is hot from just his caress over my clothes. I want him so badly it hurts. Our tongues continue to swirl together as my fingers slide into his hair, the hair I've daydreamed about touching. I run my hands through it, curling and tightening, egging him on. His hand moves to my lower back, and he pushes me flush against him.

He's breathing heavily. "So, this is the first time for both of us in a long time."

"Are you warning me that it's not going to last?"

His fingers move to my face, bringing my chin closer to his. His eyes suddenly turn serious, pinning me. Instantly, my body wakes up.

"There's no way you'll be leaving here without a real orgasm."

The promise hits me hard, and I blurt out, "I promise, I'll never lie to you." If one of his kisses leaves me gasping, I can't imagine what it'll be like to go further together.

"I can read your body if you lie to me anyway." He smirks confidently. "And baby, once we start, I'm not going to be able to stop. So I'll ask you again, are you sure about this?"

He is so compelling that, on instinct, I inch forward, impelled involuntarily by my own passion. "I've never been more sure of anything in my life."

It's one of the things I enjoy about Evan. He's not cocky; he's confident. To the outside world, he's quiet and cold, but to me, he is anything but.

My need for him is beyond desperate. I tug his shirt out of his pants and undo his buttons one by one, starting from the base until his chest is exposed.

Humming at the sight before me, my hands glide over his strong warm chest and down over his stomach. The dark hair is trimmed. His body is strong with a hint of softness that reminds me he works out but not in a I-live-in-the-gym way. The noises he makes and his shallow breathing tell me he's enjoying this as much as me.

Because this is his first time in eight years, I want this to be as good for him as he promises it will be for me. I want him to know how attracted I am to him just by how I touch and look at him.

His hands lie limp beside him, as if he is enjoying watching me remove pieces of clothing from his body. I move my hand all the way up his broad shoulders and push his shirt off too. My eyes drink in his body—up his big, bulging biceps, over his broad shoulders, down his chest that has a dusting of hair that trails down to his abdomen and stops where his pants start.

Grabbing the bottom of my tank, he pulls it swiftly over my head, along with my sports bra. His eyes bounce between my face and my breasts. I enjoy the way he looks darkly at me, a deep longing clear as day in his stare.

I'm tingling with desire, but I hold myself back. His finger reaches out to touch my side at the same time he leans forward and peppers kisses along my shoulder.

My heart beats rapidly, breaths quickening to match. "Beautiful, so fucking beautiful, Shell." His nickname for me comes out huskily as he murmurs against my skin.

My hands twitch, needing more. I grab his belt and pull it off. He removes my leggings as I unbutton his pants. They fall easily to his ankles, leaving him standing in only his briefs. I reach out and stroke his hot, taunt stomach. He whimpers when I touch him. The sound almost breaks me, but I know he needs this. When it's his turn, he'll find me wet, and that will make him see how badly I want him. I wiggle my leggings off and kick them away. Pushing my thong down, he does the same with his boxers. Now we both stand naked, breathing heavily with anticipation. His cock is big and hard. He's 6'5", with big hands and feet, so I took a guess he was big, but I take my time looking over him, memorizing it into my brain. Thankful he gave in to my plea. I've never craved someone enough to beg. But with Evan, I'd do it again. The fire in his eyes and the way he touches me make me feel special. I don't want him to ever stop looking at or touching me.

Remembering his earlier words, I step over and snatch the bottle of bourbon from the table and walk back to him.

He quirks an eyebrow.

I smirk. "My turn first."

Chapter 20

Chelsea

His dark eyes look at me hungrily. I wonder if his heart is beating as fast as mine.

My fingers grip the bottle tight. I edge closer to him, forcing him to sit on the bed. Pushing him back until he lies down, I crawl over him.

"This might not work," I say, looking at his soft white bed linen.

His eyes travel over my face and search my eyes for answers. "Why?"

There's no way the bourbon won't end up on the sheets. "It'll get messy."

His mouth twitches, and he looks at me with an obvious double meaning. "Not if you suck as you pour."

Inside my chest, my heart is hammering, and between my thighs, my sex throbs. "Don't get upset when your bed is wet."

"I won't." His wolfish smirk makes my stomach tingle. When he looks at me like that, I feel adored and I'm powerless to resist him.

With that, I focus on pouring the bourbon, starting with his toned stomach. It splashes, but I don't allow it to run on the bed. I pour tiny amounts, licking and sucking as I go. I memorize every bit of him. Taking my time to slowly explore and gently play. His body is driving me insane. The smoothness of his feverish skin on my tongue, mixed with alcohol adds to the intoxication.

A gentle but rough hand tickles my back as he groans in pleasure, "Don't stop." He encourages me along with a rasp. I continue the pattern over his sculpted chest and over his thick neck, watching his Adam's apple bobble as I pour alcohol along his throat.

"Fuck," he grunts.

His throat works when I lick and suck my way along it, moaning, his touch on my back tender. The moment I lift my lips off his neck and hover my face over his, I stare into his eyes as he throws me another wicked smirk.

"You're too good at this."

I've never done anything this crazy, but with him, I feel comfortable to be myself and to ask for what I want. I bite my lip and say on a pant, "Open up."

He growls sexily at my command and does exactly as I say. I pour bourbon into his mouth, and when I bring my lips to his and kiss him, it's explosive. The passion pouring into this kiss is something I haven't felt before. It's the feeling of being so wanted; I never want it to end. So I take my time exploring his mouth, our tongues touching, and we kiss deeply for a long time...until I'm desperate for air.

I pull back, glancing up at him with a smirk. "That was fun."

He licks his lips. "Was it now?"

"I've wondered what your lips would feel like against mine," I pant, still trying to catch my breath.

He lifts up to lay a sweet soft——all too brief——kiss on me. "And you were better than my fucking imagination. I don't want to stop. I need more of you."

Before I get another word out, he grabs the bottle and flips me with expert precision.

How he didn't spill a drop, I don't know.

"My turn," he says darkly, raking his eyes over my body hungrily, making me squirm and desperate beneath him.

My skin prickles as he moves the bottle to my mouth. I open it, and he pours a little and then kisses me hard. I've never been big on kissing, but with him, I could kiss him all night, and it seems he can't get enough of it either.

Pulling back, he brings the bottle to my throat, and I swallow hard with anticipation.

"Ahh," I breathe as he trickles bourbon down my neck and the cold liquid causes me to shiver. My nipples are already tight buds, aching with need. But now I'm desperate. A soft, long moan escapes me. Arching my back off the bed, he pours the liquid, and it trickles down my sides.

"You're making a mess-s," I stammer, trying to speak through the ache.

He sucks, licks, and nibbles my neck. Then he moves to my shoulder and chest, where he takes it in turn sucking on my nipples. When he flicks his tongue over my nipple and then bites it, I writhe and moan, "Evan, please." My fingers dig into the blanket as he continues grazing his teeth over my breast. Under my heavy lashes, I watch him kiss across to my other breast, where he squeezes and sucks before biting the other side. Giving it the exact same attention. When his lips lift for a moment, my breath hitches, watching his mouth trail kisses and bites along my abs down to the tops of my thighs. I'm breathing fast as he dribbles a little over my lower stomach, but instead of finishing there, he pours the cold liquid between my thighs.

"Evan." His name comes out on a shaky exhale. My legs spread as he settles between them.

"Yeah, baby?" he replies softly before his hot mouth lands on my clit, stealing my breath. I give in to the strong pull of his lips.

His loud groans between licking cause me to thrash beneath him. My head rocks from side to side on the mattress as I chant out, "Un-n fair," in a moan.

The touch of his tongue on my pussy is almost too much to bear. My lower back tingles and the heaviness between my thighs warms me. I'm close to coming. So close.

He holds one leg with one hand, spreading me wide while the other pours more liquor on my pussy, and the sounds of him sucking up the liquid are too much.

"Evan," I pant, my hips rocking desperately against his mouth.

He doesn't stop; he only mumbles against me, "I know, baby."

I can't stop the coiling of my muscles that are so desperate for relief.

"If you don't stop soon," I say on a shaky breath, "I'll come."

And as if that was the sign he needed, he turns it up a notch.

"Then come, baby. Come all over my mouth. I've got you. I'm right here."

His thick, warm tongue slides through and enters me.

"Oh, God," I groan. "This feels so good."

My thighs close around his head, and he's relentless with his tongue. His spare hand grips my hip firmly, holding me in place.

"Yes, fuck, Evan," I stammer as he fucks me ruthlessly with his tongue. Then, suddenly, a wave crashes through my body. I gasp at the soul-reaching sensation. My eyes flutter, trying to fight the will to close them.

But I manage to watch. With my lips parted, I grip his head tightly and roll my hips as my orgasm tears through my body. He doesn't stop gripping my hip or licking my pussy until he has every drop from me. "Fuck, you're perfect, and so beautiful when you come for me."

I go lax, finally allowing myself to close my eyes. My fingers drop from his head and my arms and legs flop from the powerful orgasm.

"Well, that was easy," he murmurs, kissing my inner thighs.

I peel my eyes open and look at him, ignoring the way my legs are shaking.

His smug grin shows me how much he loved doing that to me. And I want that same feeling in return.

"Damn it. I missed out on sucking you," I confess with a pout, hoping it will be my turn now.

His eyes widen, but he shakes his head with a dark chuckle. "Next time."

My brow furrows as I stare into his dark blue eyes. "Why? Just tell me how you like it, and I'll do it. I promise I'll make you feel good."

His fingers are on my face, in my hair, gripping me as if he can't get enough, causing these weird noises to escape my throat. "You don't need me to tell you how to suck dick. I can see in your eyes how hungry you are for my cock, but Shell baby, right now, I fucking need you," he says, kissing along my jaw, as if I'm the most precious thing in the whole world.

A desperate moan leaves my mouth as he settles himself between my thighs.

I rock my hips up, chasing him. His blue eyes are hungry as they travel all over my body.

His fingers brush along the side of my waist, causing a chill to run down my spine. Grabbing my thigh, he lifts one of my legs and lines himself up.

Another loud moan leaves my mouth.

"The sounds you're making are driving me fucking crazy." He closes his mouth over mine, as if he's trying to swallow them.

I'm so pent up and achy to have him inside me that I claw his back.

"Your nails feel incredible marking my skin." He kisses me before disconnecting to slip away, grabbing a condom, rolling it on, and quickly returning.

My hands touch his shoulders, enjoying how big and strong they feel. I love how he, in his entirety, makes me and my five-nine frame feel small.

"So pretty." His thumb grazes my bottom lip as if he's mesmerized as his eyes roam my face. "I adore your eyes. Something you do with your makeup accentuates your features beautifully and drives me even more wild for you than I already am."

I can barely breathe as he gazes at me. Does he realize what he's saying to me? My eyes sting, but I refuse to cry. Even if they're happy tears.

Instead, I pull him down, close to me, so I can bring my lips to his, and kiss him with everything that I have.

I never imagined anyone, other than my family, would find those parts of me lovable. However, his appreciation for both Pilates and my makeup sparks a profound and unfamiliar desire within me that I've never felt before.

"I've wanted you so bad," he rasps, his gaze causing a fire across my skin.

I lick my lips and stare up at him. "Don't hold back now."

His mouth moves to my ear and he whispers, "I'll make you forget about everything and everyone." Trailing kisses along my cheek, he stares down at me again.

My whole body shudders at his words. "Only you."

"I never want to see you wake up like that again." He kisses me before adding the final blow. "You're mine now."

My mouth opens and closes, but I can't speak.

I capture his lips, kissing him deeply as my hands touch his strong jaw that says those sweet words.

Words I've been dying to hear for years. *Forever*.

The first and last man to want me the way I want him. A reciprocation makes this moment more special.

As the tip of his cock hits my entrance, I part my legs farther, welcoming him in. My head falls back, and when he enters me, I sink further into his plush bed.

He pauses once he's all the way in, allowing me to adjust to him before he pulls out and repeats. My body coils tight as my body hums. It's not going to take long for me to come again.

I groan loudly and rock my body with his. We fit tight and perfectly together. Our rhythm is set at a pace that we both can enjoy.

I feel the heat between my thighs building. My back arches as I chase friction on my clit. My breathing becomes ragged.

He grunts above me. "Look at me. I want to see your eyes as you come for me."

I fight the urge to close my eyes by focusing on watching him. It's not hard when his face is filled with euphoria.

He continues his thrusts as his name leaves my lips in a chant.

I don't know how much longer I can keep doing this. My fingernails dig into his shoulders, grasping at his perspired body. He doesn't flinch.

"You feel incredible. You feel like mine."

My body is sparking like a firecracker. It feels strange, yet incredible, something I haven't had in a while. And now I'm going to have it twice in one night. I can't even do that to myself.

It's as if every fiber in my body is being electrocuted. It's the mix of him and his words. Our eyes are locked, both of our mouths parted, sucking in large breaths of air.

Suddenly, my orgasm slams into me. My body ripples like a wave, head tipping back as I call out his name on a long moan.

He's close, his body only thrusting harder a few more times before he stills. His cock jerks inside me as he grunts and groans my name. I watch the tight lines on his face as he orgasms, in a state of awe. He's breathtaking.

"Are you okay?" he asks, still only thinking about me as he looks into my eyes.

"Perfect," I answer, and a slight smirk forms on his face. "I thought you were the quiet one."

"So did I."

"Then what changed?"

"You."

Three letters that hit my core and make me fold over.

"I want to be my whole self with you. The way we share the same pain makes it hard for me to deny what we have, and how I want to be with you."

My mouth opens and closes, and no response forms.

"Loud, unapologetically me, without worrying you will hurt me."

"That's beautiful."

"Like you," he says, skimming my face with his hand.

Under hooded eyes, I watch him blink his eyes open and they are brighter now. I expect him to pull out immediately and dispose of the condom, but he gives me a shit-eating grin before kissing my lips in a bruising claim.

When he pulls back, he whispers, "Thank you."

"What for?" I ask in a daze.

"For tonight. For being you."

I stare up at his dangerous smile, because he doesn't smile very often, so I know it's special at this moment.

"You're so beautiful when you smile," I blurt out.

He shakes his head and kisses me more tenderly. "You're the beautiful one, baby. Now let me clean you up."

I nod, humming with satisfaction. He leaves for the bathroom, and I hear the tap turn on. Is he running the tub?

Peeling myself up out of his comfortable bed, I walk to see him beside it, adding candles and bath scents.

He must sense me because as soon as I hit the entry, he turns. "You ready?"

I step over to him and take his hand, moving to the side of the tub.

Sitting down, I sigh as the warm water covers me. My eyes drift closed. "Now this is going to be hard to get out of."

"Stay in as long as you want."

I open my eyes, lips forming a small pout. "You aren't joining me?"

"I need to get you some food. You haven't eaten."

"I'm not hungry," I say quickly.

"But you haven't eaten."

"It's okay."

"You'll sleep better after you eat," he says softly, yet firmly. I could get used to having someone care for me like this.

"It's fast food anyway."

"Oh, our Chick-fil-A order."

He chuckles at my high-pitched voice.

"Yes."

"Well, now I changed my mind," I say, settling back down into the tub, allowing my head to lay back on the headrest behind me.

He comes back a little later, wearing a pair of black sweat shorts, and sits on the edge of the tub.

"Is it ready?"

He nods.

Pulling the plug, I stand before him. His eyes drop slowly over my figure. He makes me feel incredible with just that one look.

"How did I get so lucky?" he says, holding a warm towel and helping me step out.

I wrap myself in the soft towel, savoring its warmth. "Mmm, thanks," I reply, patting my face dry. "And I could say the same thing."

He shakes his head. "Come on, baby. Let's eat," he says, not answering my question. Uncertainty now swarms my stomach as I grab my clothes to put back on.

"Let me get you something to wear," he says. As he walks away, I enjoy watching his toned back.

When he's gone, I towel dry. I hear a drawer open and close, then his heavy steps make their way back to me.

He returns with one of his tops. I can't deny I've thought about wearing a man's shirt many times, but this is the first time I've ever had a man give me his shirt to wear.

I slip it on, and it feels heavenly. Soft and soaked in his delicious scent.

A grumble leaves his chest. "I love that on you."

I look at him with an easy smile as the top sits on my knees. "It only works because you're taller than me."

"You're perfect for me," he says in a whisper, but I catch it.

For a guy who hasn't been with a woman in years, he sure knows exactly what to say and do.

The way he worked my body tonight was incredibly skilled. It's also nice knowing that I am not broken after not being able to come with Bobby.

We eat and watch TV in his bed, comfortable and at ease. When we lie down, I settle on top of his chest. The thump of his heart is like a lullaby and my lids close, but not before hearing more of his sweet words.

"My unique Shell. I'm obsessed with you."

I stay silent, soaking in every single word that leaves his mouth. It's sexy, raspy, and everything I've ever wanted to hear. It's sad that I've never heard them before, and I truly didn't think I deserved a life like this. Where a guy is obsessed with me. An unattainable dream. I hoped, of course. But there's something in the way that Evan says it that makes me believe him.

Bobby may have broken my heart, but Evan has pieced it back together.

I love the fact he brought back the carefree, bubbly attitude I once had. Maybe it's because he's the complete opposite of me. Either way, I'm mesmerized by him.

His lips brush my forehead as he lays a kiss there. "Go to sleep, baby. I'll be right here when you wake up."

I don't need any more encouragement because his strong arms wrap around me——his scent is everywhere, and my body is tired, so it doesn't take long for my eyes to close. I drift into a beautiful dream this time. One where I take him home and my parents love him...and he loves them.

CHAPTER 21

EVAN

SOFT BREATHS FILL THE room as Chelsea snuggles up beside me. Her legs are resting on top of mine, her hand draped across my waist, and her head lays between my arm and chest.

If she were awake, she'd hear the heavy beats of my heart.

I dip my head and peer down to watch her face, softly sleeping. She looks as peaceful as I feel now.

In this moment, there's no worry or distrust, just pure freedom. It's a weightless feeling I've never experienced before. And I fucking love it.

This is everything I've ever wanted but never allowed myself to hope for, not since I was betrayed.

As I replay the memories we've made together, I can honestly say she's always been the same person since we met. When I think about our slow progression from meeting to last night, it's been a mutual pining with no hidden agendas.

She doesn't want me because I'm rich. She wants me for me.

A guy who genuinely wants the best for her and encourages her to follow her dreams.

Being around her brings out a fun, youthful side out of me that I put away for so long. But with her around, I want to talk about everything and anything—a memory of our childhood, a dream, the future, or just our day at work.

I thought I loved my ex. But as I lie here with Chelsea in my arms, it's evident that I didn't, because I didn't feel this soul-crushing need to be around her all the time. There's still a fear that remains deep in my heart that she'll wake up and realize she deserves better, though.

Only, my thoughts disappear the moment she twists in my arms.

"You're watching me sleep. You creep." She laughs, and I can't help the deep rumble coming from my chest as she moves her hand across it.

How could someone as pretty as her like someone like me? A guy who never used to laugh, yet with her laughs all the time.

"I'm wondering if you're going to run away," I say honestly.

"Not unless you want me to go." Lifting her head, she gives me a playful smile.

I shake my head, tracing her skin with my fingers, enjoying the feel of her silky skin. "I don't want you to."

"I don't want you to either." She sighs, clearly enjoying the touch of my hand on her warm skin.

"Good."

There's something about the way her face pinches.

"What are you thinking about?" I ask, pressing a kiss to her head, and when I pull back, her eyes meet mine again.

I want to know what's in that pretty little head of hers.

"Sorry," she says quietly. Her teeth tug her lip before she answers. "But I'm just wondering if this was a one-time thing for you?"

I shake my head again before she's even finished. "No, I can't do casual. I wouldn't have let you in if I wasn't serious about you." There's no question about that, but then what made her think that?

"Did I say something that made you think I wanted something casual?" I ask, searching her eyes.

She sucks in a deep breath and lowers her head gently against my chest. "No, I just assumed. So there's no more fake relationship?"

I move my fingers from her back to her hair, enjoying her dark locks against her skin. "Well, let me make this clear. I want you, Shell. Nothing has been fake. I was kidding myself thinking it could be. Everything I felt for you was real."

I'm sure she can feel my heart racing against her chest. But I don't plan to do anything with her. I want to show her that this is more than just sex, that my heart belongs to her and, fuck, she has the power to break it.

"I want you too, and it was never fake for me either." The desperation in her voice makes me reach out and bring her face to mine, sealing our words with a kiss.

Reluctantly, I pull back, and we simply stare at each other in silence. It's as if we're just in a lust bubble. The room is quiet except for our heavy breathing.

I don't want to leave at this moment, but I know we can't stay here all day.

I tug her to me and hold her tight again, relieved almost everything is out in the open. I've never slept so well in my life. There's something about holding her in my arms as I slept that made me drift into a heavier sleep. I never want to change my sheets again, wondering if they'll keep bringing me good rest. The shades on the windows are down, blocking out the sunlight. Leaving us to question what time it is.

But when her stomach rumbles, I realize it must be breakfast time. My cheek pulls up on one side, remembering the time at the sandwich place when her stomach did the same thing. I love these moments alone.

"Let me make you some breakfast."

Her head lifts to look up at me as she asks, "Do you mind if I cook?"

"Mind? No. Feel bad? Yeah..."

Her cheeks flush pink as she shakes her head. "Don't. I enjoy it."

My stomach rumbles loudly, interrupting us.

Another deep chuckle leaves my chest, and I shake my head. "I've never laughed this much before."

The corner of her mouth tips up. "I'd say I'm sorry, but I think it's a good thing."

"It's definitely a good thing." I wink at her playfully.

Looking down bashfully, she peels herself away from me. I mourn the loss of her body against mine.

She surprises me with a kiss, tender and loving. I love her kisses. I love the feel of her lips on mine. And I groan into it.

She pulls back with a laugh. "Let's go make some breakfast."

There's not much to choose from. Most mornings, I'm at work very early, so all I have is eggs and toast.

We head to the kitchen, where she moves around my house effortlessly. Her wearing my blue shirt is distracting. Needing something to do with my hands, I start on the eggs, trying to focus on stirring them into a scramble. But my mind drifts to how I've never felt like this with any other woman. It's deeper than attraction. Feeling this connected to another person is scary, but I feel safe enough to open myself up to Chelsea and let my insecurities go. For the first time in a very long time, I bring down my walls and welcome trust back in. I never thought it would happen, but Chelsea is genuinely into me. She sees me without judgement, with an understanding that's both patient and kind. It didn't happen overnight; the attraction was always there, but she never pushed. She just stayed, waiting until I was ready to trust again. I'm not afraid she'll break my heart, as she's shown time and time again, she's honest and loyal.

"Are you working today?" I ask, wondering how much time we have together.

She nods, but keeps her eyes on cooking. "I want to set up an online booking system."

I love her determination. "I'm happy to help."

I'm not very tech-savvy, so it's going to test me, but I'm determined to figure it out if she needs me.

Her head lifts to look at me. "You mean you'll hire someone?"

She's teasing me. But I love it. And it's not like I wouldn't do that for her if she wanted. "Hey. I can actually help."

"Don't you need to work?" she says, as if I need reminding.

"I'm the CEO, whose office happens to be a few floors up from yours." I wink, offering to blur the line between work and play. Something I never would have thought I'd do. But with her, I'd do anything.

"Does this mean I get to take advantage of you?" Her teeth sink into her bottom lip as she holds back a smile.

Fucking hell, that seductive look she throws me makes me hard. If she didn't need to eat and I wasn't cooking, I'd lift her on my counter and have my way with her.

"I wouldn't turn that down," I hiss, trying to restrain myself.

She doesn't say it, but she looks happy with my reply, as she comes beside me, holding onto my arm.

Just a simple touch, but it's enough to show me how much she cares about me.

I turn the burner off and look down at her.

She screws her nose up. "I'll make the toast." Spinning around, she grabs the bread.

"I'll set up the table." I move to the kitchen drawer, where I keep the placemats.

She throws out a hand and shakes her head, pointing at the counter stools. "You don't need to set the table for me. I'm happy to sit at the island counter."

As much as her easy-going attitude is appealing, I continue moving through the kitchen, grabbing the placements. "You deserve to sit at the table."

Her mouth parts slightly, like she's at a loss for words. I love seeing her stunned by simple gestures that my gram ingrained in me.

I grab silverware and glasses. "Tell me more about the online system, and maybe we can brainstorm some ideas."

She blinks at me, pausing mid-task.

"What?" I stiffen, wondering if I said something wrong.

Her face softens and her lips twist up. "You've been a nice surprise and someone I didn't know I needed, but I'm very grateful you're in my life."

It's exactly how I feel about her.

"Likewise," I agree, feeling the weight of our admissions.

She turns and moves toward the toaster, and I shake my head, returning to serving up our food. I try not to get too lost in her, but everything about her distracts me.

We sit at the table beside each other. Neither one of us wants to be apart, even if we don't say it.

Grabbing the ketchup, she drowns her eggs in it.

My face scrunches up at her food on her plate. "I don't think there are eggs left."

"Don't knock it until you try it." She shifts her egg-sauce combo to my lips.

I shake my head, my response fast and firm. "I'll pass."

"Your loss." She shrugs and dives into her food.

I stare at her, loving how much she eats. Not self-conscious at all. But I guess she needs it to fuel her body. Especially prior to that awful, torturous class that she calls Pilates.

"I'm surprised your phone isn't constantly ringing." Her words pull my gaze up to her face, wondering where that came from.

"I switched it off."

"He switches it off," she mumbles under her breath. Not missing the way her eyes narrow to her plate.

"When I'm with you, I don't want anyone to distract me. I want you all to myself," I reply boldly, lowering my silverware and sitting back in my chair and watching as her head lifts.

Her eyes find mine, and I find them glassy.

"Work is not a priority," I add, leaning my arms on the table so I'm closer to her, knowing she needs to hear it.

"It's not a priority," she repeats, nodding to herself.

She's thinking about Bobby. We're two different people. Because when she's with me, I don't want to be consumed by work. I've built my business where it should run efficiently. I hired the best staff I could find. Hence why I would love to get rid of Bobby, but unfair dismissal won't let me do it.

If I want to be with her, I can be with her. I've given up so much for work. It was my choice. And now, it's like I am ready. Healed and open to a relationship. It's all thanks to the strong friendship we built first and how we grew from there. I never thought I'd be here, so yes, she deserves my undivided attention. It's a simple but important thing for her.

"You ready to drop me off at home? I need to get ready for work."

I lean in close to her soft, delicate skin, enjoying the mix of her faded perfume and my cologne as I lay a kiss and whisper, "Are you sure I can't change your mind?"

"No, mister. Stop distracting me, otherwise you'll make us both late."

"I don't see the problem with that. Isn't that the perk of being the CEO?" I rasp against her skin.

CHAPTER 22

CHELSEA

A few days later

"Do I look okay?" I ask, adjusting my outfit.

Evan's blue eyes slide slowly and seductively down my body. "You look more than fine."

Happiness fills me at his gravelly tone. "Thanks. We kinda match."

He gives me a wolfish grin. "I hadn't thought about that."

Every day, my attraction for him deepens. Now it's my chance to take in his handsome body. He's wearing a navy button-up shirt, undone at the top, and his shirt isn't tucked in. His blue jeans fit so well on his thick thighs, it has me salivating already to get them off. His dark boots make heavy sounds with each step, resonating through my bones. It's a sexy swagger I can't get enough of.

We walk the few steps to Evan's gram's house. Surprisingly, I'm not nervous. It's probably because I met her over a year ago. But even if I was, he's reassuring me with his touch. I squeeze his hand tighter. As he tilts his head, and I flash him a smile, and his lips turn up in response. He kisses my temple before ringing the doorbell. His affectionate ways have me on cloud nine. I wanted to feel loved and cherished, and now with Evan, I realize this is the first time I'm truly experiencing it.

There's also peace in the fact I am meeting his gram. I'm meeting his family. This never happened with Bobby. I wasn't good enough for that. With Evan, I'm good enough to be here on his arm. My heart sings with delight.

The door opens to reveal a woman with short dark hair. I notice the flecks of gray as the light hits it.

"Saylor," says Evan, his gram's housekeeper.

"Come in. Gram is out back in her garden," she says, opening the door wide.

She looks at me with a warm smile, so I give her one back.

As we step into the house, it smells delicious. The waft of cake hits my nose. I can't wait to taste whatever is baking.

We wander through the house toward the back door, and Evan opens it. Hearing sounds coming from the left, we walk down until we find Gram sitting in a chair, under the shade. The afternoon sun is gone, but her frail, thin skin still needs protection.

"Hey, Gram," says Evan warmly.

She glances up, a smile stretching on her face. "Evan. Chelsea."

"Hi," I say as butterflies fill my stomach.

There's a gleam in her eye. Evan releases my hand and leans forward to lay a kiss on her cheek.

She holds his cheeks in her hands.

"You good?" he asks.

"I'm good." She pinches his cheeks, and he steps back to stand beside me again.

"What are you doing out here? Aren't you cold?" he asks.

I peer down and notice she's in a short-sleeve pale green dress. Her hair is immaculately styled, but the gust of wind flattens it.

"Why don't you go grab me a coat and flick the kettle on, and I'll have a little chat with Chelsea."

"Is that wise?" Evan asks, but there's a softness to it.

She rolls her eyes and shoos him. "E, be a good boy and go."

His gaze drops to me, waiting for my permission. "I'm fine. Listen to your gram and go on."

A little flicker of heat deepens in his eyes.

I bite my bottom lip, watching him exhale a big breath and turn around to leave. Then I take the empty space next to her.

"How are you and Evan?"

She gets straight into it, doesn't she?

"Wonderful. He's such a gentleman."

My eyes lift from her assessing ones to the garden that is very well-kept. I bet she has a gardener every day. The yard reminds me of my parents' place. It allows my body to sink into the chair, relax and talk openly with her.

"He's reserved, but he's very sweet inside."

A wrinkle forms between my eyebrows as I glance back at her. "Everyone keeps telling me he's quiet, even he does. But I don't get that from him."

A soft, easy smile lifts on her lips. "He's comfortable with you. I can see that."

"You can?"

She nods slowly. "Yes, dear. When a man like Evan opens himself up, it means he feels safe."

I take a minute to let her words sink in. "I guess I hadn't thought of it that way. I just see this incredibly generous person."

She reaches over and pats my hand. "You bring out the best in him. We can all see that."

I smile, feeling a warmth spread through me. "Thank you. He brings out the best in me too."

Leaning back, her gaze turns to the garden. "You know, when I met my husband, he was the same way. Quiet and reserved. But with time, he became my best friend. My son is also like that, so I'm not surprised one of my grandchildren turned out the same."

I appreciate her sharing her story. It helps me understand the family and Evan on a deeper level.

Her eyes shift back to me, and I share what's in my heart.
"You give me hope for the future."

She smiles softly. "I can see a very promising one for you
and Evan. Just keep being yourself."

Evan arrives back, cutting our conversation short. She
excuses herself inside and encourages us to take a quick
walk in the garden.

I admire the white flowers; they are the same ones from
his balcony. "I love these."

"Gardenias."

"Oh, someone knows his flowers." I poke his ribs playfully. He captures my finger, and he pulls me into his arms.
I land into his strong, hard chest. His arms hug me, and I
settle my head on his chest, staring at the gardenias.

"I'll tell you a secret. I used to help Gram in the garden.
It was our time."

He rests his head on mine as my chest warms, imagining
all the time he's spent with his gram.

"What's your favorite flower?"

"I don't have one. I'm more of a tree guy."

I snort. "What type of tree?"

"White oak."

I frown as my eyes search the garden. "There isn't one
here."

"I know, but my parents had one in our backyard when I was little. They were so big and beautiful."

"Like you."

His head lifts, and he's staring longingly into my eyes. Something passes between us.

"The only beautiful thing I know is you."

I peer down briefly before batting my lashes at his compliment.

"Th——"

His lips capture mine, and I sink into his body. Our kiss is slow and all-consuming, so much so, my toes curl inside my shoes.

He breaks our kiss, leaving me panting.

"We better get inside before Gram gets upset." He winks.

"I've heard her desserts are amazing."

I'm ready to taste her baking. Nova hasn't stopped raving about it.

He nods. "The best."

We turn and begin walking back through the garden.

My fingers graze something, and a sharp sting hits my forefinger.

"Ow."

I look at my bleeding finger and suck on it.

"Let me look," he says, turning me to face him.

"No."

"You're bleeding."

"It's fine. Don't worry about it. Just a scratch." I try to wave it off.

"No, come, let me fix it."

My lips lift into a smile at his gruff command. I don't bother arguing because Evan will get his way and, honestly, I like this nurturing side of him. It's foreign and endearing.

He takes me to the bathroom and turns on the water, guiding my finger underneath it. His focus is on my finger, but my focus is on his side profile. The strong jaw, crooked nose, and dusting of a five o'clock shadow make me ache.

"I shouldn't have taken you out there," he grumbles.

"It's a garden. It's my fault for not paying attention."

"Next time be careful."

"Do you know how sexy it is when you get this worried about me?" I whisper.

He stops the water and grabs a bandage from under the sink, putting it on and adding pressure.

Stepping in front of me, his eyes hold mine, backing me so my ass hits the sink, causing my pulse to skyrocket.

"I more than worry about you." He leans forward and runs his nose along my neck, and my skin prickles with goosebumps. "I like you."

"I like you too." My voice is breathy, giving away just how much I want him.

"You're a bad girl right now."

I nod slowly. There's no denying my desire for him.

He brings his fingers to my neck, gently squeezes, and whispers, "Later. I'll show you just how much I like you."

The promise in his voice leaves me shuddering. He steps back, and I close my parted lips, swallowing a whine. Without another word, he finishes dressing my cut, leaving our tension surrounding us.

"Now it won't get infected."

"Thanks."

"Better?" He quirks an eyebrow, but it's the grin on his face that tells me he's teasing me. And I want to tease him back.

"You know what will be better?" I breathe.

His head tilts to the side. "What's that?"

I move my lips to his ear and whisper, "If you could make me come now." Pulling my head back, I bite back a grin.

His eyes widen, and he grips my chin, laying a bruising kiss to my lips before he pants on my lips, "Fuck, Shell. As much as I want to, I fucking can't."

"I know. I'm teasing."

He shakes his head and grunts. "Naughty girl. I'm going to make you pay for that tonight."

There's no playfulness in his tone; he's serious and that makes me giddy for what's to come later.

I turn and grab the door handle, pushing the door open and welcoming the fresh air that hits my lungs. In that space, all I could inhale was his spicy scent, and I was drowning.

We move to the kitchen area and see Gram sitting at the table, nursing a cup of tea.

"Sit, and I'll make you a tea," Evan says as his hand grazes my lower back. My gaze drops to his lips. He licks them, knowing I'm transfixed, before he removes his hand and strides away. Taking a breath, I turn to sit down. My heart drops when I see Gram watching us.

I hope she didn't hear or witness anything inappropriate.

I slowly slide into the seat. She sips her drink and then lowers it, her silence killing me.

She leans forward. "He's falling for you."

I don't hesitate to answer her. "I'm falling for him too."

The corners of her lips lift. "I can see that."

My eyes drift where he left, expecting him to walk in any moment.

"Just be patient with him."

I'm about to ask what she means when he walks back in, holding two cups. He lowers one in front of me. "There you go."

"Thanks."

He takes the seat next to me.

"What were you two talking about?"

"Just how you two are in love."

"Jes——"

He stops himself before he swears. Nova warned me that Gram is strict.

"What happened to your finger out there?" she asks, changing the subject.

I smile. "I had a fight with a rose thorn."

Gram laughs. "You're funny."

I take that as a compliment because I don't see myself as a funny person.

"Your grandson made it better, though." I offer him a knowing smirk as he sips his coffee.

Her house is large, but with Evan, he makes the room feel small. He takes over every sense.

I sip my tea and let Gram talk about her garden.

"Which was your favorite?" she asks.

"Your white gardenias."

I jerk when his hand reaches onto my lap and settles there. It's sitting mid-thigh, and I'm growing hot. I hope he doesn't try to make me pay for my comments because I'd say sorry if I have to.

Gram has moved on from talking about the garden to her daytime soap, and I know the one she's talking about. Evan grumbles beside me and inches his hand up higher. My body freezes, and I keep my hands above the table so she doesn't think there's anything going on. I have no idea if she can see Evan's hand, but I want him to quit teasing. Thankfully, we're interrupted by Saylor.

The famous dessert is a chocolate sponge cake, and it looks mouth-watering. She's popped sprinkles on top.

I take a picture of Evan and the cake, then upload it to my social media pages.

Picking up my fork, I stab a piece, unable to wait any longer for a bite. But I lose my appetite the moment Bobby sends me a text.

> **Bobby:** I should have known you were an untrustworthy slut but why did you have to choose my boss and one-up me?

My heart lurches to my throat as his words break me momentarily. But as much as the desire screams at me to text him back and say, *fuck you, leave me alone,* I do what I should have done but forgot to do...I block his ass via text and all social channels and then refocus on the cake. I don't want Gram or Evan to realize Bobby has bothered me. Instead, I choose to ignore his insults and stay strong.

The pillowy cake is incredible. Gram is a great cook. The cake is not too sweet and not too bland. It's the perfect mix.

Evan finishes his slice in four bites. He even managed to do it one-handed. That's right, he refused to move his hand from my leg. Not that I'm totally complaining, because it's like he doesn't want to let me go. Keeping me within reach because he wants to, and I revel in it.

I feel full and like I could be rolled out of here. Drinking my tea, I drag my chair out so I can clean up.

"No, dear. Leave it. Saylor will do it," Gram says.

I don't want to argue with her, so I remove my hand and sit back down. But I notice Evan starts cleaning up with Saylor and it makes my heart swell.

As much as I've enjoyed being here tonight, I'm ready to head home. Ready for him to finish what we started in the bathroom.

As if Evan can read my mind, his hand reaches for mine. "We should get going, Gram."

She looks at her dainty gold watch on her wrist. "Yeah, it's getting late."

I stand, and Gram brings her walker with her.

"Gram, you can go sit down. We can see ourselves out."

"No, I've got my walker, I can do it," she says, as she walks us to the door.

We follow closely behind. Evan looks like he's ready to catch her when she falls. I think my heart melted a little more. Is there anything more beautiful than your man doting over his gram?

Evan pulls the door open. He kisses and hugs her before stepping into the doorway.

I copy him, giving her a kiss and briefly hugging her. I touch her bony shoulder; having noticed her smaller frame when I first met her. Nova told me all about her cancer. It's awful, and I worry who Evan will become if he ever loses her. Will he withdraw further into himself? Or fill the void with work? What would he do?

Shaking off those dark thoughts, I smile at her. "It was lovely to see you again."

"Same, dear. Now go make some babies."

Evan fires back fast with a grimace. "Grams, please."

"Well, practice then." She winks, which makes me chuckle. "You know what they say, practice makes perfect." Gram's eyes move to mine.

I don't know how to respond, so I just remain silent. Luckily for me, Evan speaks.

"Alright, goodnight, Gram, I'll call you tomorrow."

"Goodnight, Evan and Chelsea."

I wave and take a few steps down, returning to Evan's car.

Reaching his car, I expect him to do what he always does and open the door for me. But tonight, he pushes me against the car. His hands on my hips as he presses his body against mine. My body has memorized his so it already softens beneath him, succumbing to him, like it knows he will give it the pleasure it's seeking.

"You killed it in there."

"I did?" Nothing I said or did stands out. I'm lost.

"You just fit in so easily."

I blink up at him, trying to understand why that's so special. "She's so easy to get along with."

"She means the world to all of us."

"I can tell she's special," I breathe out as he leans in and kisses my cheek.

"She is, but so are you." He kisses my lips briefly before saying, "Now good girls should be rewarded."

"I thought I was naughty." I lift my eyebrow in a silent challenge.

"Get in that car before I do something that will cause my gram to whip me with her wooden spoon."

I laugh. "You guys are petrified of her."

"You have no idea. Growing up, she was the boss."

She still is, I want to say, but instead, I keep it light.

"Get me back to yours so you can show me who's the boss."

A sexy smirk settles on his lips. "Now we're talking."

CHAPTER 23

CHELSEA

THE NEXT DAY I arrive home from a walk to find Nova visiting. Summer and Nova both turn to look at me as I enter.

Their faces are bright with curiosity.

"What are you girls doing?" I ask, though I suspect they're here to find out about my time with Evan.

"Nothing, we're just wondering where you've been."

I drag out a chair and sit down, noticing the teacups in front of them.

"Well, I've been officially dating Evan."

"I fucking knew it," Summer shouts, causing me to giggle.

Nova smiles knowingly at me. Now that they're eager for my news, it adds to my excitement. I can't wipe the smile off my face.

"It's so good," I say, trying to downplay the flutters in my stomach when I think of Evan.

"You like him." Nova smirks into her tea.

"She's smitten, you mean," Summer adds.

"All of the above," I reply with a grin. These are my best friends. I tell them everything; we've been through thick and thin together since school.

Both girls stay quiet as they eagerly wait for me to discuss what happened with Evan.

They've been through everything with Bobby, so it's nice to have something positive to say.

"At first, you know how he suggested we date to piss off Bobby...Well, then we forgot about it, and just started hanging out and realized we both liked each other."

"I'm glad he's treating you good," Nova says.

"God, he's everything I've ever wanted. Plus, he's an old-fashioned gentleman," I gush in a ramble.

"Why is old-fashioned good?" Summer asks, her face pinched.

Nova wears a knowing smile——she is dating his brother, so she knows exactly what I mean.

"He opens doors, makes sure I've eaten, and that I'm warm. He makes me feel cared for."

"Yeah, men these days suck. They don't open doors. They don't even pay the full bill. They lie," Summer replies with a sigh.

"That's why he's so different," I say.

The girls look at me with the same awestruck expression I wear. They're happy for me.

My phone chimes, interrupting our conversation.

The girls drink their tea, and Nova tells Summer how the boys must have learned a lot from their parents and Gram.

I check my phone and see it's a text.

"Is that him?" Summer asks.

"Yeah," I reply, laying my phone back down without opening the message.

"Read it," Nova says.

You don't need to tell me twice. I'm dying to know what he's written.

I pick it up and swipe my finger across the screen to read it.

> **Evan:** *My house feels cold without you.*

My teeth dig into my bottom lip as my stomach flutters.

> **Me:** *I miss you too.*

After hitting send, I put my phone away. But my mind is still high from the idea that he misses me. It's only been twelve hours, and I'm already getting a text.

"You deserve this," Nova says.

"About time," Summer adds. "Now, tell us more."

I clear my throat before replying.

"It just kind of happened. Like, we've been avoiding it."

"Until you can't take it any longer," Summer interrupts, wiggling her eyebrows at me.

I laugh. "Exactly. We snapped, and it was perfect."

I feel my cheeks tingle from the memories of the orgasms he gave me. It's been a long time since I've had one with a guy. Now being with Evan, I'm craving it.

"When will you see each other again?" Nova asks.

My phone dings again, but I keep my gaze on Nova's inquisitive eyes.

"I don't know. We didn't make plans."

I didn't think that was an issue, and his text message confirms I don't need to worry about that with him.

I check my phone.

> **Evan:** *When can we see each other again?*

A bubble of laughter leaves my chest. I turn the phone over to show them the message. "Looks like he's thinking what you guys are thinking," I say, letting them read his text.

We're both missing each other, which is nice. It's good to feel wanted. He's so different. He asked to make plans with me again. It's not me making the plans or seeking him out.

He wants me. He wants to hang out with me.

The girls talk amongst themselves, so I text back.

Me: Tonight?

Evan: Come over to my beach house. I'll arrange the ride.

I put my phone down and announce it to the girls. "I'm seeing him tonight."

"Where are you two going?" Nova asks.

"He's suggesting we just go to his beach house," I tell them.

"That sounds nice," Nova comments.

"Sounds hot," Summer adds with a smirk.

"We've been out a couple of times already, so it'd be nice to just chill. Maybe watch a movie or something," I explain.

"Damn, girls, where do I find one of these men?" Summer jokes.

"They have two..." Nova starts.

But Summer interrupts her. "I'm not interested in one of the brothers."

"Your time will come. Don't rush it," I advise.

"You'll know when the person's right," Nova adds.

Summer sighs heavily. "Well, let's hope it's not too long. You know, I would like to have kids at some point."

I understand that feeling. I've always wanted kids and marriage. I haven't asked Evan what he wants because it feels too early. I'm sure it will naturally progress just like our relationship has so far.

But I'm hopeful because it's been a dream of mine since forever. And the quick flash of the future makes me smile as I imagine Evan standing in a black tux, waiting for me at the end of an aisle, makes my stomach flip.

"Well, girls, I need to go meet Jeremy soon," Nova says, pushing her chair out and putting her cup in the dishwasher.

My phone pings again, and I struggle not to read it because I'm not used to my messages blowing up from a guy.

"I might head to the studio and get a workout in. Summer, do you want to come?" I ask.

Both of them laugh.

Summer snorts. "No chance."

"That's my cue to leave," Nova says.

"I'm not just working out; I need to build my website too."

"You need to pay someone to do that," Summer says.

"You're taking on so much," Nova says.

"I'm not, it's fun, and if I get stuck Evan will help me," I tell them.

Standing, I walk with Summer to the door, where we say goodbye to Nova.

I get ready and head to the studio. I feel much better from stretching and taking myself through one of the workouts I plan to teach. After I open my computer, I begin playing around with the website and the booking system.

After half an hour, I'm a little hot and sweaty. It hasn't been as smooth as I originally thought.

My phone rings.

Looking at the screen, I see Evan's name flashing.

I smile, unable to believe that this guy keeps calling and messaging me.

"Hello."

"What are you doing?" he asks.

"I'm in the studio, trying to add the booking system."

He must hear the stress in my voice. "You okay?"

I blow out a breath, trying to calm myself down so I don't cause him to panic. "Yeah, it's just a little tricky, that's all."

"I'll come and help you out."

"I don't want to disturb you," I say in a rush, trying to prevent him from helping me instead of doing his work.

"You're not." The sincerity in his voice has my shoulders dropping in relief.

"It would be nice to have some help," I admit, smiling to myself.

"I'll be there soon."

He hangs up, and I sigh in relief.

Ten minutes later, he knocks on my office door.

I remember that he has a key to let himself into the top floor but not inside my studio. Getting up from my desk chair, I move to the door and open it up for him.

He's looking freshly shaved, and I take in his designer gray and white pinstripe suit and matching gray tie. There's not a hair out of place from whatever styling gel he uses to keep his waves secured. During my inspection, he bends to capture my lips with his in a hard but brief kiss.

"Hey, Shell."

"Hi," I breathe.

I look up at him with new butterflies filling my stomach. My mouth is wide open as I stare at him for a moment, still unable to believe that he's here to help me.

"Come inside." I gesture to the studio. He strides in, and I close the door as he moves straight to the little office where my white desk is. I don't even have to tell him; he's already clicking the mouse and typing on the keyboard.

I stand beside him, watching in awe.

An hour goes by, and I'm all set up.

"Maybe I should test it for you. Book a class from my phone."

"Good idea. I'll do that too."

So we both jump on the website and book a class.

"Have you thought about an app?"

"I thought about using a third-party app because it's cheaper and easier than setting up my own."

"I could give you the money. And you can hire someone to set it up straight away."

As much as I love how sweet of an offer that is, I can't take it. This is my journey. It's a dream for me, so I want to do everything on my own. I don't ever want to rely on a guy again.

I don't have the kind of money or mental capacity to take on something as big as designing my app. It also reminds me how things come easy to him compared to me.

"Thanks for the offer, but right now, I'm happy with the website. Maybe in a few months, I'll look into the app."

"Well, it looks like it all works."

I touch his arm, leaning into him. "Thank you. I'm sorry for bugging you again."

He twists to face me. "It's my pleasure. It's nice, helping you and doing something other than the same things I do every day."

We leave my studio and head downstairs. His hand interlaces with mine, and I rest my head on his shoulder, the gravity of how tired I am hitting me now.

We kiss before parting ways.

A few hours later, I arrive at his modern coastal two-story beach house in the Hamptons by helicopter. He had surprised me by organizing it.

His house is stunning. It's all clean lines, large windows, and a mix of natural wood and stone. I wonder if the inside is just as pretty, but as I join him on the porch, where it's decorated with a comfortable seat and potted plants, he suggests a beach walk.

With our hands entwined, we head to the beach, where I kick off my sneakers to sink my feet into the cold yet soft sand. The shoreline stretches for miles in both directions. I follow his lead as we head right. Soaking in the beautiful sight and the sound of waves constantly crashing, occasionally avoiding seaweed or seashells. It feels like heaven having the wind in my hair and the smell of salty air around us.

As kids laugh with their families and dogs, that hope of my own family one day makes my insides vibrate. The impossible might be possible now.

"How often do you come down here?" I ask.

He sighs heavily. "Not as often as I'd like."

"Would you live here?"

The atmosphere here is so relaxed compared to the hustle and bustle back in New York. Taking a glance at his bliss-filled face, I look down at our joined hands before back to the people soaking up the sun.

"No. I like it as a summer house, but it doesn't feel like home."

I get that, because some houses and areas give you a vacation feeling, not a forever feeling.

"What about retirement?"

He chuckles as we turn around to head back to his place. "I haven't thought about it. Are you telling me I'm old?"

I giggle. "No, just asking."

After the leisurely stroll, we enter his house and it's just as I thought—coastal.

My eyes widen at the high ceilings, neutral colors, a fireplace, and modern appliances. But my nostrils flare from the smell of something cooking. My stomach grumbles. It smells a bit like onion and garlic and slow-cooked meat.

My eyebrows pinch. "You started cooking?"

We wander into his kitchen. I follow, grabbing the back of the stool, and put my bag down.

"I marinated some chicken and placed it in the slow cooker when we were messaging. It should be done. I've just got to pop the veggies and the potatoes on. Then put some bread out."

"You've done a lot," I say quietly, amazed by how much he's done for me.

"It's not much."

He thinks that way, but to me, this is a lot.

"Has no one ever cooked for you before?"

"Yeah."

"Of course they have," he says, his tone a little darker. I sense a hint of jealousy. Only, he doesn't know that it's not a male.

"My parents and roommates," I say, smirking.

"He didn't?"

With a sigh, I shake my head.

He must sense my sadness and changes the subject.

"When was the last time you saw your parents or your family?"

I try to think back a while.

"A few months." I shake my head, lips pursed. "Have you been to Connecticut before?"

"No."

"I'm surprised," I mumble.

"Why?"

"You seem to be well-traveled, and it's only a two-hour drive away."

He nods. "I am worldly to some degree, but only when it comes to work. I used to travel a lot for work, but now I leave it to my employees to do."

"Why?"

"I prefer to do it for pleasure, not for work."

For a moment, I picture him in Connecticut.

The quiet town. Simple life. I think it would suit him.

It would probably bore him after a little bit, but I could see him enjoying it as a break stop. It has the same feeling here gives you...peace. Growing up, I'd enjoy nature walks along the tracks, the fireplace in the living room, the open space in the yard, where I'd play games with my sister or study for high school exams. The sun and air kissing my skin, life was so much easier then.

"I'll see my parents when I've set up my studio, and I can trust the staff to lead without me."

Then maybe I could go for a weekend-long break.

"Family is important," he says in a serious tone. His voice makes me think he's talking about his own.

"I love how close you are with yours."

"They're very important to me. No matter how annoying my brothers are. Holidays, birthdays, any celebrations, we are always together."

I smile, but I wonder what it would've been like growing up with three brothers. Noisy, I bet.

"Has it always been like that, or just since your gram got sick?"

Nova has told me and Summer about his gram's because that's how Jeremy and Nova connected. Gram has breast cancer and Nova's dad has colon cancer.

"We've always been close," he says. "Do you want a drink with dinner?"

"Sure. I'll grab it," I offer, wanting to help.

He smiles. A devilishly handsome one and points to an area. "Glasses are in that cupboard. Wine is in the cellar. Take the stairs on the right and you'll see it."

I follow the directions and enter the dimly lit cellar. I admire the wall that's full of rows of bottles on wooden racks, stretched out with a variety of shapes and sizes. The air is cool and heavy with the rich aroma of aged wines. "Wow, this is crazy," I mumble to myself. The lights cast a warm glow over the stone walls, highlighting the labels as I try to find something that looks good. He could have warned me he had this type of selection. I'm a little lost. I must've been there for a while because a warm hand snakes around my middle.

"Oh," I breathe.

As his other hand wraps around my stomach, he snuggles into my neck, his heavy breath in my ear. His voice is low and quiet as he asks, "What are you looking for?"

The electricity of his touch makes it hard to talk. But I use the energy he projects to find my voice.

"Wine."

He chuckles, digging his fingers into my ribs, making me squirm in his arm. "Naughty girl."

"You have too many to choose from."

As his nearness kindles feelings of fire, I focus on breathing deeply through my nose, but it also means I'm inhaling his delicious scent.

A hot ache grows in my throat. "Spicy."

"Spicy? Huh. Good choice."

When he moves, I mourn the loss of the heat from his proximity.

"This is the one, then."

I grab the bottle of red from his hands, reading the red wine label as he continues talking.

"This peppery Shiraz will go well with our dinner."

I expect to leave the room, but his arms tighten around me once again. He kisses my neck, and I swallow a moan, concentrating on holding the bottle and not dropping it.

My knees weaken when he runs his nose up and down my throat to the side of my neck.

"You make me crazy." His voice, deep and sensual, sends a ripple of awareness through me.

"Later," I breathe, clutching the bottle as I twist in his arms.

He doesn't move his face from mine. I gaze into his dark, broody eyes. He's thinking, and I don't get long to wonder what he's thinking about, because he reclaims my lips, crushing me to him.

I sink into his strong arms and enjoy the velvet warmth of his kiss. It flows through my veins. I'll never get sick of kissing him.

I'm clutching the wine in my hands between our chests, while his hands explore my lower back.

When we pull away to take a breath, he whispers into my hair, "Let's go eat dinner."

His hand pushes my lower back gently, encouraging me to walk, embracing me the whole way back to the dining table. Only then does his hand leave my body.

I put the bottle in the middle of the table and take in all the food.

"I think you've cooked for a family, not just for us."

"I wanted to make sure you have enough to eat." He reaches over and twists open the bottle and pours wine into our glasses. "You can take leftovers to Summer."

I smile, knowing Summer would love that. She'd love him more than she already does.

We take our seats across from each other, and I feel a knot in my throat form at the thought of how lonely living alone would be. At least I have Summer.

I concentrate on eating, and afterwards Evan ushers me outside to his deck, where chairs sit facing the ocean. If I thought it was beautiful during the day, it's absolutely captivating at night. With the wind rustling the trees, insects and sea birds making noises, and the ocean waves crashing, it's the perfect place to relax.

"Thank you for cooking for me tonight."

His mouth curves into an infectious grin. "Anything for you."

His disarming smile makes my heart thump erratically.

But as we sit in silence, my mind can't let go of the missing facts I have about his past. He knows everything about Bobby, and I feel like I barely know a thing about his ex. We touched on it briefly, but I still have unanswered questions.

"Can I ask you something?"

His head turns to look at me. "Of course."

"How long were you and your ex together?"

He doesn't blink. "Five years."

"And you were engaged?" I probe further.

"Yes," he responds with a tight jaw. It's the only uncomfortable sign he's shown tonight.

"Would you ever get engaged again?" I ask, my curiosity piqued.

He looks out to the ocean, taking a few minutes before answering. My hands are tightly resting on my lap, waiting eagerly for his reply.

"No, honestly, never again," he says firmly.

My lips press into a grimace as I lower my head. Inside, my heart is shrinking. I always envisioned my father walking me down the aisle in my big dress to my husband-to-be. The celebration going all night, starting with our bridal waltz to the speech where he declares his love for me in front of all our family and friends.

So where does this leave us?

A tense silence envelops the air.

"Would you want to get engaged?" he asks, staring over at me.

I flick my eyes back up. Ignoring the cold knot that forms in my stomach, I dip my head. "Yeah, I see myself getting married one day."

Color drains from his face, and I can't control the trembling of my body.

With Bobby, I thought I was close to that, and he crushed my dreams. Now with Evan, he's telling me I will never get it. I feel as if a hand has closed around my throat.

Would I be willing to give up all my dreams when I've always wanted to get married and have children?

I have a much stronger guard up now. Because no, I don't want to give up my goals for somebody else.

I keep doing that. I keep giving up everything I want. It's not anyone's fault. Definitely not Evan's, and I get it. But it's also not my fault. I didn't cheat. I didn't hurt him. Do I deserve to be punished?

No. I don't.

The looming silence is like a heavy mist and is making me uncomfortable, so I decide to enjoy the ocean waves while I take a moment to think.

"Are you okay?" he asks.

"Yeah. I just have a lot on my mind, and I'm tired."

Which isn't a lie. My mind is going around and around in circles, and now, suddenly, I'm exhausted.

He stands and holds out a hand to me. "Let's go lie on the sofa."

"What about the dishes?"

"Later," he dismisses my concern.

I don't argue and take his hand. We walk back inside to the sofa and sit down. When he drags my body close to his, I snuggle in, trying to get warm. He reaches behind me and pulls a blanket, throwing it over my legs.

I wrap myself in the blanket. "I'm going to fall asleep; this is too cozy."

His fingers stroke my hair. "Sleep then. I'll be right here when you wake up."

He flicks the TV on and tries to find something to watch. In the meantime, my body becomes heavy, and I close my eyes, surrendering to the darkness.

I wake when I feel weightless in his arms. I'm being carried as if I'm light as a feather. His strong arms support me.

"Evan?" I say groggily.

"I'm right here. Sleep, baby," he reassures me.

This moment of Evan carrying me in his arms reminds me of how a man carries his bride. Of how it would feel if Evan was my husband. I swallow hard and bite back tears, remembering he doesn't want the same future as me.

We arrive in his bedroom, and I kiss him in a frenzy, trying to clear my mind. I don't want to think about it tonight. I can think about it tomorrow after I've slept on it. Maybe I can talk to Summer and Nova about it. Right now, with tears of bittersweet pleasure, I want to enjoy our final moments together because they might be our last.

CHAPTER 24

EVAN

WE'RE TEARING EACH OTHER'S clothes off as we enter my bedroom. It's a frenzy I've never experienced before. She seems to be feeling the same way as she tries to rip at my shirt.

Why are we so impatient tonight? It's as if that first time wasn't enough. But I don't overthink it; I just give myself over to this moment.

My pants are unbuttoned and she's fiddling with my zipper before she pushes it down.

Her eyes travel hungrily over my body. My gaze doesn't leave her face, and I enjoy the way she soaks me in.

Restraint snapping, I rip off her dress, revealing a sexy purple lace bra and a matching thong.

My semi is now a full hard-on from the sight of her, knowing she wore this for me tonight.

She licks her lips, and my heart pounds harder when she grabs at my briefs and pushes them down.

My hands are on her breasts through her lace, the fabric soft and delicate just like her. A sexy sigh leaves her mouth as I squeeze and rub.

I'm quick to remove the bra. Even though it's so pretty. I just need her already. I'm desperate to get my fill of her.

I bend to bring my mouth to one of her puckered nipples. Sucking on one, then move to the other, giving it as much attention as the first. Her body vibrates underneath my touch as her fingers grip my hair in a vise.

When I move my fingers to the sides of her thong, shaky breaths leave her lips as if she is about to come.

Sliding her thong down her long legs, I see evidence of her readiness.

I grunt. "You're wet."

"Evan," she whimpers.

"You're incredible," I say, running my eyes slowly over her body, soaking in every inch of her.

Both of us stand naked. Our clothes scattered along the floor. We don't speak. Our heavy breaths fill the air. I'm so feral for her, ready to have her. But as much as I want to take her here on my bedroom floor, I want to fuck her in my bed. She deserves to be cherished like the beautiful woman she is.

I lift her up and lay her on my bed. And fuck, she looks incredible stretched out on my mattress.

She parts her thighs, and I know I'm going to come quickly so I sit between them. Her pretty pussy makes a rumble leave my chest. "Fucking hell, baby. You're killing me."

Skimming my hands up her inner thighs, I enjoy her smooth skin until I reach her core. I flick my gaze from her hooded eyes and parted lips, down to her pussy that's glistening for me, begging to be touched. Moving one hand from her inner thigh, I touch her clit, while my other hand keeps her legs parted so I can look at her when she takes my fingers.

"You're so swollen and so fucking perfect for me."

She bucks her hips, trying to get me to finger her. "Evan. More."

I smirk, but I keep rubbing her clit in hard circles. Wanting to slow down a little to have her come once before I fuck her. "Soon. I promise. You're doing so good, baby."

After another couple of slow hard rubs, I drag my finger through her wetness and slide two fingers straight inside her. Her walls clamp down at the intrusion, and I watch her eyes roll back into her head. Pulling out slowly, I then re-enter her.

"You feel amazing," I hiss, increasing the pace.

Her body rocks, meeting my rhythm, as she keeps her eyes closed.

Every time I'm all the way inside, she tightens. It's fucking incredible. Her body is so responsive to my touch. Feeling needy to be inside her now, I curl my fingers down her front wall and rub my thumb over her clit.

Her eyes snap open, locking onto mine. "Do that again," she begs.

My cock pulses, loving her begging, and the plea in her honey-colored eyes.

I do it again but slower. "Is that what you want?" I ask huskily.

"Yes," she pants, urging me on.

She arches her back, but I keep fingering her. To help her come, I bring my mouth down on her clit and twirl my tongue hard on it, which has her gasping for air. "Evan." My name leaves her lips in a high-pitched cry.

She's so fucking close. I hum against her, unable to talk with my mouth buried in her pussy. I can't get enough. I'm relentless.

I can feel her tension on my fingers, and her thighs tighten around my head, suffocating me, but I love it, and I don't bother trying to keep them open.

I want her to smother me with her pussy. I keep going and she's rocking her hips, chasing her release.

"Come, baby." I slide one more finger into her pussy.

She moans loudly. Her pussy tightens around my three fingers, and she calls out my name in one long pant. It's seductive and almost poetic. "Evan-n-n."

She's quivering underneath me, coming as hard as she possibly can. But I don't stop, I keep going. My cock throbs at the sight of her coming undone.

When her body finally goes limp, I slowly sit back and lift my head to gaze up at her. Fuck. Her face is exquisite.

"I liked that," she rasps out in a weak voice. Her bright eyes gleam. I love this post-orgasm look.

"I've only just started," I warn with a wicked grin.

I lie on the bed beside her, where she's melted into the mattress, all cute and lust-drunk.

"Was it that good?" I ask, my eyes roaming her face.

She rolls her eyes and shoves at my chest. "Don't fish for compliments."

I chuckle. "I'm serious."

Her head rocks side to side on the mattress. "You know it was good. You just want me to boost your ego."

I tickle her side as she writhes and giggles beneath me. "No, I'm reminding you I can make you come multiple times."

Instead of rushing up to kiss and fuck her, I take in every inch of her skin, admiring her toned body. Starting with her inner thighs and then moving up to kiss a path along her middle until I reach the base of her neck. She tips her head back, welcoming my lips on her delicate skin.

Lifting my head up, I hover my face over hers. When I gaze down, I find heated brown pools staring back at me. It matches my own burning need. I'm so hard I could blow any second.

She's looking at me like I am her everything, and it's scary. Scary that I could trust this girl. But I don't let the cloud of doubts ruin this moment. I grab a condom from a new box I picked up at the store today and roll it on.

I shift, so my back is leaning against the headboard, my legs long out in front as my erection stands tall. Her eyes stare at it as her tongue pokes out and skims her lips, the sight making me growl. "Come here and ride my cock, baby."

Her eyes lift and widen at my command, but she doesn't hesitate, instead she moves closer to me, shuffling until she's straddling me. My palms immediately skim her thighs until they settle at her hips. "You do it."

She rolls her hips, and I grunt.

Digging my fingers in her hips, to still her, I whisper. "Grab my cock and put it inside you. I want to watch you fuck me."

She grabs onto my shoulder and lifts her hips, and with her other hand, she grabs my dick and lines me up. My cock hits the outside of her entrance, and I jerk. Fuck.

I take a deep breath as she lowers and I slide deep inside her tight, wet pussy, watching her mouth part. Our eyes lock as I watch her taking all of me. She's so tight and fucking perfect.

Both of her hands find my shoulders.

"You ready?" I grit out, as her pussy stretches around me.

She hums. "Yes."

"Keep your eyes on me. I want to see you fall apart."

She answers me by rocking her hips, and my chest swells.

Fucking hell. She feels like home.

I can't help but use my hands and help lift her and watch her slam back down, her pretty tits bouncing each time.

"You take me so well," I say, as her walls adjust to me. Every time she clamps down, strangling my cock, I have to fight myself not to fucking blow like a damn teenager who's never had sex.

"Fuck, Evan." Her back arches on a moan. The strangled sound unhinges me. In a new frenzy, I rock my hips, meeting her rocking, and quicken the pace, desperate to watch her come undone.

I want to give her the best sex of her life, to thank her for giving me everything that I didn't know I needed.

She fits so perfectly with me. She's consuming me and she doesn't even know it.

Her body shifts with every thrust.

On the next drop, she tips her head back. Her pulse pounds in her throat. My lips curl into a smile as my hand comes up to touch it, fascinated by it. It goes higher and her own lips lift into a seductive smile. "Yes," she moans, as she tightens her walls around me.

I drop my hand beside her again, needing to steady myself for a second.

"Keep your eyes on me, Shell," I rasp, as the sounds of our skin slapping against each other fill the air.

"Oh my God," she chants on an airy groan.

Bliss is written across her face. It sets me off and she fucks me harder.

Fuck, I need her to orgasm now.

"You're so fucking perfect for me," I ramble, as if my brain is talking on its own.

My fingers grab her hips to help her. Her pussy clamps me, and I know as she screams the words, "I'm coming."

Her hands move from my shoulders to my neck to still her. As she moans out her orgasm, her fingers dig into my skin.

"Yes," I growl back, but I continue rocking my hips up into her. I want to come at the same time as her, so I pump a little harder. My balls tighten, and I choke out, "Fuck! I'm coming."

When she finishes, I still, and my cock jerks, emptying inside her. Spots come in front of my eyes. Fucking hell. I haven't come like that in a very long time.

She collapses on my chest, her body quivering on top of me. "Are you okay?" I ask breathlessly after I come down from my high.

"Yes, that was perfect," she breathes out so quietly I almost miss it.

I stroke her back as she sucks in a deep lungful of air. "So fucking perfect," I say.

She sits back, her eyes are blazing so much brighter. "Just like you," she says in her breathy voice.

"Come here." I curve one finger toward her.

She giggles, as if I'm crazy for thinking she'd want to go anywhere else but here, lying with me. The sound is so light and sexy. It's the sound of letting go and just enjoying the moment.

We kiss, but I want to hold her in bed, so I roll her onto her back, pull myself out, and discard the rubber. Returning to the bed, I push back the blankets and help her under. I hold her around the middle as I curl up behind her. Keeping her safe and close in my arms, as if that's the only place for her.

I lay a kiss on her temple to whisper in her ear, "Do you have to let Summer know where you are?"

She lifts her chin to meet my eyes as her cheek pulls at one side. "No, she knows I'm with you."

I poke her flushed nose and wink at her. "She knows I'm good for you."

She giggles and smacks my chest. "You're cocky some-times, aren't you?"

"I'm definitely confident," I answer at the same time she yawns.

I kiss her forehead, then her lips. "Go to sleep, baby."

She blinks her eyes rapidly, fighting her tiredness. "What will you do? Watch me again?"

I kiss her lips again, because I'm a sucker and I can't get enough of her, then I move my lips to her ear to whisper, "I'll sleep here with you."

She doesn't bother protesting as her eyelids flutter closed. I enjoy the heat of her body and her scent, but sleep evades me. My mind drifts back to our earlier conversation about engagements and marriage—the way her face paled and her chin dropped at my response has me tied up in knots. Could this be the beginning of the end for us?

CHAPTER 25

CHELSEA

"I SEE. WELL, THANK you for your time," I say with a forced smile, closing the door as I finish up with another disaster instructor interview back in the city. With the opening so soon, I'm becoming a little stressed. Why can't I find more competent instructors? I massage my temples, feeling the beginning of a headache. There's a stack of resumes on my desk with notes. I'm also overseeing the construction of the locker rooms, making sure they get finished on time while managing everything else. There has already been a delay in the building because the wood material I needed is on back order. I chose one that would match the rest of the studio, but I won't budge. I wanted that exact one; it's what I envisioned. I won't sacrifice what makes me happy. It's my name on this business so I want to be proud.

"Come on, Chelsea, you can do this," I mutter, moving away to have my lunch break when I'm interrupted by my phone ringing.

An unknown number flashes. I frown. *Who could that be...*

"Hello?"

"Hi, Chelsea," Bobby replies casually.

"What do you want?" I snap, as my stomach churns at the sound of his voice.

"I'm calling to ask if we can have dinner together?"

He's talking to me in a voice he's never used before. It's soft and kind. So unlike him.

"No chance," I say, his words seeping like rot through my bones.

"What do you mean?" Now his voice has a hint of annoyance. The real him is slipping back in.

I grip the phone tighter. Every fiber of my being feels stronger now that I am away from him. "We aren't together. I'm not interested in you."

I'm not going backward; I've come so far. Slowly building my confidence back up.

"You won't give me a chance to explain," he chokes out. "I even sent you roses."

Is he fucking kidding me? He decided to buy them after we broke up. Jerk.

"There's nothing to explain." I exhale heavily, moving around the studio and cleaning up. I discard the roses that he bought immediately. The builders are out to lunch, and they'll be back to make more of a mess, so what I'm doing is pointless, but I need something to do while I talk to him. It seems to be calming down my irritation.

Taking a big inhale, I decide I need to be honest with him. It may get him to leave me alone once and for all. "You need to move on and leave me alone."

He makes a disapproving sound in my ear before sneering, "Is it because of him?"

Pausing, I hold on to the Pilates ball that fell from a box. Squeezing the PVC tight in my hands as perspiration coats my skin. *Evan...*

I close my eyes, controlling my next word so it sounds unaffected. "Who?"

I'm not stupid, he wants me to say his name.

"Don't be dumb, Chelsea," he insults me.

I drop the ball in the well of the Pilates bed and straighten. "I'm not dumb. Don't call me that." My own voice rises as hurt shoots through me.

"Well stop acting like it, Chelsea. Do you have feelings for Evan?"

"It's none of your fucking business," I bite back, pacing the office as a new spike of adrenaline hits me. He's in my past now. I've already moved on with my life. "Leave me the fuck alone!" I say, hanging up, happy I got the last word in. It feels like a win. Finally, I stood up for myself.

With trembling fingers, I block his new phone number. But I need to rid him from my mind.

I'm supposed to be having lunch, but I can't stomach food right now. My belly is in knots. So I walk to take a seat in my back room, which I call my office. It's not big or glamorous. Definitely nothing like Evan's grand floor upstairs. The tiny wood desk and chair are enough to do my basic administrative tasks. I begin sorting through the files and booking new instructor interviews. But five minutes later, the distraction is not enough to rid me from the anger of Bobby's call or the anxiety I feel about the fact that Evan doesn't want to get engaged again.

I know I need to hear my mom's voice, so with a heavy squeeze of my heart, I call her.

"Chelsea?" Mom says, when she answers the phone almost immediately.

"Hi, Mom," I reply, struggling to keep my voice steady.

"How are you doing today?"

It's the same question she always asks, but this time, it hits me differently. My eyes fill with tears, and my voice cracks when I answer her. "Not so good."

"Oh, darling, what's wrong?"

"Setting up the studio has been a bigger task than I thought it would be." Once I start, I can't stop. "I started dating someone, and I really like him, but I don't think we want the same things. Then there was a delivery that went to the wrong state. I haven't been sleeping. The list goes on."

"Oh, darling. I'm so sorry. But let's start with one thing at a time. What's bothering you the most?"

I pause, her question easy. "The guy I'm falling for...he doesn't want to get engaged again."

"He actually said that?"

"Yes. And you know how much I've always wanted to get married."

"I do," she replies, and I can hear the smile in her voice. "You've been obsessed with weddings and babies since you were five."

Tears leak from my eyes, her words hitting me hard as I realize this isn't some silly childhood dream. It's deeply important to me.

"I don't want to give up my dream for a guy again, Mom."

"I don't want you to either, darling. You'll never be truly happy if you do."

"So what do I do about it?" I ask sniffling.

"Relationships are about compromise, but not at the expense of your own happiness. Talk to him, share your feelings, and see what he says. But remember, you deserve to be with someone who shares your dreams and values."

I take a deep breath, letting her words sink in. She's right, I can't ignore what's important to me.

"Thanks, Mom," I say softly, wiping away the last tear that trickles down my cheek. "I needed to hear that."

"I'm always here for you, Chelsea. Just remember, you deserve the best, so don't settle."

"I will," I reply, feeling a new sense of clarity and calmness. "I think I know what I need to do."

Chapter 26

Evan

I'm talking to the security firm. They set up cameras at the new office.

I'm trying to pay attention, but my focus is on the person on the screen. Bobby's on the sidewalk of my new office building.

"Can we get audio?" I ask without moving from my position. I'm leaning on the desk, my hands curled into fists, and I continue watching the computer screen with a hard-set jaw.

Bobby's wearing black jeans and a gray shirt. One hand is in his pocket, and the other's holding his phone to his ear.

I run my hand through my hair. Why is he there?

"Yeah," the security guy answers calmly, then hits something, and Bobby's voice echoes in the room.

"I'm calling to ask if we can have dinner together?" Bobby asks, walking in circles on the concrete.

I frown, not only at the words, but his tone.

The awfully fake seductive tone that I hear around the office.

But as I let his words sink in, my stomach drops. Have Bobby and Chelsea been talking behind my back? Would she be interested in him again?

My brain continues to come up with a million scenarios until he speaks again.

"What do you mean?" he says, pausing on the spot, clearly annoyed.

I'm holding my breath, waiting for her to prove she's just like my ex, and I shouldn't have believed Chelsea would be different. But his next words have me standing up.

"You won't give me a chance to explain?" Bobby snaps, pacing the sidewalk again. His hand is out of his pocket now. "I even sent you roses."

I fucking knew it was that slimy bastard.

"Is it because of him?" he says as his hand flies out of his pocket and punches the wall.

My eyes bulge from their sockets at his angry outburst.

"Don't be dumb, Chelsea," he says.

My heartbeat pounds in my ears as my body grows hot.

He called her dumb. She's not dumb. He's fucking dumb.

A throat clears behind me. I turn my head as he asks. "Do you still need me?"

For a moment, I forgot the security guy was still here.

"No, I need to go," I mutter, spinning back around and taking a final look at Bobby on the screen. He's pissed, but I'm fucking outraged at what I just witnessed. As much as I want to continue watching, icy fear grasps my throat at what could happen if I don't get down there. I take off down the stairs, not bothering to see if security followed.

I tell Gabby as I pass her desk that I'll be back. I don't wait for her reply. The elevators are too slow, and I don't want to get stuck talking to anyone. Pushing the heavy metal door, I take the fire exit stairs. I get outside, where I welcome the cool air on my perspired skin. Opening the door of my car, I tell the driver to drive as fast as possible to the new office.

I peel off my suit jacket in the car, tossing it to the side. Then I remove my cufflinks and unbutton and roll up my sleeves.

Five minutes later, I push the door open before the car is completely parked and call out, "I'll be back."

I storm the pavement and, thank fuck, Bobby's still here. He's not on the phone anymore, though. So why is he still here? Is he waiting for her? Will he hurt her? I shake my head, not letting that happen. I'll handle this.

When I storm closer, my heavy footsteps and labored breaths give me away. His head lifts and his eyes widen slightly.

Gotcha.

"You weren't expecting me, were you?" I say, my voice dripping with venom.

"No," he replies calmly, crossing his arms over his chest.

My lips curl as I sneer. "You're meant to be down on Broadway covering the firing of the princess's bodyguard. Instead, you're here calling to talk to Chelsea."

"I wasn't," he lies.

My rage claws to the surface. I try to keep the anger inside and stay professional. I point to the camera. His head turns to follow my finger.

"I could see and hear you," I say smoothly, my lip curling.

He twists back to me with a frown, unbothered. "Why were you watching me?"

His accusatory voice irks me. I'm the CEO. I don't have time to watch employees. Does he actually think I have nothing better to do?

Through a tight jaw, I spit out, "I wasn't watching you. I just had these installed and the security firm was showing me the setup when I saw you."

Not that I had to explain myself to him. I'm not in the wrong.

He squints his eyes at me, as if assessing if I'm lying.

I move closer to him. "You're stalking and harassing her, Bobby." My voice is quiet, as I see a group passing us and staring.

"I'm not!" Bobby shouts, his hands flying out and making a scene. "I'm on my way to take pictures."

I freeze, eyes wide at his outburst. Suddenly, I realize his composure is slipping. His usually neat hair is messy and oily. His eyes are bloodshot like he has been drinking all night.

I take a deep breath, trying to regulate my breathing and gain control of the situation before Chelsea comes down. "You're going in the wrong direction for that."

"I'm going now."

The tone of his voice makes my jaw twitch. He's being a smartass.

I check my watch, which adds to my disappointment. Keeping myself calm, even though inside I'm vibrating with anger, I answer scathingly, "It's too late."

"It's not," he spits.

My temple throbs from the conversation, the dull ache growing with every word he spews. He's arguing with me now, and I can't take a moment more of this, of him. I worked too hard for him to ruin everything.

"You know what, I've had enough. Your behavior is unacceptable," I grumble, annoyed by his lack of professionalism.

An alert comes through my phone. Pulling out my phone, I curse. "Are you fucking kidding me!" Our competition has photos and an article covering the firing.

"What are you saying?" he asks, his shoulders dropping as realization dawns on him.

"You're fired. Go pack your shit, and I'll call HR." I lift my chin, clutching my phone tighter. I'll have to deal with the fallout later.

"What about the pictures?" he asks, dropping his arms, but his body remains rigid.

I rub the back of my neck, frustration building as I take in his bleeding knuckles, a reminder of his outburst. "Fuck the pictures. You've missed her anyways."

I turn my phone and show him the article with the headline glaring back at us. His eyes widen, and his face turns white as paper, his shoulders sagging further. He knows he has no leg to stand on. But just as I thought I won, he spits one last remark.

"Fuck you. Enjoy my sloppy seconds."

I squeeze my fists, hold my breath, and stand still. I'm telling myself not to punch him in the face. That Chelsea is not sloppy fucking anything. She's a graceful, intelligent, bubbly person, who deserves love, not a cheating scumbag like him.

When he realizes I'm not biting, he turns around and walks away.

Letting go of the breath I was holding, I call HR as I climb into the car. I urgently need to restructure our photography team and rehire a replacement. His sudden departure will disrupt the department by adding more work to some employees, but it won't be for long, and I'll give them all bonuses.

But fuck, I'm happy. I finally feel like the dead weight has been lifted. That's what he brought to the company. And fuck, I kept him longer than I wanted to. But harassing and stalking his ex on my time is unacceptable. But it's even more than that. He's hurting the woman I'm falling for.

CHAPTER 27

CHELSEA

My heart lodges in my throat as tears well up in my eyes. I hold my phone with a trembling hand, staring at my screen. There it is——a photo of me splashed across the Industry News section of Evan's newspaper, The New York Press.

Not just any photo, but an old racy lingerie picture I once sent to Bobby when we were first dating.

I want to curl up in a ball. *How did it end up here?*

I haven't heard from him since he called me two days ago. I've put that awkward exchange behind me. But now this disgusting, vindictive revenge act makes me think he hasn't moved on and that he's trying to remind me he still holds all the power.

I'll never be rid of him.

The tears brim in my eyes uncontrollably as pain crushes my chest.

My family, friends, clients——everyone will know about this. And Evan...Surely, he didn't approve this?

I brought this disaster upon him. I should never have agreed to get revenge on Bobby. Now, this humiliating image is out there for the whole world to see. My phone starts buzzing; it begins with Nova, then Summer, all flooding me with calls and then texts saying, "Call me."

Evie walks into the studio after I begged her to come in early due to an emergency.

Her face drops as she sees me, arms opening wide as she steps closer.

There's no point denying a hug, I really need one from a friend. I wrap my arms around her, sobbing into her neck. One of her arms encircling my shoulder, the other rubs my back, as she whispers tenderly, "It's okay. It'll be old news tomorrow."

I sniff, feeling the tears still slip past my lashes as I pull away from her. Grateful she was able to meet the cable guy for the finishing touches on the locker room because I didn't have it in me. I don't want to face anybody today.

I want to hide.

A part of me wishes I could jump in my car and drive straight to Connecticut.

But I have my grand opening for the studio to prepare for. I can't let myself down. I can't be a coward. I've come too far with this studio.

I'm sure after a week, I'll be old news, right?

A half-naked woman on the front of Evan's gossip section. I haven't even read the article. The headline, "The New Mrs. Lincoln Media" is bad enough.

I know I shouldn't, but I can't stop myself. After I detangle myself from Evie, I slump in my office chair and open the article on my phone to read it properly.

The New Mrs. Lincoln Media

Image: *Chelsea's lingerie picture.*

Concerns rise over Evan Lincoln's leadership and professional conduct amid his relationship with Chelsea Macfarlane.

There's been growing concerns about Mr. Evan Lincoln, the CEO of Lincoln Media.

His new relationship with Chelsea Macfarlane, a Pilates Instructor, has raised questions about his professional judgment.

Employees report experiencing a significant change in his behavior, which many attribute it to his new relationship.

One long-time employee shared, "It's like he's become a different person."

These issues have been raised with Mr. Lincoln, but according to insiders, he's shown no interest in addressing these concerns. "We've tried to bring it up, but it feels like we're being ignored."

What's more troubling to some is Miss MacFarlane's apparent financial interest in Mr. Lincoln's company. She recently acquired a new Pilates studio conveniently located in the same building as Mr. Lincoln's private office, leading to speculation about her true intentions. "It's too convenient to be a coincidence," remarked one employee.

There are growing fears that Miss Macfarlane may be more interested in Mr. Lincoln's wealth and business than in the relationship itself. This suspicion is reportedly causing tension within the company, leading to low morale and a potential loss of key employees.

"It's hard to stay motivated when you feel undervalued and disrespected," said one employee.

The issues surrounding Evan Lincoln's leadership and his relationship with Chelsea Macfarlane highlight an immediate need for intervention to protect the company's future.

Tears stream down my cheeks as I read. Finishing the article, I drop my phone and cry into my hands. Sobs wrack my body.

My phone buzzes again. I blink back the tears, but my vision remains blurry as I pick up my phone. Evan.

Another sob slips at seeing his name. I can't talk right now. I'd sound like a strangled cat, or worse, I'd be a blubbering mess. I need a moment to collect myself, so I let it go to voicemail. But he calls again. And again. Each time, making me cry harder. After all the failed call attempts, he texts.

> **Evan:** *Call me.*

I force myself to get up, needing to leave. Grabbing my bag, I exit my office and pass Evie. "Will you be okay to drive?" she asks, wearing a worried expression as she walks toward me.

I must look like a mess. So I wipe my tears and clear my throat. "Yeah. I'm sorry."

She offers me a sympathetic smile. "Don't be sorry. It's not your fault."

I give her a half one back. "Thanks for helping me out."

"Anytime, boss."

My heart swells a little from the nickname *boss,* but I'm unable to completely enjoy it because of the disgusting image of me splashed in the media. I leave the studio and head home.

As much as I want to drive straight to my parents' place to run away, I don't.

When I arrive home, I find myself alone. Summer left me a note to tell me she's out. So I throw my bag on the table and rush to my room. Collapsing into my blankets, I cry out the remainder of my tears.

"Chelsea?" Summer's voice sounds distant, as if she's underwater.

I sit up, rubbing my face as she enters the room.

"What time is it?" I ask, blinking at her.

Her gaze roams my face. "Six. Were you sleeping?"

It's still bright outside from daylight. I'm surprised I was able to fall asleep with the blinds open. I must have passed out from crying so much.

"I must have," I say, looking down at my hands tangled in my lap.

"I saw the article and tried to call you. Are you okay?" She moves to sit beside me on my bed.

"Not good," I reply on a shaky breath.

"Do you have any idea who did it?"

I turn to look at her, swallowing my shame. "It was Bobby. I sent him that picture."

"I always hated him."

I try to laugh, but it turns into a snort. "I know. I should've listened."

She leans her hand on my white blanket. "What did Evan say?"

I run my teeth over my bottom lip and stare at my white dresser across the room. I'm too embarrassed to meet her gaze. "I haven't spoken to him."

"Do you think he had anything to do with it?"

I shake my head as the answer falls easily from my mouth. "No."

She raises an eyebrow at me. "Then you should call him."

I sigh and let her know what I've been thinking. "We want different things."

"What do you mean?" she asks softly.

"He's so organized, and I'm kind of all over the place." I point to myself and peer up at her from under my wet lashes. My face feels puffy and sore. I'm sure I look as miserable as I feel.

Her eyebrows draw together. "He's not perfect, and I'm sure he doesn't expect you to be either."

"I brought this mess to his company."

"Bobby did, not you!" she argues.

But that's not the only reason I'm crying. I know that Evan and I won't be able to have a long-term relationship.

"That's not all. He doesn't want the same future as me," I admit. "Summer, I don't want another relationship where I give up my dreams for a guy."

Her face falls as she understands. "Well, that fucking sucks."

I nod, my gaze dropping to my hands as I pick at the skin around my nails. "Yeah, it does."

She shuffles on the bed, grabbing my hands to stop me picking. "You shouldn't have to give up anything."

I look up at her. "So what do I do?"

"It sounds like you need some space to think."

It's exactly what I want, and I keep coming back to the same conclusion. "I was thinking of going home for a few days after the studio opens."

She nods. "No, you should go now."

"But the studio——"

She shakes her head and squeezes my hand. "Can wait a few days."

I nod, knowing she's right. There's only a cleaner due to come before the grand opening, so a few days won't kill me.

"You need to talk to Evan before you go, though," she adds.

Even though all I want to do is avoid him, I can't ignore him forever.

She rubs my shoulder before squeezing it and standing.

I watch her walk out, softly closing my door behind her.

When she leaves my room, I pick up my phone and notice a few missed calls from Evan. I call him back. He answers on the first ring.

"Chelsea."

My heart pounds in my ears every time I hear his voice. "Hi."

"I've been worried about you." His voice is so sincere it makes me squeeze the phone tighter.

"I'm sorry I haven't——" I stop talking because I don't want to admit I've been crying hysterically over my idiot ex.

"I'm sorry that was printed. Please know I had nothing to do with it."

I shuffle on the bed until my back is against the headboard. "I know." I release a heavy sigh. "It was Bobby."

"I fired him and I'm trying to find out how he did it," he says angrily and continues talking. "But he isn't answering my calls." A grumble leaves Evan. "I'll find him."

"Thanks."

It's so silent between us, you can hear a pin drop, but then he speaks.

"Did you want to come over tonight?" His voice is so raw and tender it causes a lump to form in my throat.

I swallow hard, hating what I have to say next. "No. I'm going home."

"Connecticut?"

"Yes," I whisper.

"Why?"

"I want to get away from this mess, and this will be the only time off I get before the studio opens."

"Did you want me to come?"

My chest hurts. Really aches, because even though I've come to realize I love him, I need this time away to process everything. I deserve to have the future I want, and he should have the one he needs, and the only way to do that is give ourselves time apart.

"To be honest, I need to think about us too."

"Right."

Hating how he doesn't ask me why, I feel the need to explain. Because I don't want to end it like this, for him not to know the reason. He didn't know why his ex cheated, and it messed him up for years. I don't want to cause him more pain. He doesn't deserve that.

"You don't want to get engaged again, and I've always dreamed of a big wedding and a happy marriage." New tears fill my eyes as I continue to say what's in my heart. "I gave up everything for Bobby. I-I don't think I can do it again." I stumble over the last few words.

More crushing silence envelops me. I pull the phone away from my ear to check he's still on the line.

When I bring the phone back, his voice finally breaks the silence, softer now. "I get that. Thank you for telling me the truth."

"It's not that I don't care about you," I say, though it's strained. Tears spill down my cheeks, my heart shattering with each new salty tear.

"I care about you too," he says, filled with a mix of understanding and sorrow.

My throat aches and constricts until words get caught. Is this the end of us?

"Are you busy?" I hear in the background. My heart cracks a little more, knowing our conversation has been cut off already.

"I'll let you go." I hesitate but close my mouth, stopping the words, *I'll speak to you soon,* because will I? I doubt it. He knows we both want different things in our futures.

"Okay. Bye, Chelsea."

"Bye," I whisper and hang up.

My head falls, and so do fresh sobs.

CHAPTER 28

CHELSEA

THERE'S STILL NO NEWS about Bobby, but I find myself in the car to Connecticut. Anna picked me up, and she's been talking the whole time about her professor. It's a nice distraction.

Evan, well, he's gone radio silent. No calls or texts. But I haven't reached out to him either. Deep down, I wish he'd change his mind about getting engaged, but I can't expect him to change for me.

"You're quiet. Are you still thinking about the article?" Anna asks.

I grimace, remembering my semi-naked picture plastered for the world to see. Not that I permitted Bobby to do it.

"Yeah, a little."

"What's going on?"

I stare out the car window, watching the houses pass us by. We don't have much longer before we're with my parents.

"I haven't heard from Evan."

Her head whips to me, smirking. "You like a guy?"

I rub my makeup-free face, sinking into the seat. "Yes, but why is my life a mess?"

"It's not a mess. It's life. Nothing you love ever comes easy."

"I love him," I say quietly. Expecting her to lecture me about falling so soon after Bobby, but her next words leave me shocked.

"I know."

My head turns to look at her. Her lips twist into a small smirk.

"You knew?"

She tilts her head, meeting my gaze for a brief moment. "Of course."

"How?"

"Mom told me all about him helping you with the studio."

Of course she did...

"And what do you think?" I ask, knowing she has opinions on everything.

"I like him."

I exhale. "He's better than Bobby."

"Not hard to beat that." She laughs.

The sound of her laugh makes my lips part in the first true smile from me in twenty-four hours. "True."

"Will you press charges against Bobby for invading your privacy?"

It's suddenly cold in the car as I think about her question. I hadn't given any thought to it. I was too embarrassed to think clearly.

"Maybe."

"You're too nice."

"I'm not," I argue.

She doesn't know I broke things off with Evan because I chose me. My usual pattern of letting people's life choices become mine is gone. As much as I'm hurting, I know I couldn't keep doing it.

She pulls up into our parents' long drive, and another smile breaks free across my face. Trees and flowers line the driveway. My parents' wrap-around porch and house remind me how big the land is here. The garden is spectacular. I can't wait to sit out here and think.

Think about my next steps. And also unwind before my studio opens.

I don't even get a foot out before the wire door opens. I'm practically pulled from the car by my mom.

"Mom. Hi," I say, as she wraps her arms around me in a tight squeeze.

"I'm so glad to see you."

Her warm body and thumping heart relax me instantly. I needed her. I may be an adult, but I still need my parents' hugs sometimes.

"I missed you too," I mumble into her shoulder.

"How was the drive?" she asks, pulling away to hold my cheeks in her hands.

"Good. We talked and listened to music."

Nothing about love; I didn't want to cry again.

"Have you eaten?"

"Yes."

Not much, but I don't need her asking questions.

"Okay, come and sit down." She touches my arm, guiding me toward the chair. She speaks as if I've been traveling all day, even though it was just a two-hour drive.

"I might put my bags down and walk through the garden, if you don't mind."

Her eyes roam my face. "Of course not. Do you want some company?"

I put on a fake smile. "Maybe next time."

"Okay, enjoy." Mom winks.

I take my bag from the trunk, but my dad's already there, taking it from me.

"No daughter of mine is carrying her bag."

"Thanks, Dad," I say, giving him a big hug.

He brings it inside, so I turn on my heel and walk toward the garden. It's a slow wander, and I take in the sounds of the birds, wind, and trees. The air is warmer here. My dad must have cut the grass today; it's got that fresh-cut smell.

I take a big inhale through my nose. My childhood memories coming back. My sister and I would swing in a tire from that big oak tree. It's still there because my dad refuses to remove it. He says one day the grandchildren will play with it like me and Anna did.

The memory makes me shudder. Children. I feel like that's getting further out of reach every day.

Of course, when I finally find a guy worth sharing my life with, he doesn't want it.

Just my luck.

And it's as if the tree is mocking me by being his favorite. I remember that time at his gram's and being in her garden.

I keep wandering along the path when I come to the open area. I remember practicing Pilates out here when I was eighteen. My passion started at such a young age. My parents always encouraged me to pursue it, and it helped me dream big. In a way, they are so similar to Evan. He allowed me to follow my goals and supported what I was passionate about. Never once did he look down on me. He was always encouraging. Am I ready to throw that all away?

I need to clear my thoughts, so I take my old spot on the grass and do some stretches. Moving my body feels incredible. I end up doing a mixture of yoga and Pilates until my sister comes out to tell me it's dinnertime.

It's only been half a day, and although I'm getting what I came here for, I miss Evan. It will take a lot of self-talk to stop me from messaging him tonight. I owe myself a few days of no contact to do what I said I was coming here to do. Think.

So I message Nova and Summer to tell them I arrived, with a picture of the garden and a message to let them know I'll speak to them in a few days. Then I do the hardest yet the most important thing, turn my phone off and put it in my bag. I promise myself this time to take the space I need to think without distractions.

CHAPTER 29

EVAN

IT'S THURSDAY NIGHT. POKER night. My brothers and friends are gathered at my place. I offered to host due to the need to fill my house so I'm not alone to think about Chelsea with each passing hour. I've thought about texting and calling her, but I don't want to hurt her; the pain in her voice in our call mirrored my own. I couldn't speak because I knew what she wanted to hear, and I couldn't say it.

I should be happy, right? I didn't trust women. Didn't want to fall in love and get married again. I got what I wanted. But instead of feeling relief, I feel lost. Completely lost without her. No one to talk to. No one to share my days with. No one to kiss. Fuck. I'm so fucking lonely without her.

"Have you heard from her?" Jeremy asks, sitting opposite me at my green round poker table for six. The room is painted green with a TV on one wall, a bar cart to the side, and windows lining the opposite wall. It's dark outside, and so the single chandelier hanging above the table is lighting up the room.

My head lifts, my gaze moving from my cards to his face. "No."

"Nova said she's back with her parents for a while," he says, leaning back in the dark green leather chair.

I nod.

"You were better with her," Harvey mumbles, then throws down a bet as he gives me a pointed look.

"Less fucking grumpy." Oliver leans over and shoves my shoulder.

I bite the inside of my cheek to prevent myself from snapping back. I know I've gone back into my shell, but I'm trying to find that slimy fucker, Bobby. He's disappeared off the face of the earth. The investigators I hired are doing everything they can to track him down. I wish they would hurry. He shouldn't be roaming the streets. He stalked Chelsea and then put an intimate photo of her in my newspaper, behind my back.

I briefly spoke to Shyla on the phone, and she confessed to me how she and Bobby were in a relationship. She got wrapped up in his games and thought with her heart and not her head. So when he pushed her to post the article he had written, she did it. She's lost her job, but I plan on having a meeting with her to tell her.

How could that bastard do something so disrespectful and think there'd be no consequences? Does he remember who I am? I have the means to track him down and get him thrown in jail. This is one of the times I'm so fucking grateful to have money. Most people wouldn't have the police——even with evidence——looking into these cases so quickly. It's sad but true. The police are often over-whelmed with high case volumes and resource constraints.

The photo was not for anyone else to see. The rage bubbling inside me makes me want to gouge every guy's eyes out and scream she's mine, not theirs to look at, like some fucking idiot. I don't know what came over me, but it was like an out-of-body experience. I'm not a violent man, but my mind was going savage.

Bobby illegally posted it. As soon as I find his where-abouts, I'll alert the police. She shouldn't let Bobby get away with it or he'll never learn. He deserves to be pun-ished for humiliating her. The pain in her voice during our last phone call broke me. Her raw and honest conversation about needing space made me proud of her for putting herself first. I just fucking miss her so incredibly much. I wonder if I could get past my fear of commitment. Because not having her in my life has been so hard, so much harder than my ex cheating on me.

My phone buzzes, and I stupidly think it's her.

"She's in Connecticut. Due back tomorrow," Jeremy says nonchalantly. "I raise the bet to $35."

My head lifts, and my eyes meet his.

She's coming back.

"Right," I reply and return to my cards.

When it's my play, I end up tilting. I'm letting my emotions about Chelsea get the best of me. My usual control is slipping.

"Gabby, can you tell the officers to meet me in my office in an hour?" I say on the phone the next day.

"Yes, sir. And I'll order some coffee and bagels."

Her attention to detail is precisely why I need her. Feeding people isn't my priority, but I need to make a good impression. Besides, it wouldn't hurt to get some food in me. I've barely been eating this week. My diet has only consisted of coffee and sleep deprivation. Every spare moment, I have been scouring everywhere for any evidence of Bobby. The need to stay busy consumes me.

"Could you go there and meet the delivery? I have to meet with Shyla quickly."

"Sure."

She doesn't ask questions, which is another thing I appreciate about Gabby. She doesn't try to pry into my social life, she just does her job and does it well.

I decide to add a big bonus in her paycheck this week. It's almost Christmas, and she's a single mom. She deserves it for dealing with my grumpy ass again.

I hang up and enter the elevator.

It's been a few days since Bobby was fired and already the overall morale in the office has significantly improved.

So, as I ride the six floors up, I check my emails for potential replacements for Shyla and Bobby. I can't afford to have a weak link on my team. What would it say about me? I've worked so hard for so long that I don't want any more unreliable workers at The New York Press.

The doors open, and I walk to see her at her desk, typing a new article.

"Shyla."

Her eyes lift, noticing me, and she pushes away from the table to face me. "Mr. Lincoln."

"We need to talk."

Her face falls, but I keep my expression neutral, not giving away where her position in the company stands right now.

She drops her gaze back to the computer and saves her work before closing it.

When she's finished, she stands.

"Let's go to the meeting room." I stride to the empty room and hold the door open.

The frosted glass will stop any other staff from looking in.

"Take a seat."

Closing the door, I take a seat opposite her. Her back is ramrod straight, blonde hair tied up in a ponytail.

Her eyes are misty. I peer down at my empty hands that are open on top of the wooden table, taking a moment before looking back up to meet her pleading eyes.

"I need you to explain."

"I'm sorry, Mr. Lincoln. I thought-t he..." She exhales a shaky breath. "I thought he loved me."

My nostrils flare. "And he doesn't?"

I know he still loves Chelsea. And I hate the idea of anyone else having strong feelings for her. I'm still a mess trying to figure out what my feelings mean. All I know is right now I'm fucking miserable.

"No."

"How do you know?"

A single tear leaks from her eye. "He told me I was just a fling."

Standing, I grab a box of tissues from the console table and hand it to her.

"Thanks."

She pats her face with the tissue.

I give her a moment before I ask the big questions.

"Did he tell you to post that particular..." I run my finger inside my collar, pulling on it until it feels like I can breathe. "Picture?"

"Yes."

I drop my finger, and a heavy sigh leaves my chest. "Why would you do it?"

"I was pressured. He made it clear if I wanted to progress with our relationship, I needed to do this, or we were over." More tears leak as she shakes her head vehemently.

"I'm losing my job, aren't I?" Her bottom lip wobbles.

"Yes."

Her shoulders drop slightly.

"The few chats we've had, I was impressed——"

She brings her hands together and clasps them at her chest. "If you give me another chance, I promise..."

"No. Sorry, Shyla, but there's no second chance. But I need to ask, are you still in contact with him?"

She shakes her head. "No."

"Do you have a way of contacting him?"

"Yes. He has two phones."

A fresh idea comes to me. "I need you to give me both numbers."

She nods as new tears fall while pulling out her phone to find them, then she gives them to me. "I'm sorry I broke your trust."

I should tell her that once you break my trust, there's no way I'll forgive you. And it hits me like a hammer to the heart. Chelsea has never done anything to hurt or break my trust. If anything, she has done the opposite. She only wants one thing in the future.

Can I get over my hang-ups to win her back?

I rise to my feet in a rush. "I've gotta go to my office. Let me know if you hear from him."

Dashing out of the room, I head to the office to meet the police.

Bobby broke Shyla's trust, and I know exactly how that feels. I can help take him down, and I have just the plan. Ready or not, here I come.

CHAPTER 30

CHELSEA

I COUNT TO ONE hundred before I roll out my purple yoga mat, which I found in my closet. Under the dark sky and light wind, I decide to step out onto the grass with bare feet. Breathing in the fresh crisp air feels different in my lungs.

I'm glad I decided to keep stuff here for when I visit. I swallow the lump that's lodged in my throat at how that has slipped over the years.

Not anymore...

I do some single-leg stretches on each side before sitting up to drink water. It's still dark out. I couldn't sleep, so once it hit 5 a.m. on my alarm clock——and after half an hour of tossing and turning——I got dressed. Then I quietly trekked through the house on my tiptoes and snuck out without waking anyone up.

After running through my stretches and breath work, I roll up my mat and sit in a chair on the porch.

Watching the sunrise out here is exactly what I needed. The cool breeze and the birds chirping are the perfect morning tune. There's nothing better than this.

The door creaks open, and I turn my head.

It's my dad. I smile at him, but when he steps out with two cups, my lips stretch even more.

"Thanks," I whisper, taking the cup from him.

Immediately sipping the coffee, I settle back into the chair.

Dad sits in his spot next to me, and we look out onto the yard. Neither of us speaks; we're just content to sit here and drink our morning brew. Even the coffee tastes different. Or is it because it was made with love from my dad?

I cradle my half-empty mug in my hands and look over to the flowerbeds, noticing how he has recently been in there. It reminds me of growing up and helping him. Anna and I had our own gardening gloves and tools to help him. And I'm sure we ended up making more mess than if he had done it by himself, but he never said anything.

"Are you ready for the opening?" he asks, breaking my trip down memory lane.

"Definitely. It's been a long time coming." I tilt my head on the back of the chair to face him, meeting his proud gaze.

"You've taken your time doing it. I think it'll be the best in New York."

I smile at his enthusiasm. "That's a big call."

One of his eyebrows edges up in a challenge. "I'm a big guy."

I shake my head and roll my eyes. Dad jokes are the worst, but God, it's what I need right now. Sitting here with my dad and reflecting causes a splinter of pain to pierce my heart. I've missed them all so much.

"Do you need me to come back with you?"

I know he's referring to New York.

Shifting my eyes back to him, I ask, "You'll be there this week for the grand opening, right?"

He touches my shoulder and squeezes it. His eyes are bright. "Wouldn't miss it for the world."

I let out the breath of air I was holding, suddenly thinking he wasn't able to come. "Did Mom tell you I broke up with Bobby?"

"She did," he replies simply.

I sigh loudly, feeling as if the burden has been lifted. I'm not mad at Mom. I wouldn't have wanted to tell my dad. I feel like it's the same as admitting I failed. I don't want to let either of my parents down but, specifically, my dad. He's so supportive and encouraging. He would've hated to know how little Bobby supported me. And how he belittled my passion for Pilates.

"Are you okay?" he asks softly.

I wonder if he's talking in general, about Bobby, or the dreaded half-naked image of me. He hasn't mentioned the newspaper. My dad reads it every day. I'm sure he saw it. I just hope he doesn't bring it up. So I'm going to assume he asked about the breakup, and I feel fine discussing that with him.

"I should have done it a while ago," I confess, shifting in my seat to get more comfortable.

His eyebrows rise a fraction. "Why do you say that?"

"He never met you guys," I say, lowering my gaze to my coffee.

It's something I regret more now that I'm back here. There's nothing shameful or anything bad that's happened here. It's a beautiful place, just like my family. He should've been honored to have met them. I'll never let that happen again. The next guy I date must come to Connecticut. Respect me and my family. Love me and my family. I shudder inwardly at the realization that I haven't experienced it. I was close with Evan. I had just started to rebuild when everything fell apart and left me shattered.

Our futures don't align. And that kills me. I'm more heartbroken over Evan than I was about Bobby. And that's so fucking sad. I was with Bobby for two years, so that says just how little I truly felt for him, and how hard and fast I fell for Evan.

My dad hums. "It's the lack of effort. He should've visited. Or when we came to New York, he should have come to dinner."

"He never did," I add, recalling the times I came to the restaurant alone, telling them he had to work. Now I doubt it was work.

"And he hurt you. In a big way."

I slip down in my chair as if it can hide me. He's referring to the gossip article. But I have to swallow my shame and learn to move on. If I can do that with the people I love, I can do it with strangers. Holding my dad's eyes, I nod. "He did."

I settle in, expecting him to ask questions about it.

"Did you want to go to Saville Dam?" He changes the subject unexpectedly.

We used to go regularly as a family for picnics when I was growing up. We'd often watch as people hiked the woodlands, fished or boated. I haven't been in years. The thought of seeing the scenic views and soaking in the quiet while hanging with my family before I head back sounds perfect.

My lips spread wide as excitement warms me. "That sounds like the perfect thing to do before I head off."

"Let's get a start on the picnic," he says as he stands from his chair.

Dad and I have always been the early risers in the family. Anna and Mom love to sleep. We will have the picnic rug and basket packed and in the car before they wake.

My heart feels less heavy today. I'm so glad I came.

There's a fear that when I get back, I'll revert to having a heavy heart. The article and Evan still remain in the back of my mind. But I can't hide forever. My studio is about to open, and I still need to finalize the menu, the music, and the decorations.

I'm so ready to open the doors to my new career. I've waited a long time for this moment. I can't let anything take that excitement away from me.

Chapter 31

Evan

It's Saturday, and I've already run ten miles with Harvey, worked for an hour, gone to the gym, eaten, and showered. But when I check my watch, I curse...it's only nine fifty-five.

What am I going to do now?

I pace my home office, running my hand through my hair, trying to decide how to spend the rest of today. I can't work, because it just brings back memories of her, and I'm giving her the space she needs.

Needing someone familiar and wise, I grab my keys and head to my car. I know exactly who I need to see.

After the short drive, I arrive at her house, but she's napping. For a brief moment, I think about leaving, but the smell of fresh bread and the comforting familiarity of her furniture make me want to stay. I take a seat on the sofa and find something to watch.

I must have drifted off to sleep because, in my dreams, Chelsea is there——happy——and we're together.

"Evan?" a voice calls out.

I blink my eyes open, and reality hits me hard as I remember where I am. Chelsea isn't here, and we're no longer together.

I sit up and walk over to Gram, kissing her cheek as she maneuvers her walker to her usual spot to take a seat.

"Can I get you anything, Gram?"

"No, but you're staying for lunch, right?'

"Yes, I hear today's the classic chicken noodle soup."

She nods. "I feel like I'm coming down with something, so I asked for it."

My stomach drops with worry. "Are you okay?"

"Yes, just a cold."

"Enough about me. How are you?"

I drop my gaze to my hands clutched in front of me and let out a heavy sigh. "Alright, I guess..."

My gaze lifts back to her assessing one. Her eyebrows lift high to her freshly brushed grey hair. "What does 'I guess' mean?"

My eyes shift to the garden, where Chelsea had formally met Gram. I watched from inside, in awe of how effortlessly they chatted. Then, at the next Sunday family dinner, Gram told me how lovely Chelsea was.

I brought Chelsea into my life, so I feel like I owe it to Gram to tell her what's happened.

"Chelsea asked for space."

"That's not good. What happened?" she asks, crossing her ankles and settling back into the sofa.

"She wants marriage and kids."

Gram smiles.

She actually fucking smiles.

"What's that look for?" I ask.

"Get over your fear," she replies simply, but that only has my nerves heightening.

"How do I do that?"

"You try. Do you give up at work if on the first try you fail?"

"No," I say tentatively.

"Well, relationships are no different."

I remain silent, mind spinning, so she continues.

"Is she worth fighting for?"

I nod without a second's hesitation. "Definitely. But I don't know if I can give her what she needs."

"Let's try something. Close your eyes."

I follow her order, then she continues talking. "Now picture her married to someone else and baring another man's child."

My eyes snap open, my temperature rising, turning my nerves to a raging mix of longing and jealousy.

"Close them, Evan," she warns.

"I don't want to see it."

"But if you don't get over your fear, that's what will happen. She's an intelligent, kind, strong, beautiful woman who deserves a man who loves and trusts her."

I squeeze my neck, tension building there as I wrestle with what to do.

"Is she someone you want to lose and let someone else marry?"

"No, but——"

"There's no 'but.' It's either you let her in, or you let her go...forever."

A life without Chelsea. Her married to someone else? Baring someone else's child. No fucking chance. I curl my fingers into a fist, and I swallow the curse that's sitting on the tip of my tongue.

Gram gives me a knowing smile. "Don't let that good woman go, E. You'll regret it for the rest of your life."

I sit up straighter. "I won't, Gram." And as I say it, I feel it in my bones, the truth of it.

"Make sure you do something special for her."

"Well, I actually have an idea, but I need you, Mom, Dad, Oliver, Jeremy, and Harvey too.

Her eyes light up, her excitement palpable. "What is it?"

CHAPTER 32

CHELSEA

I'VE BEEN HOME FOR a few days, and since I've been back, I've thrown myself into work.

The grand opening is this Sunday. The food, drinks, and entertainment are organized.

There are still a few finishing touches like artwork and plants to add, but overall, everything is done. My family will fly in early on Sunday, and I can't wait to pick them up. I've been sending photos or video calling them as it all comes together. I live for their emojis and excitement.

I'm cooking beef mince on the stove when the doorbell rings.

"Are you expecting anyone?" Summer asks from the living room, throwing the blanket off her legs. She stands abruptly and walks to me.

My eyebrows draw together. "No."

She opens the door and a small gasp leaves her mouth. "Officers?"

Police? My stomach bottoms out as worst-case scenarios flood my mind. Is my family or Summer's in trouble? She rarely talks about her parents who are separated and with new partners. Both sets live in New York. She has four step-siblings who she sees at family events and frequently calls, but her work and college hours make visits difficult.

I turn my head to see what's happening, but I can't leave the food unattended, so I just listen in.

"I'm Officer Fletcher, and this is Officer Maverick. Are you Miss Macfarlane?"

"No, she's inside," Summer replies.

The door creaks open, and heavy footsteps enter. I turn off the burner. My blood pressure rises at the sight of two middle-aged officers stepping into the room.

"Hi, I'm Chelsea Macfarlane," I say, stepping forward to shake their hands, pretending that I'm not panicking inside.

"Hi, Chelsea. Can we take a seat?" Officer Fletcher asks.

"Sure," I say, sitting down opposite them.

"Did you want a drink?" Summer asks. At least one of us remembering our manners.

"No, thanks," the officers answer in unison.

Summer sits beside me, bringing me a small amount of comfort.

"We're here to get your statement about Bobby Cox," Officer Fletcher begins. I suddenly feel nauseas.

"What about him?" I ask, glancing between the two officers.

"We have received a statement indicating that he was stalking and harassing you, and he also distributed an intimate image without your consent. To proceed with charges, we require your detailed account of these incidents."

"You found him?" Summer asks. Taking the words right out of my mouth.

"Yeah, but he's out on bail."

Of course.

I'm sure his parents bailed him out, but I doubt they realize what kind of person he's turned into. He surprised me, so they likely would be too.

As I sit with the officers, a sense of calm washes over me. This is my chance to stand up for myself.

"Since we've broken up, he's called me several times and has sent a few texts. I blocked him, but he called from a new number. He also sent me roses, but that's all I have." My face flushes with embarrassment as I discuss the image. "It was an old photo I had sent him while we were dating, and he chose to share it without asking me."

"Thank you for that information. We already have a statement that contributes to the case, but we needed to hear your account as well, Miss Macfarlane."

"Evan. Sorry, I mean, Mr. Lincoln pressed charges?"

"Yes. He also provided a video of Bobby outside your building on May 19th at 11:30 a.m. Do you remember speaking to him?"

I sit back and look at the table, trying to recall that day. "We argued. I told him to stop calling."

"Did you know where he was?" Officer Maverick asks.

"At work," I reply.

Officer Maverick takes notes as Officer Fletcher continues.

"He was supposed to be, but he was outside your building instead. Can you confirm you had broken up with him?"

Why was he outside my building?

"Yes."

"There was a delivery of yours that was tampered with?"

I frown. "What do you mean?"

"There was a delivery that ended up in the wrong state?"

"Yeahhh," I breathe out as realization dawns.

"Bobby changed the address," Officer Fletcher states.

"I had no idea." I'm trying to wrap my head around all this new information.

"Is there anything else you would like to add?"

"No, officers."

"Thank you, Miss Macfarlane. If you think of anything else, please don't hesitate to contact us."

They slide their card to me and stand to leave. Summer and I walk them out. Closing the door, I turn around with my head full of confusion. I wasn't expecting that. But I'm glad it happened. I haven't heard from Bobby, but I wanted to press charges against him. Now I have.

"Are you okay?" Summer asks, touching my shoulder.

"I think so…"

"At least Evan pressed charges too. It'll help build a case against him."

"He was stalking and harassing me. They have that on film," I say, needing to hear it out loud to believe it's true.

"He probably realized what he lost when Evan came into the picture."

When I hear Evan's name, it hurts. I thought by now the pain would have lessened. It's not like I was with him for a long time. But it seems he made a huge impact on me in such a short period.

"I doubt Bobby could see past his own reflection."

"Touché." Summer sets the table for dinner.

"But why didn't you tell me he was still calling you?"

"I didn't think it was important."

She walks up and wraps her arms around me, holding me tight. "You can tell me anything. I'm here for you."

"I love you, Summer."

"I love you, too."

We pull back from our hug and her eyes are watery. "Go get on the sofa. I'll clean up and bring us wine."

"I'll put on *Love Actually*."

The corners of my lips lift, and I set up the movie on autopilot, grateful for her company. The police, Bobby, and Evan are weighing heavily on me, but I need to push it aside and focus on all the good things in my life. Like my friends, family, and my studio opening.

CHAPTER 33

CHELSEA

TODAY IS THE DAY. I take a deep breath and blow it out slowly, ready for the grand opening of my studio.

This week has flown by. I haven't had enough time to sit and reflect. I've been in and out of meetings. The walk into the office is hard now that I know Bobby has been here. But it's not just that. The anticipation of bumping into Evan is the main reason for the turmoil running my nerves ragged.

I haven't seen him despite being at the studio on Friday and Saturday. Friday, I had a staff meeting/get-to know-each-other day. And yesterday, I organized and prepared for today. Not once did I see him. And I have to admit it burns a hole in my heart.

Summer insisted she would guide my family, arguing with me about how I should be here in case anyone turns up early.

I pace back and forth, ensuring that every spring, weight, band, and box is in order. Glad that the deliveries all made it in time, including the one Bobby tried to sabotage. I shudder at the lengths he went to just to hurt me. But I won't let him take this moment away from me.

When the first buzz sounds, I see the food is here. I can't help the stupid grin that transforms on my face.

I open the door and let them in, showing them the table I want it set up at.

Once they leave, the balloons arrive, and I arrange them around the signs. Then the DJ comes in and sets up in the corner of the room.

The sounds of my favorite 90s pop songs play through the speakers at a soft volume.

Next, my family and Summer enter. Their lit-up faces and proud expressions make my eyes misty, and the hugs from my parents and sister fill my heart. For some reason, I shake, but it's not from nerves anymore, it's with relief.

The studio begins to fill with instructors, my old colleagues and boss come to celebrate too. It's nice to have their support.

I look over as Nova enters holding a piece of paper, and I think I'm hallucinating.

But I'm not.

Following her are Jeremy, Oliver, Harvey, Eliza (Evan's mom), Sebastian (Evan's dad), and Iris (Gram).

But that's not the person who causes my heart to beat outside of my chest. No, it's the tall, broody man wearing a delicious beige suit with piercing blue eyes who captures my attention. He's holding a massive bunch of white gardenias. His presence drowns out all the noise in the studio.

When Summer speaks to me, I shake my head, trying to pay attention. "Sorry."

Nova's next, shoving her doctor's clearance into my hands before hugging me and whispering in my ear. "Surprise."

"I'm going to kill you later," I mumble back into her long, wavy brown hair.

I can feel the heat of everyone watching us, and I pull back with a smile.

Nova steps aside to allow others to say hello. First up is Harvey as he steps forward. "Congratulations, Chelsea."

He steps away rather fast, and I don't get long to think about it because Oliver is next. He gives me a charming smile and a quick hug. Next in line to say hi to me are Evan's parents.

"Mr. and Mrs. Lincoln, thanks for coming," I say and kiss both of their cheeks.

"Congratulations, love," Eliza says, her eyes sparkling as they look from me and then around the studio.

"This is great," Sebastian says, before pulling away to stand with Eliza.

"Hi, dear," Iris says.

Today, her pale cheeks are hidden behind some powder. The effort she's put in for me makes it hard to breathe. My own grandparents aren't able to be here because they have both passed, my gramps being the most recent loss, just three years ago.

I will not cry.

"Hi, thanks for coming."

Her soft smile reaches her eyes. "Thanks for inviting me."

I can't say I didn't, so I just smile and dip my chin.

All his family is here. For me. I take a second to let that sink in.

A supportive family is what I've always wanted in a partner.

What I've craved.

Then why can't we want the same thing in the future?

My eyes shift to his, and my heart thumps in my ears. The way my body responds is nothing like I've experienced before.

"Hi," I say, keeping my voice even to hide the way his presence affects me.

His lips lift into a tender smile. "Hi."

We stare at each other, but knowing I have an audience makes me think on my feet.

"Come, everyone, I want you to meet my family."

I turn and walk to my parents and sister. "Mom, Dad, and Anna, I'd like you to meet Sebastian, Eliza, Oliver, Harvey, Nova, Jeremy, who is Nova's boyfriend, Evan, and Iris."

They exchange pleasantries.

I watch the dads shake hands and then start up easy conversation. My mom takes Eliza and Gram around on a tour. Then the brothers slip away, leaving Evan and me alone.

I don't know if it's on purpose, but he doesn't waste time. "Congratulations. I'm so proud and happy for you."

His soft gaze and the flowers have my knees buckling. I take the gardenias and smell them, their sweet fragrance filling my senses. Peering at him from under my lashes, I murmur, "Thanks. You didn't have to."

"I did," he replies firmly, his eyes locked on mine.

I lower the bouquet, clutching them in my hands in front of me. "I still can't believe it's finally happening."

"I can. You worked hard."

His compliments fluster me, and I look away, biting my lip. "You did help."

"I didn't do much. This is all you."

My fingers tighten around the bouquet as my stomach flutters. "Your designer. And you helped me with the booking system."

"I'm glad I could help," he says, stepping closer. His closeness sends a shudder through me, and I feel a lump forming in my throat.

My heart bleeds. I want to say, *I don't care about marriage and kids. I want you back.*

But the other part of me says, *you've come so far, don't let yourself down now.*

"I——" he starts, his voice hesitant, as if he's about to say something important.

"Sorry to interrupt," Iris says, coming to join us.

I twist to face her. "You're never interrupting."

"I'll come back later," Evan says. My eyes flick to him and watch him walk away to join his brothers.

Returning my attention to Iris, I take in her white mid-length dress with a collar. It's the perfect style for her. It looks comfortable and yet trendy. Her slip-on shoes add the touch of casual needed for the event. No one is overdressed except for the Lincoln men. All of them are in suits of some kind.

"I love your dress," I say, needing to tear my attention away from one Lincoln in particular.

"This silly old thing. I've had it for years."

"I know the feeling."

"It's nice to see a woman in a blazer. Very classy."

I shift the bouquet up a little, hiding the small cleavage that's visible from the top.

"I've had it for years too."

In fact, I've had these blue jeans and this black blazer since I was twenty.

"What's happening with Evan?"

Uneasiness swarms my body. I've not been asked this directly before. How much can I say to his gram?

"Um..."

I sense a pair of eyes on me. Looking over her shoulder, I see him watching us, a deep wrinkle between his eyebrows.

"You can tell me. Is he grumpy?"

My lips part, and I bite back a laugh. "With me, no."

"What is it, then? He was happy before."

"I was too."

Her gaze drops to the gardenias. "He's never brought a woman flowers."

His family is well aware he's not been with another woman since his ex.

"We want different things for our future," I admit.

"He's fallen for you, dear."

Hearing those words makes my heart crack. It's supposed to make me feel better, but it doesn't. "I've fallen for him too. But I want what my parents have. Since I was little, I dreamed of that fairy tale love."

"You know his past."

"I do."

"Then things will work out the way they're meant to."

I give her a small smile as hope flares in my chest. "I hope you're right."

I miss him.

"I can see why he likes you."

I wait for her to explain because I don't.

"We're so different."

"Exactly. You're fun. Yet caring. He needs your energy to bring him back to life."

"What was he like growing up?" I ask curiously.

"My boy was caring and cautious." Eliza stands beside Iris, joining our conversation.

"He's still the same," I say with a smile.

"With you, he's the old Evan, but the last few years, he's been withdrawn." His mom's eyes wash over with sadness.

Iris's mouth flattens. "His ex wasn't very kind."

Iris is so polite. I'm sure those aren't the words everyone else would use for her, but I love and respect Iris's opinion.

"Excuse me," Summer interrupts. "Chelse. Do you want to do the speech now?"

Checking the time on my watch, I see Summer came right on time.

"Oh yes, thanks. Sorry, ladies."

"Go." Eliza waves her hand, encouraging me.

I head off toward the DJ and explain I'll do a quick speech. I put the flowers down and stand at the front of the room.

With the mic in my hand, I suddenly take a mental picture of the full room. All the support for me to succeed. It gives me the push to tap the mic.

Everyone's chatter silences.

"Hi. Thanks, everyone, for coming today. I was just looking at you all and thinking how lucky I am to have all your support. I hope you're all having a good time. There's plenty of food and drinks. And now is the time to let your hair down and dance."

"You're first," Oliver's loud voice calls.

The room applauds.

I shake my head.

The DJ starts the music, and the moment "Photograph" by Ed Sheeran plays through the speakers, I turn to Evan, wondering how he knew. I scan the crowd until I find those bright blue eyes.

It's the song he and I danced to the night of his work function.

My parents take the dance floor, then so do Jeremy and Nova.

But my feet are frozen on the spot. Evan moves between people, weaving through them until he's in front of me. He slips the microphone out of my hand and hands it to the DJ.

"I believe this is our song."

My heart is in my throat. To touch him again. Have his hands on me. God, just the thought sends a shiver down my spine.

"We shouldn't," I whisper.

He frowns. "Why?"

"We're not together anymore."

"It's just one dance."

"Go on," my mom encourages from her spot on the dance floor.

"If I was your age, you wouldn't be able to get me off there. Me and Gramps loved a good dance floor," Iris says.

My eyes flick from my mom to her.

Where did she come from?

Iris and Sebastian move slowly around the dance floor.

When she says it like that, I have no reason not to. The encouragement from our families makes it hard to say no.

Evan stretches his hand out, palm up in a clear invitation. I slip my hand in his, and I shake my head at the applause around us.

Do they not understand we can't be together?

As much as his hand feels so good in mine, it's just a tease. There can never be an us.

His hand closes over mine and he tugs me gently to the floor.

Eyes flaring with fire, he glances over me, starting at my body and sliding up to my lips.

Don't, my heart whispers. Eyes up and away.

Our bodies sway closely, following the beat of the music. My head is close to his shoulder, but I resist resting it there. "I haven't seen you."

"I know." His breath tickles my hair.

My eyes close momentarily. "Is it too hard?"

Time passes before he breathes out, "Yes."

That one word echoes my own crushed heart.

"You found Bobby," I say, my voice barely above a whisper.

His grip on my waist tightens ever so slightly. "I did. Shyla actually helped."

"She did?" I tilt my head to look up at him, trying to read his eyes.

"Yeah. But I had to let her go."

I nod, enjoying being here in his arms again, even if it's only for a short time.

The song ends, so I step out of his embrace, needing to clear my head. I see my group of instructors talking and join them. Looking over my shoulder, I spot Evan on the opposite side of the room with his dad, his eyes firmly on me.

I twist around with my heart in my throat and pay attention to the group.

The afternoon comes to an end. People slowly say goodbye. I thank them for coming, and I only have my family and the Lincolns left.

"We need to head back," my sister says.

I look at the room and then my watch.

"Summer will see us out, she's leaving too," Mom adds, seeing the wheels turning in my head.

There are still trainers and Evan's family here. I'm backed into a corner.

"I feel awful, Mom," I admit.

"Why? We'll see each other again soon." She kisses my cheek and hugs me.

I wrap my arms around her, thanking her and Dad silently for the support to open my dream studio.

"Thank you for everything."

"Of course. We're so proud of you," Mom says, eyes shining with pride.

"I'll be back home soon."

"We look forward to it," Dad says as he squeezes my shoulder.

I hug them all and thank Summer, telling her I'll see her later at home.

The Lincolns come over and I smile at them naturally. They've been like a second family.

"Thanks again for coming."

"Of course. It was a great afternoon," Eliza says.

I say goodbye, hugging Iris last. Of course, she whispers in my ear, "Don't give up on him just yet."

I pull back and stare into her eyes, seeing her truth.

With no idea how to respond, I simply smile and nod.

"Where did you get the painting?" Oliver asks with a deep wrinkle between his eyebrows.

"The designer found it. Why?"

He shakes his head. "No reason. Thanks for having me, and congratulations again."

I smile and thank him.

Evan is the last to say goodbye. Luckily for me, we have an audience. So we have to keep it short and sweet.

"I'm so incredibly grateful to have met you. I may not do another class, but I'm sure I'll pass you in the elevator sometime."

"Unless you avoid me." I wink, but I feel pained by this exchange. I don't want to be just passing acquaintances.

His lips turn up into a small grin. "No more hiding."

"Okay, I'll hold you to that."

We grin at each other. Staring into his eyes, I wonder why he makes it so hard to let go.

He steps forward, and I quiver the moment his arms wrap around me. I hold back my emotions. This is the end of us. Only fleeting elevator rides now.

I step back, and a shaky sigh leaves my lips. Waving, I watch them leave. Evan is the last. He looks over his shoulder one last time. I clutch my hands together, and when they are out of sight, I spin and look around my now-empty studio. Yes, it's messy. In fact, I should have been more panicked that I have to clean up by tomorrow, but thankfully I decided to splurge and hire a cleaner.

I begin to tidy some of the pieces the cleaners aren't expected to do, like folding up the trestle table the food was on. I have a few minutes before they are due.

There's a noise at the door, as expected; the cleaners must be here. But when I look, I do a double take. My heart plummets and my body temperature rises.

Bobby.

CHAPTER 34

CHELSEA

THERE'S NO ONE ELSE here but me and him. Suddenly, the room feels oddly still and cold. I've never feared for my life until today. The way his pupils dilate sends a chill down my spine.

I concentrate on breathing slowly and steadily, so he can't see how rattled I feel.

"What are you doing here?" I say, keeping my voice steady and in control.

"No hello?" he sneers, goading me.

Straightening my shoulders, I bite back. "You put a private picture of me in the newspaper, so I think we can skip the pleasantries."

He steps closer to me, eating up the space between us like I'm his prey. "Chelsea, Chelsea, Chelsea," he mocks. "There's no need to get snappy."

My heart pounds powerfully, but I keep my back ramrod straight. His feet continue to step closer, but mine stay glued to the floor.

I can see the purple under his eyes, his hair limp and without styling products, his top has a coffee stain, and he's wearing a pair of basic blue jeans. This image of him before me is so unlike him. His usual immaculate image has fallen from grace.

"Why are you here?" I ask.

He flashes me a deranged smile. "To see you."

He's in front of me now. I should run. But I freeze the moment his hand touches my arm. I try to tug it out of his grip, but it makes him squeeze it tighter, and my eyes prick with tears.

"You're hurting me," I whisper-shout as a tear leaks from my eye. My strong facade falls as soul-deep fear courses through my veins. Is he going to kill me?

Tears sprinkle my cheeks, but an inaudible gasp leaves my mouth when I see a blurry Evan behind him.

A new thought hits me. Evan's going to kill him. No. I can't have Evan go to jail.

Evan holds his index finger to his lips in a *shh* motion. My eyes flutter and roll as the hold Bobby has on me is bruising; he's never inflicted this much pain before.

My heart rattles inside my chest like I'm sprinting instead of standing here, unmoving.

Tears continue to roll over my cheeks and down into my mouth. I taste the salt.

"Why are you crying? I thought you loved me?" he taunts, his voice tight and strained.

I hold his eyes as I say, "I thought I did."

His face darkens into a scowl. "You loved me before he had his turn with you," he spits venomously.

My heart is racing so fast it causes pain to hit my chest. I feel like I need oxygen; I'm lightheaded.

In the distance, heavy footsteps enter the studio, and an unfamiliar deep voice speaks. "You are under arrest, Mr. Cox. Anything you say can and will be used against you."

"You fucking bitch," he snarls, sending a spray of saliva in my face. I wince as it hits me, recoiling as sobs rack my body.

Someone touches my arm, and I instinctively try to hit it away, terrified it's Bobby. I thrash around in panic.

"It's me," a voice repeats over and over.

Evan's voice penetrates through the noise. I stop flailing and wipe my face one last time.

Blinking, I turn toward him. "Shell, it's me, baby."

My body is overtaken with a fresh wave of uncontrollable sobs.

"You're safe now."

He sits on the floor in his suit.

"You're going to ruin your suit."

"Fuck my suit. All that matters is you."

His words sting, but it's a different kind of pain. I want him, but one touch will make it harder to leave.

"Come here. I've got you. Lean on me." He guides my arms around him. His familiar touch and spicy scent wash over me like a warm blanket.

My arms circle his neck, and he wraps me in his embrace. He holds me until there are no more tears, but my breath is still shaky.

When I'm spent, I slowly peel myself away. Our faces are an inch apart, his eyes scanning mine. His hands gently cradle my cheeks. I stare into his familiar handsome features, his square jaw visibly tensed.

Old familiarity and yearning crash into me. His lips part, revealing his white teeth, and I realize he's talking.

"Okay?" I catch the end of his sentence.

"Better now," I tell him.

He nods. "Are you ready to go home?"

He must sense my hesitation.

"My house. I need to hold you."

I need to stay strong and say no.

"We sh——" I start.

His eyes call to me, making him irresistible. "Please. We can just talk. I can-n..." he stammers, shaking his head and running a hand through his hair.

If I thought Bobby shook me up, the pained lines on Evan's face and his rigid posture show he's struggling with what happened too.

"Let's talk to the police, and then I'm taking you home."

"Okay."

"Okay?"

I nod. "Take me to your place. But——"

I can talk to him. A hug would be nice too.

He tilts his head when I leave him hanging.

"Bourbon and Chick-fil-A are also required."

His lips twitch. "You got it, baby."

His affectionate words seep into my body, bringing a warm welcome I've been craving from only him.

CHAPTER 35

EVAN

WITNESSING BOBBY'S FILTHY FUCKING hands hurting her and then the spitting in her face sent the pulse in my temple ticking and my hands curling into fists. He's so fucking lucky the police intervened; otherwise, I would've beaten the shit out of him. What a deplorable human being.

Thankfully, my security guys have been keeping an eye on him and alerted me. They called the police first. I was walking my family to their cars before I was going to go back and talk to her, when I received the call and rushed back inside.

Chelsea's fearful face flashes before my eyes. I hold her closer in the back of my private car, taking in her sweet scent. A sense of comfort washes over me, but it's still not enough to just hold her. I need her to be okay. I can't let her go.

Marriage. Kids. We need to talk about it, in the safety of my home.

My heart pounded at the sight of her happy face earlier today. She saw the people who want her to succeed. And then fucking Bobby comes along and ruins it all.

She deserves to know there are many people who love and support her.

She's slumped beside me, as if she needs me to hold her up. It's like the adrenaline has worn off and her body is fatigued.

I cradle her like a precious shell in the ocean—Unique, gentle, and beautiful.

She shines a light on me. I was in the dark ripple of the sea, unable to see or feel my way out of it. Now I found her, like my way back to the shore. She's the one I can't live without.

Her body shakes with fresh shivers. "Are you cold?" I ask, pulling her closer, letting her nuzzle into my body.

She moves her head. "No," she murmurs, her breath tickling my neck.

The car arrives at my house. "We're here," I whisper against her.

She pulls away to sit up, looking a bit dazed and very tired.

"Wait there," I say, quickly exiting the car and rushing around to her door. In a hurry, I rip the door open and sweep her up in my arms, carrying her like a delicate flower. A whoosh of air leaves her mouth, but she doesn't resist. Her head rests on my shoulder.

I carry her through my house, taking her to the bathroom next to the basin. She stands, frowning as she looks at me in question. "What are you doing?"

"Cleaning you up."

I get a washcloth, run it under warm water, bring it to her face to wash it, and then I repeat. With my body close to hers, she tips her head back and closes her eyes. I push her bangs up with one hand and hold them out of the way while I wipe lightly with the other. Washing away Bobby's disgusting saliva. When I finish, I watch her straighten, her eyes fluttering open. All her makeup is removed, leaving only her bright wide eyes.

"Better?" she asks, raising an eyebrow.

"Yeah. Are you okay?" I ask, still trying to calm my simmering anger. I hate Bobby fucking Cox. He will be ruined. No matter what happens between Chelsea and me, I'll never let him near her again.

She lifts her lips in a half smile. "Surprisingly, yes."

I'd like to think I am the one making her better, but I doubt it.

I take her hand and lead her to the kitchen, lifting her tall, graceful body onto the counter.

My lips part when I close the distance between us, standing between her parted legs, gazing into her intoxicating brown eyes. Only a small space separates us now. My eyes drift to her mouth. I want to kiss her, but I know one kiss wouldn't be enough. I wouldn't be able to hold myself back. Her sweetness, presence, and attention are powerful, and I haven't had any of that for so long.

Fuck, I've missed her.

It's the first time since my office, when I stood between her legs, desperate to kiss her. My breathing is becoming ragged.

I rub my hand over my face, knowing I need space so we can talk first.

"I'll get you a drink, order food, and then we can talk."

She exhales heavily. "Sounds good."

Stepping away, I move around my kitchen, preparing our drinks and ordering our food. I hand over a glass of bourbon, which she takes and sips.

"Thanks," she mumbles, staring over the rim of the glass with clear, compelling eyes.

I stand in between her thighs, but not as close as before, clutching my glass to keep from touching her as we talk. Keeping my gentle gaze locked on hers, I speak from the heart.

"Chelsea, my life felt empty without you. You are such an important part of my life, and when you were gone, it left a hole that nothing could fill. No amount of work, family, poker, exercise——" I lift the glass up. "Alcohol can fill that void."

"My life isn't the same either. I had to go to Connecticut to get away from painful reminders. Even something as small as the damn building reminded me of you. I went away to try to detach myself from you." She looks at me with a faraway look, as if remembering the times we shared.

"I'm sorry I hurt you," I tell her, keeping my eyes on hers.

Her eyebrows draw together in an agonized expression. "Where does that leave us, Evan?"

"I love you." The words tumble easily out of my mouth.

She stares blankly at me with her lips parting. "I love you too, but it's not enough."

I sip my drink, wetting my dry mouth that this conversation has given me. I found someone who I love for the first time, who loves me back. She's the first woman who truly loves me. I can see a future with her. Something I haven't thought would happen to me. I thought that door was closed. Fuck, locked with a key even.

"I choose to trust you because I don't want to be stuck in the same place, and I can't keep doing this. I don't want to lose you because I'm scared."

Her eyes soften as her frown deepens. "You're scared?"

I step closer so my body hits the front of her. "Of you hurting me? Yes, so fucking scared."

"I won't do that. You can trust me with your heart."

My heart is beating so hard at her words, trust, heart, love...it all mirrors what I feel for her. With that, I set my glass on the counter and rest my hands on top of her thighs, feeling the muscles twitch underneath. "I love you so much that I'd marry you today to prove it."

A smile as intimate as a kiss trembles over her lips as she nods. My hands slide up to her waist as hot tears slowly find their way down her cheeks.

"I want that so m-much," she stammers as tears choke her voice, and she lowers her glass next to mine. Her hands touch my shoulders, reminding me just how much I've craved and missed her during our time apart. It fucking killed me.

Closing the distance between our mouths, I smother her sob. I kiss her with all the hollowness I felt without her, allowing her kiss to rebuild the sadness with new beginnings. Her lips are wet, sweet, and demanding.

This moment of soul-searching makes all the doubts and fears disappear. There's something about the way I feel with her that quiets the voices. Her words were sealed with a kiss.

The door sounds, and I reluctantly pull back. She touches her lips with her hand like she's in a dream. Unable to get enough, I sear a path down her delicate neck. "Stay here, I'll be right back."

I keep my eyes on her as I head to the door. Reluctantly, I tear my gaze away to open the front door to retrieve our food. Quickly, I return to the kitchen.

She grips the edge of the counter, and her body slides down. I hold out my hand to stop her from moving any farther.

"Stay there," I command.

She rolls her eyes. "I can walk and sit at the table."

Leaning forward, I lower my lips to her ear and whisper, "I know, but I want you here."

I like standing between her legs. She looks down at me with a glimmer in her eye, like I'm the rarest gem she's ever seen.

She shrugs as if she doesn't have the energy to fight me.

I open the bag and pull out the sandwich, unwrapping it for her, ready to hand it to her.

Her eyebrows lift. "Are you going to feed me?"

I wasn't, but if that's what she wants. I shrug. "If you want."

She giggles at me. "No. I can't believe you were, though. You're insane."

"No, I'm in love with you, Miss Macfarlane."

She accepts the food from my hands and takes a large bite.

I feel like right now is the first time in over a week I've felt alive.

Such a mundane task, but caring for her is a need. It gives me a purpose in life. I want something that makes me feel alive. Risks and all. Heartbreak or not. I'm giving her my heart and soul. There's no way around it. I'm all in with this relationship.

I pick up my food and eat. We both must have been hungry because we don't speak in between bites, only look at each other like we're the most interesting show.

Once the food and bourbon are finished, I offer her another drink, which she declines.

"Take me to bed and hold me, Mr. Lincoln," she orders.

"I thought you'd never ask," I reply, pulling her off the counter and close to the planes of my body. In long purposeful strides, I walk to my room, lowering her to the bed and climbing in beside her.

Drawing her legs up, I bring my body behind her. We fit snugly together. My hand grips her waist as her hand slips over mine and holds me there.

I lift my head and kiss her temple. "You're safe. Rest, baby, I'm right here if you need me. I'll never spend a day without you again."

She sighs and shuffles into me. Her in my bed makes the scars fade as I realize how much I've grown over my fears to ask her to stay. Stay for life.

With those thoughts, I hold her tight and fall asleep with the sounds of her breaths as a lullaby.

CHAPTER 36

EVAN

I'VE BEEN AWAKE BUT lying here quietly for at least half an hour. I'm too comfortable to move, enjoying the way her luscious body wraps around mine. How and when did that happen?

The morning light seeps through the curtains. What time is it?

It's the first time I've felt this refreshed. I have a feeling it's due to the sexy brunette in my bed. The heat of her body with mine helped me fall asleep.

Her hand slides up my abdomen, and I hiss, enjoying the way her hands slowly trail along the lines on my body. She moves her fingers lower, tracing the top of my boxers, and a deep grumble leaves my chest.

Slipping her hand under my boxers, she grabs my cock. I jerk at the hot, firm touch. But then she slides under the covers, settling between my thighs.

Fuck.

She grabs the top of my boxer briefs, trying to tug them down, and I throw the blankets off. Her eyes lift to lock eyes with me, the corner of her lip lifting in a smug smile.

"You're desperate to suck my cock, aren't you?"

She nods as her tongue skims her bottom lip. I growl at the movement, but my brain misfires when her pretty pink tongue darts out and licks the pre-cum leaking from the tip like a fucking lollipop.

"Fuck, baby. That's so good."

Her hair falls and it partially blocks my view, so I reach my hand out and push her hair back as she licks my cock from base to tip, needing to see everything.

"You're such a tease," I say through my heavy breathing.

Unable to look anywhere else but her lips moving to wrap around the head, a small whimper leaves my chest. I'm so close to begging it's pathetic.

Thankfully, she takes me deeper and swallows, causing my fingers to tighten in her hair. Her mouth is perfection. And when she unexpectedly takes me to the back of her throat and swallows hard, I just about lose my restraint. I focus on breathing in through my nose and out through my mouth, trying to slow myself down. Her hand grips the base and works it up as her mouth follows. "So fucking good."

Eyes fluttering up, she continues to suck me, and I realize she has all the power right now.

Her moans and shifting on the bed make me think she's turned on by sucking my cock.

"You've been dreaming about doing this, haven't you?"

"Yesss," she says, her teeth scratching along my length, and I just about fucking blow. She smiles around me.

I thrust up into her hot, needy mouth, chasing my orgasm, because after this, it's her turn. If she hasn't figured out I'm a pussy eater, she's about to. I fucking live for her crumbling apart as my mouth is on her.

Just thinking about it has me fucking up into her mouth. "Keep going."

She moans and twirls her tongue, sending me fucking crazy.

When I feel my orgasm hitting, I try to pull her up, but she swallows me farther.

"I'm going to come down your throat if you don't get off now," I warn in a hoarse voice.

She grips my cock tighter, her cheeks hollow as she sucks harder, and I slow my thrust as I blow. "Fuck!"

My grip on her hair softens as I come watching her swallow me down. It's a fucking sight I'll remember forever.

Wiping her mouth, she drops back down beside me, panting heavily.

I freeze momentarily, before twisting around to face her. The white sheets tangle around our feet.

With a grin, I run my hands through her bangs, which are all bent and wild now. She looks just as good in the morning as she does all done up. Her messy sleepy hair and sexy smile are heaven. "How are you feeling?" I ask.

The corner of her lips curves up. "Much better."

I shake my head, unable to fight her sultry plea. "Fuck. I've missed you like crazy."

The air feels like it's being sucked out between us. I can't deny her. Leaning forward, my lips capture hers in a new passionate kiss. A whimper escapes her, and I swallow it down.

She digs her teeth into my bottom lip, then she glides her tongue over the top. I growl at the sharp sting that's soothed by her tongue, before shifting my body over her so she has to roll onto her back. I kiss her harder before peppering my way along her jaw and neck. She's only wearing her bra and thong. Sometime during the night, she must have removed her dress. I kiss my way to the middle of her chest, down over her toned stomach until I reach her core.

"Evan," she breathes.

I sit back on my heels, loop my fingers in her thong, and drag it down. But I want to savor this moment. I can see the wetness between her legs, and it makes me painfully hard all over again.

"Are you wet from sucking my dick?"

"Yes," she says, smirking proudly.

"I'm going to eat this beautiful pussy, make love to you, and then I'm taking you to work where you'll think about me all day."

"Then what?" she asks on a shaky breath, an eyebrow quirked as she leans up on her elbows with a smoldering look.

"I'll pick you up after work and take you home."

"Summer will send out a search party."

"She knows exactly where you are."

She grows still.

I stroke her inner thigh as I explain. "I told her she needs to find a new roommate."

"What-t?" she stammers out from my touch.

"You're with me now," I say matter-of-factly, sliding my hands to the crease of her thigh and apex.

Her whole body shudders, and a ripple of goosebumps covers her skin.

Her reactions to my touch make me feral. I run my fingers through her wet pussy, causing a long moan to leave her lips and her back to arch. Her skin is feverish to the touch.

I groan at the sight before me. "Fucking hell, baby."

My right hand glides over her stomach to her breast, where I find her bud taut. I run my thumb back and forth over her nipple. She's bucking her hips, loving the rough touch on her breast. Which is a small handful. Perfect for me. Her whole fucking being is perfect for me.

I move my fingers to her other nipple, giving it the same treatment. When they're both sensitive, and she's thrashing around, needing more, I dip down the bed and lay wet kisses along the inside of her thighs. Her hands grip my head as she tries to push my mouth onto her.

"What do you want, baby?" I say, as I explore her pussy with my fingers, rubbing hard circles over her swollen clit.

"Eat my pussy, please-e," she pants.

I touch her wetness, but I don't enter her. Just teasing her opening, watching as it clenches with need. "Are you going to come if I do?"

A dazed and lustful look settles on her face. "Yes."

"Good girl."

But I continue to tease her with my fingers, which earns me a plea. "Hurry up and do it."

I chuckle, loving her new confidence in speaking up. Body wise, she's always been confident, which I fucking love. She never hides or asks for the lights off. So with the morning light illuminating her features, I push one finger inside her. I watch her breath catch as I hold my own, watching her crumble in my hands. Her head falls back into my pillows, face is open and glowing, making me want to kiss her all over again.

I curl my finger as I draw along the front wall. But as much as I want to watch her come on my fingers, I want to taste her even more. Before she has time to open her eyes, my mouth comes down on her clit. Her sexy long legs squeeze my head. I'm going to make sure she comes twice as hard as she ever has before. Then I'll fuck her until she's achy and spent. I want her to remember who was between her legs this morning with every step she takes. I've never cared about a woman as much as I care about her.

I want to treat her like the precious thing she is. Remove any of the hurt delivered to her yesterday. Enjoy watching her grow into herself more. Now that it's unlocked, I wonder what else she'll do next. She's capable of great things and I'll be honored to be there every step of the way. Encouraging and supporting her. I've been fascinated by her since day one.

She writhes when I lick from bottom to top. She's so sensitive now. I keep my eyes up, observing her every move.

"More," she hisses.

I smile before giving her what she wants.

Dragging my tongue from her clit down to her opening, I enter my thick tongue inside her. She clamps down with her legs as her hole tightens. I grumble a deep, guttural sound at the feeling. She feels and tastes like heaven. I've missed this. I'm harder than I've ever been in my life. High on her.

"Yes-s," she stammers.

Her hips rock and roll in a wave. She's so close.

I pull my mouth off her. Her eyes flutter open, and she looks at me with wild eyes. "What are you doing?"

I smirk like the bastard I am. "Do you want more?"

"Don't come up for air until I come on your face."

I blink in disbelief at her.

"You got it," I answer before bending down, and this time her legs cross over my back. She locks me in place, hips shifting so her pussy rubs all over my mouth. She's pulling me closer. Her scent is strong.

"Don't stop."

As if I could.

I grip her thighs, spreading her and thrusting my tongue inside her. Over and over again. Her muscles twitch under my hands. I remove one to touch her swollen clit.

My jaw aches in the best way. I couldn't care less if I bruise it.

I rub in hard circles as I fuck her. Her body quivers, and I keep thrusting my tongue and twirling my thumb on the bundle of nerves until she clenches and cries out. "Ah. Yes. God. Yes."

I love hearing and feeling her fall apart. It makes me harder.

When her body goes lax, I pull away to find her head on my pillow. All the tension is expelled. She's boneless and sleepy. I take a moment to drink her in. She's real. She's back with me. Right where she belongs. I won't do anything else to fuck it up. She needs to stay here, in my house and my bed.

I lean forward, giving her a quick kiss. Staring into her eyes, I smirk at her lust-filled expression.

"Have a nap. I'll make you breakfast."

"No chance." Her eyes pop open. I know that look. She pulls my head close to hers. "Evan, I need you to fuck me. Take that second orgasm I know you can give me."

My eyebrows shoot up in surprise. She's not mocking me. We've seen I've been able to do it before. I now get to watch her fall apart once more. It's one thing to feel it on my tongue, but to see the ecstasy on her face as she comes around me is something else.

"Don't need to ask me twice."

I shift off the bed, quickly removing my boxers, grab a condom, put it on, and then I settle between her legs.

Her eyes drop down over my body and come back with so much longing I can hear the loud pounding of my heart in my ears.

Lining myself up, I inch forward, easing myself inside her.

My eyes drop to her body, watching her chest rise and fall. Needing to read her clues, and when she relaxes, I inch in farther.

I bring my eyes back to hers, staring as I push inside her one last time. Once I'm all the way in, I pause.

Her pouty lips are parted, and a whimper leaves her mouth. "Mine," she whispers as vibrations rack her body.

And I go still inside her for a moment. If that's how she feels about me, she has no idea how I feel about her. I need to show her.

With my hands on either side of her shoulders, she feels incredible.

"More. Please. Ev——"

I slide out and slowly work inside her more easily this time. She's warm and adjusted.

My heart races as I watch her ripple with a shudder beneath me.

Her hands move to my shoulders. Her spot. But it's when her hips tilt that I feel like I'm all the way inside her.

Every thrust, she clenches around me. I grit my teeth, holding back my orgasm to make sure she comes first.

Her breaths are louder as she cries out, "Don't stop."

"Never," I grunt back, thrusting harder now.

Her back arches, and she cries out my name as she orgasms. I keep going to ride out her release, and then when she's almost done, I stop and jerk inside her.

My breath catches in my lungs like a burn. When we're finished, I kiss her lips and whisper, "I love you, Shell."

This is it. My dream girl is mine.

CHAPTER 37

CHELSEA

EVAN SLIPS HIS HAND into mine and pulls me to his car—black, sporty, expensive. Not in the least bit surprising. After a good night with him, I'm on my way to my first class in my own studio. Evie held the morning classes, and I'm going to take over for the afternoon.

I knew the early morning classes after a grand opening would be too much. I'm thanking myself for thinking ahead.

He pulls the car into the lot, and we take the elevator up. I hit my level, but he doesn't hit his.

I turn to face him. "You don't have to drop me off at the door."

He moves his lips to my ear. "I do."

My teeth skim my bottom lip. "Okay."

The doors open, and we arrive in front of my glass doors. He unlinks our hands, and his fingers grab something from his pocket.

My eyebrows knit together, wondering what he's doing.

"My office keys," he says, opening his hand to reveal a set of keys.

My eyes flick between the keys and his eyes as a smile breaks out on my lips.

"I guess you'll need mine."

He nods.

I grab his keys and wind them on my keychain before opening my purse and looking for my spare.

Spotting it, I hand it over. *We exchanged office keys.*

We gaze at each other. Does he realize how monumental basic things like this are for me? I craved such silly little things like this, and with Evan, he initiates it.

He steps into my space, reaching for my chin to tip it up. The touch and the deep soul-searching stare make me quiver inside.

"Have a great first day." He kisses me in a slow, drugging kiss. His hand slips to my throat, and my pulse beats widely against the pressure. When he pulls away, I'm in a daze.

"See you after work."

My brain snaps awake. "You don't have to wait for me."

"I want to."

"Well, who am I to argue?"

"What time do you finish?" he asks.

"Nine-thirty."

"Pick you up then. Stay here, don't go downstairs." His voice is firm, with a hint of warning.

"Never." I give him a knowing smile and head inside the studio.

My eyes are fixed on the class stretching. My chest swells at the sight. How good it looks in here with a full class. I snap a few photos for socials later, as if sensing him watching. Spinning around, I see him. His eyes are on me before he slips away.

Some might think he's too much. But after what I've been through, I want to feel smothered. It's an intoxicating love I desire.

I move out back to put my bag away, check my emails, and make a coffee for Evie and me.

"Hey," Evie says.

I hold out a coffee cup. "You angel."

I smile. "How were the classes?"

"Amazing. Everything is so fresh."

"Any hiccups?" I ask.

"None."

I sigh. "That's a relief."

"Do you need anything before I go?" Evie asks.

I peek around and see everything is clean and tidy.

I shake my head. "No, I'm working on the website until my class starts."

"Well, I'll let you go. I'll see you tomorrow."

I alter the website with next week's classes.

Twenty minutes pass, and I get the room set up. Clients begin to enter. I didn't check the names until now. But I giggle as I see Jeremy, Nova, Summer, Oliver, Harvey, and Evan come inside.

"Why do I feel like this was a planned attack?"

"Because it was, baby. Everyone in your first class is someone we know. Gabby. Kirstie, who is Jeremy's receptionist, Esme, who is Harvey's, and Cora, who is Oliver's."

"I feel cheap," Summer pouts.

"Why?"

"I don't have a receptionist."

"Hey, neither do I," Nova calls out.

"Yeah, but Kirstie is Jeremy's, so technically she's yours too."

"Hate to break it to you, but she isn't."

Nova shakes her head. "Listen, I wouldn't say no."

"See. I need a rich guy with a receptionist."

My eyes cast to Harvey and Oliver. Something is up with Harvey, but Oliver is single.

"Don't you dare," Summer spits under her breath.

"What?"

Her eyes narrow, but her lips are tipped up. "No chance. He's not my type."

"How do you know?" I ask, looking at Oliver, who is talking to Harvey, almost as if he's calming Harvey down. He probably doesn't want to be here but was dragged by Evan.

"He's too nice. I like my men rough."

My eyebrows shoot up. "Rough? Like dirty?" Nova interjects.

"Yep. Hands dirty, not a keyboard tapper."

"Ouch," Jeremy says.

Summer shrugs. "You boys are lovely and all, but I want a hands-on guy."

"Handsy, you say?" Jeremy looks toward his brothers.

"No. I just told Chelsea no way." Summer exhales heavily, annoyed.

"Relax. I'm playing." Jeremy smirks.

"Alright, you all ready?" I shout, watching them all sit on their beds and turn to face me. Harvey's wrinkled face makes me almost burst out laughing.

He doesn't want to be here. So, you bet I'll make this class hard for him.

"My name is Chelsea, and I'll be your instructor for the next forty-five minutes," I say, walking around the beds. "Lie on your backs. Calves on the bar, and let's take three deep breaths. Let all the day's problems go."

I pause in front of Harvey's and Oliver's carriages, noticing Oliver closing his eyes. "You too, Harvey."

He sighs and finally closes his eyes.

I move to Evan. He must sense me because he opens his eyes. I mouth, *Thank you.*

I love you, he mouths back.

"I love you more."

"Impossible." He closes his eyes, having the final say.

I start with simple arms-in-strap tricep pull-downs, warming the boys up to Pilates.

By the cool down, sweat is dripping from everyone. Summer and Nova are wearing only crop tops and short shorts, so they're a bit better off than the guys.

Jeremy mumbles that he will come back with Nova just to watch her work out in those tiny clothes.

I smirk while Harvey winces. Oliver laughs.

Summer and Nova are unfazed.

My heart is so full.

"Thanks for joining me. I gave you all some wipes, if you could wipe the beds down, please. And if you have any feedback or questions, come and see me."

I stand by the door, ready to say goodbye to them. I decided to treat them like usual clients to practice. During the class, I couldn't help the way my gaze dropped to Evan's, his strong muscles bulging and skin perspiring. It's a massive turn-on. My two loves combining. The first time he did this, it was for a different reason. The support he's continued to show is real love. I wonder how I can make it up to him. I have one idea. I double-check my classes and see the gap I need. I'll pay him back in a good way. Because this was a good present, so I want to reward him with one back.

As they leave, they each thank me for the class. Oliver winks. "I surprisingly didn't hate that."

I laugh. "Good to know."

"But I won't be back," he adds.

The fact he came means a lot to me.

Harvey's next, and he grunts at me. "That isn't a form of exercise." He shakes his head. "It's a form of torture, and I'm sure I've pulled a muscle in my hamstring."

"Get over it." Jeremy shoves his shoulder.

Nova hugs me. "Congrats, girl."

"Thanks," I reply as she follows Jeremy out.

"I'll see you Saturday. Please tell me you told lover boy?" Summer whispers.

I twist and see Evan. I nod to answer her. Summer, Nova, and I have a planned dinner this Saturday night at the old house before Summer moves.

"Do you need anything?" I ask.

"Nope, just you."

I smile. And that's everyone out of the studio except Evan.

"I thought it would be easier a second time." His hands settle on my waist as he steps in front of me.

"When you do it routinely, it is."

"I would rather have a different form of exercise with you." His eyes smolder with a fire that melts my insides.

I laugh. "I bet you would."

"I'd do anything for you." He brings his nose along my neck and lays a kiss on my lips, nipping at my bottom one.

"Mmm...tempting."

"Do you have time?" he mumbles between kisses, as his hands dip to my ass and squeeze, bringing the front of me to him. I feel his hardness. I know exactly what he wants.

"No, I have ten minutes until the next class starts," I say breathlessly. He has this effect on me. One touch and I'm putty in his hands.

He brings his lips to my ear. "I can make you come in five." He bites my ear, and a shiver runs down my spine.

"I know you could. But there's no time."

"You could make time."

As good as it sounds, it's my first day, and I'm not about to have clients walk in to find us.

"I wish I could, but I can't."

He groans, and it's a sexy deep rasp.

The door sounds, proving me correct. The clients are exiting the elevator, so he steps back with a groan.

"Saved by the bell." I wink.

"We'll see about that," His eyes hold mine as he retracts his steps. I allow my gaze to drop over his visible biceps. The green tank should be illegal. It looks that good.

I lick my lips and see him watching me. Shaking his head, he mouths, *You will get your payback.*

Then he retreats to the elevator, where he will head upstairs to his office. An office I have the key for. He won't know what hit him at four-thirty today.

I'm tidying up the studio after finishing the class before my dinner break.

My phone rings, and I rush to my purse, thinking it's Evan.

But I see it's my lawyer, Hayden.

"Hi."

"Chelsea. How are you?"

My heart pounds harder. I wish he would just deliver the news already.

"Good, good. What's the latest?"

He chuckles. "Straight to the point, I get it."

Hayden was referred to me by Evan. He recommended him because he's proven to be a good and trustworthy lawyer. I can't disagree when all he wants to do is to protect me. I want to feel safe too.

"He pleaded not guilty, and he's been refused bail and is waiting for his trial."

"When's the trial?"

"December 11th."

"Okay," I exhale.

"Miss Macfarlane, he will be found guilty."

I hope so...

"Thanks, Hayden."

I hang up and shake off the scared feeling that thinking of Bobby gives me and head upstairs to the man who can wipe Bobby from my mind.

The elevator ride gives me butterflies. No matter how much I see him in a day, it's never enough.

I open his office door slowly with the key he gave me.

My fingers wrap tightly around the door handle as I see him sitting at his desk while on the phone. He hasn't noticed me yet. I rest my head against the door, needing a moment to soak him in. My powerful, protective man.

He's changed his outfit, swapping his athletic wear for a black suit with a white shirt, no tie. His hair is messier than usual, and I know it's from my class earlier. His tousled waves are more prominent now.

When his eyes flick to mine, they widen. My lips quirk, loving that I've caught him by surprise.

I lift off the door and close it. All the while, keeping my eyes trained on him.

His hand lifts to his jaw as he rubs, probably wondering what I'm doing.

I step around his desk, and he follows my movements. I'm impressed he manages to continue talking without a change in his voice.

Coming beside his chair, his hand reaches out to grab my waist. He tries to pull me down onto his lap. I shake my head and push the chair and turn it to face me. Then I drop to my knees and hear a sharp intake of his breath.

Unfastening the button on his black pants, it's followed by his zip. His eyes darken with lust as his hand reaches out to touch my chin. His strong thumb grazes my lips as if he's already picturing what I'm about to do to him.

Pulling down his pants and briefs, I reveal his cock. His big erection jutting out of his suit makes my mouth water. Staring at his cock, and then up into his deep blues has me shuffling on my knees, as moisture pools between my thighs. I want to do this for him.

I lick my lips, and his eyes follow the movement.

He continues to talk in a calm voice and look at me with a steady gaze. How he's able to do that is incredible. But I want to break him. With an evil glint in my eye, my mouth comes down, and I take his tip between my lips. I swirl my tongue around him, enjoying the way his smooth skin and the salt of his pre-cum make me moan. I keep it quieter, but I need him to know I'm loving this. I want him to come in my mouth, then I'll leave and return to my classes.

He says bye to whoever it was on the phone and drops it onto the desk. His hands move to push my bangs out of my eyes.

"So pretty," he mumbles darkly. I take some of his thick cock in my mouth and release it, repeating that motion as I moan.

"That's it," he grunts. His words encourage me. I take him farther and suck harder.

A knock on the door sounds. "Fuck," he curses under his breath. "I forgot about Harvey dropping in."

I shuffle so my body is hidden under his big wooden desk. "Stay right there," he whispers. "We're not done."

Oh, he thinks he's the boss now, does he?

The office door opens, and I hear the heavy stomp of feet. I shift so I can see Harvey's shoes on the other side of his desk. I roll my lips to prevent a giggle.

Harvey sits in the chair. So much for this being a quick visit.

I cross my legs and lean my back on one side of the desk. I may as well get comfortable so I don't get a foot cramp.

"You can't go ahead with the article about Recaredo Events."

There's a panic in Harvey's tone that I've never heard.

"Why?" Evan asks, and I can see him slump in the chair folded forward, elbows on the desk to hide his erection.

"I need her name kept out of the paper."

"What am I supposed to do with that slot? It's due to go out tomorrow."

"I have another article drafted."

"The princess leaves to run away with the bodyguard? How did you get this information?"

"Not just information. I got a picture too."

Harvey slides what must be an image to Evan.

"How?"

"Does it matter?" Harvey asks.

"Is it legal?" Evan asks in a tone full of suspicion.

He huffs. "Of course."

It's quiet for a moment, and I lay my head on the wood. "Thanks."

"Anytime. I gotta go to a meeting across town."

"What about Jemima?"

"I'll keep you updated." Harvey's heavy steps leave. And the door opens and closes.

I peel my back off the wood and crawl out. Once I stand, I stretch my back.

"Sorry, I didn't expect him to be here that long."

"That's okay. I surprised you."

His lips lift into a smirk. "You did. Now we can return to it."

I shake my head and wince. "Sorry, there's no time now. I have a class that starts in five."

I saunter off, but he comes around and slams me against his door, his hot breath on my ear. One hand on my hip, the other on my neck, he says, "You think this is funny? Google edging, baby, because that's what you're getting tonight."

Epilogue 1

Chelsea

A few months later

I only have a few minutes left before I need to be outside for Evan to pick me up. I finish typing the last sentence in my draft of a new eBook. It's going to be a beginner's guide to mat Pilates at home. After taking on the studio, I realized I wanted to offer more. All my classes are full with waitlists. I needed to figure out a way to help more clients.

The books will be available through my website for purchase. I'll also offer new guides for pre-and post-natal pregnancy. It will take a few months to make each eBook, but I'm having fun making them while the trainers teach the classes.

I've been able to take a step back into a managerial role, and I only teach a few classes a week because I'm not ready to give up that part of my life yet.

I quickly close my computer down, put my coat on, grab my suitcase, say goodbye to Colby, and head downstairs.

Evan's car isn't here yet. I check the time on my watch and see it's exactly ten in the morning.

He's due any second.

His driver pulls up and Evan exits the side door, holding a bunch of white gardenias.

I smile immediately.

"Hey."

"Hey, Shell baby. Are you ready to go?"

I nod and step closer, grabbing the gardenias from his outstretched hand. His hand grabs my hip, careful not to squash the flowers, and kisses me.

For a moment, I forget where we are until his lips leave mine.

He takes my bag and puts it in the trunk. As I climb into the car, he slips in beside me.

I keep the gardenias in my hand, a little confused by the flowers because he asked me to pack for a holiday.

"Where are we going?"

"There's only one place at Thanksgiving I would love to visit."

"Will your family be there?"

"No."

"But your gram."

"She's encouraging this."

My forehead wrinkles. "Okay. So where?"

His eyes wrinkle from the irresistibly devastating grin he's wearing.

"Connecticut."

Unable to hold back my glee, I throw my arms around his neck and kiss him. I whisper into his coat, "Thank you, thank you, thank you."

His hand rubs my back up and down.

"You're welcome, baby," he says. "Now buckle up, we have a helicopter to catch."

I sit back in the leather chair and swiftly buckle up. I give the gardenias to his driver to give to his wife.

The ride was smooth and fast. It was a better experience because I was in a helicopter. It was my first time, and it was better than I had ever imagined. I don't know how I'll go back to the cabin after this.

When we exit the helicopter, holding hands, I scan the floor for Anna or my parents.

"I told them I wanted a guided tour before we arrived at the house."

He gently nudges me, which brings me back from my daydream—him calling my family.

"Well, Mr. Lincoln, I'd love to be your tour guide."

"I hired a car, so let's grab our bags and then find our car."

The genuine sounds of excitement in his voice sends a thrill through me.

On the way to my parents' place, I detour to show him landmarks like the New England Air Museum, then the Old Newgate Prison and copper mine, and the Northwest Park.

He was interested in everything, asking questions when he needed to. It made me feel closer to him. Even though I've seen it all a million times, it never gets old. It's breathtaking. I enjoyed watching him experience it for the first time. It was way more special doing it that way. We're here for a week, so we have plenty of time to explore and visit more of my favorite places.

"The drive just up on the right." I point to the house.

"I can't wait to see where you grew up."

I can feel my throat constricting as tears well in my eyes. This moment is huge for me. I'm bringing a man home. A man I love.

As we make our way along the driveway, I can hear his sharp intake of breath. "Incredible."

"It is. It was a great place to grow up in."

"Would you ever move back?"

He turns off the car, but neither of us moves. We twist in the chairs to face each other.

"No. I have my life in New York now."

He nods, but his eyes drift as he thinks about the house. I'm desperate to know what's running through his head.

"What?"

"Would you be opposed if I looked at a property for us?"

I frown, head tilting at that question. "But my studio."

"I get it. It's new, but for now, it could be a vacation stay..."

"But?" I push, hearing the hitch in his voice.

"Maybe one day we could live here?"

He means when we have a family.

I gulp hard, trying to stop new tears from choking me.

"I'd love that, but our businesses..."

"We could work remotely. Not be hands-on, just the owners. Hire more people to manage."

I sit back in the chair and let all this new information process in my brain.

It's a lot. A lot more than I dreamed of.

Move back here? And he's willing to do it with me.

"I have a great team," I say, sitting back and staring out the windshield.

"You do. But listen." He grabs my hand, and I twist around to face him.

"Nothing is happening fast. You set the pace."

"It might take a while to find a house," I murmur.

The words feel strange leaving my mouth. But I don't hate it. It's just unexpected.

"Let's go inside. I want a tour."

I giggle, exit the car, and move to the trunk.

His tan-colored coat and blue jeans with matching tan boots make him stand out in the best way. The wind blows his wavy hair onto his forehead, and I can't help but push it back. Refocusing on the task, he grabs all the luggage and heads to the door.

"You've lived here your whole life?"

"Yep."

The door opens, and Mom, Dad, and Anna stand there with large smiles on their faces. Their eyes automatically go to Evan.

And when they move to mine, the same gleam is reflected in their eyes. As if I didn't already know, now I'm certain they approve of him.

I step forward and hug them each. They all say hi to Evan.

"Would you like tea, coffee, or a cold drink?" Mom asks.

My sister and Dad are already exiting to the living room.

"Let me take our luggage to the rooms and give him a tour of the house first."

Mom smiles as she slips away.

I turn to Evan. He is wearing a humorous expression, but his wolfish grin knows exactly what he's thinking.

I shake my head. "Not happening." I walk off, and he follows behind, listening as I give him the tour.

We arrive at my childhood bedroom.

"Nice. You still have posters on the wall."

He wanders through my room with interest. Coming to the side table, he picks up the frame sitting on it. It's a family photo of me on my twenty-first birthday.

"Mom won't take anything down without me. But when I come home, I love this."

"I love seeing the young Chelsea."

"I'll show you around this week. You can meet some of my childhood friends."

"You don't talk about them much."

I sigh, feeling the heaviness of that knowledge weighing me down. "I know. I don't see them much. Most are married with children."

"You moved away. I get it."

"Exactly." I take the luggage from him and move it near the closet, and Evan whispers in my ear, "Does it squeak?"

I swallow the giggle trying to escape. "Probably."

"What do you mean, probably?"

I bite the side of my lip. "I haven't..." I don't want to say the words out loud. I don't need my family to know those things about me.

His eyebrows rise to his forehead. "We will be changing that tonight."

My bottom lip drops as I see the fire burning in his eyes.

My body temperature rises. *The tour...*

"Let's get back to the tour." I take his hand and walk him out. He and I in my bedroom is a very dangerous thing.

"You have so much room here," he says, his voice is full of disbelief as I take him out the back door. I know what he means. The lots here are much bigger and so is the square footage. Here houses are more affordable for privacy, yards, and gardens.

It's vastly different from New York. Connecticut is more colonial, capes, salt boxes, whereas New York is apartments, brownstones, townhouses, and high-rise buildings. Neither is better, just different.

We walk toward the white oak tree. Suddenly, he stops mid-step, and I turn to check on him to see him staring at it. After a good minute, he turns to me.

An expression I can't read sits on his face.

It's the tree. His favorite tree.

"Crazy, isn't it," I murmur.

"Not crazy...just unbelievable."

"I assume in a good way?"

"Yeah." He clears his throat. "You were meant to be."

I rock back and forth on my heels, knowing exactly what he means.

His hands slip into mine, and he pulls me toward the tree. "Does the tire still work?"

Tilting my head, I stare into his eyes. His eyes suddenly fill with mischief.

With his youthful face, I couldn't turn it down because the tire is at least twenty-eight years old.

"Let's see." I jog toward it, pulling him along.

A light laugh bubbles from my chest. The pure joy and freedom of sharing this special place with him.

I jump in, but it's awkward. "This isn't as comfortable as when you're younger and shorter."

His eyes drop slowly over my legs. "I'm not complaining about your long legs."

That one hungry, admiring look sends goosebumps scattering over my body.

We stay out here for a while before we decide to have a coffee with my family.

Entering the house, I amble to the wooden table where Dad has the paper out and the front page catches my eye. He's not here, so I move the paper toward me, and read the front where there is the current whereabouts of the princess. The paper's been keeping up with the princess's whereabouts.

The picture of her holding hands and looking up at her bodyguard on an island makes me smile.

The way the wind has picked up her dress and her dark blonde hair looks effortless in beach waves, makes me reflect on my happiness with Evan.

Everyone deserves to have this feeling.

"Are you looking at *my* paper?" Evan creeps up behind me, wrapping his strong arms around me. He holds me tight.

The PDA in front of my family is new. My sister winks at me before turning to the kitchen, giving us privacy. I silently thank her. He already had her seal of approval, but now I think she may like him more than me.

"I'm happy she found her happily ever after."

He nuzzles his nose into my neck. "She did. And so did I."

I twist in his arms, my hands behind his neck, gazing lovingly into his eyes.

"You didn't want this..."

"I was an idiot."

I shake my head. "No. You just needed to find me."

"I needed you."

As I stare into his eyes and hold him close, I realize, not for the first time, how completely besotted and in love we are.

EPILOGUE 2

CHELSEA

A few months later

"YOU LOOK INCREDIBLE," EVAN says as he walks toward me.

I'm standing in his bedroom, looking into a floor-length mirror. My mouth opens as I turn, but before I can speak, he grabs my hips and brings me closer to him. My words turn to dust as he kisses me. He doesn't care that I've just finished getting ready. My makeup is heavy, just how I like it.

However, my lipstick is probably smeared now, but it doesn't stop me from kissing him back hungrily. I'll touch it up before we go.

It's my 28th birthday, and we are getting ready to go out for dinner. I requested a quiet and intimate place.

We break our kiss, and his eyes cast downwards, inspecting my outfit and licking his lips.

I do the same. He's in dark blue jeans, a white shirt, no tie, and brown boots.

His hair is that perfect yet slightly tousled wave I love and can't wait to mess with later at home.

I'm totally and utterly obsessed with him.

The way he's looking over my simple black dress, you'd think he was going to eat me.

"We better get out of here before we change our minds." His infectious grin sets the tone.

I shove his shoulder playfully. "You change your mind, you mean."

"No, I want to take you out and spoil you." His fingers on my hip tighten.

Those words and his possessive touch make a large smile stretch across my face.

"I won't stop you." I spin and touch up my lipstick. It hasn't smudged much...

"Before we leave, I need to give you a gift."

My eyebrows pull together, wondering what it could be.

He hands over a brightly-colored paper bag. I take it and pull out a wrapped box. Tearing at the paper, I see it's a jewelry box. Too small for a ring, but still, my heart pounds in my ears. Gifts are another thing he's outdone himself with over the months we've been together, something Bobby never did.

Speaking of Bobby, he was convicted of publication of an intimate image, stalking, harassment, and assault. He'll spend the next two years behind bars, which is helping me sleep peacefully at night.

I open the paper with shaky fingers. And then open the box. A gorgeous shell and gold necklace stare back at me.

My eyes sting and fill with unshed tears. "Evan," I choke out.

"Do you like it?" he asks, his voice laced with concern.

As if I wouldn't. It's classically beautiful.

"I love it."

"Let me put it on."

I remove it from the box and hand it to him.

Spinning around, I lift my hair, and he puts the necklace on me, his touch feather-light. When his lips touch the back of my neck, my breath hitches, and my nipples tighten.

As he pulls away, and I shiver from the loss of his warmth. I drop my hair to swivel back and face him. My hand immediately reaches up to touch the shells sitting around my neck.

"You're my Shell," he says.

I peek up at him from under my lashes, loving the way he's looking at me with so much longing. "Always."

We share a sweet kiss, one I could melt into and end up not leaving the house over.

"We should go," he breathes across my lips.

"Let me fix my makeup."

His smile slowly grows. "Okay, baby. I'll be waiting for you in the living room."

Getting ready for dinner is so different from last year. The devastation and tears on this same day just one year ago are in complete contrast to how I feel tonight.

I'm not the same person I was back then. Now, I live the life I want to, with a man who supports me.

Spending tonight with just him and me will be special. The restaurant Evan booked will be grand. I'll be treated like a queen. I already have a house full of white gardenias in not one, but both houses.

The one we bought in Connecticut one month ago is under construction because the two-story house was older inside, but the land and location were perfect. It's fun changing the house so it's a blend of us. We wanted to make the house 'ours.' Some of the pieces will be kept——like the fireplace and the hardwood floors.

We've already planted our own white oak tree, and we plan to put a tire on ours too. More white gardenias still need to be planted in the garden, but it's getting closer to being completed.

I don't know what that means for us taking another big step, but for now, this is enough to prove to me we are on the right path. We're building a future together.

During the drive, we slipped into our usual quiet but comfortable place. My mind on our renovations. His? Well, I have no idea, but sometimes I wish I knew.

We arrive outside a fancy New York Italian restaurant.

He walks me inside, and I'm hit with the warm aromas of garlic, cheese, and onion.

"You didn't," I whisper, staring at a big wooden table running down the middle of the restaurant. There's no one else here, just our closest friends and family. They all wear excited and reassuring smiles.

I take a moment to appreciate the intimate setting he's created for me. The restaurant's rustic yet elegant charm, with its exposed brick walls and soft, ambient lighting. The table has fresh gardenias and candles, casting a gentle glow around the room.

"Thank you," I breathe, my voice wavers slightly from emotion.

He kisses my temple as my eyes remain on the guests here for me.

His hand on my back encourages me to enter, but I need a moment.

My eyes glaze over with water. He organized this. I refuse to cry and instead rejoice that they are here ready to celebrate me.

"You know I'm not thirty yet," I whisper so only he hears.

"I'm aware. I've already started planning that."

At his confession, my feet stop moving and I turn to face him. "You're kidding."

"No."

"What if I've already planned it?"

His eyes squint, trying to get a read on me to see if I have.

"We could have two."

Laughing lightly, I shake my head at his over-the-top ridiculousness. "I haven't done a thing. I can't believe you have."

"I love seeing the face you make when I give you something."

"I'm going to have to pull a blank face from now on."

"Good luck with that," he says and leans in close to my ear. "There are other signs than on your face."

My lips part as I can feel the way my breasts feel heavy and my nipples so tight from the ache growing between my thighs.

"Unfair," I pout, but it turns to a smile.

"Let's go say hi. And get you a drink," he says with an infectious grin.

I won't argue with that. The first person I say hi to is his gram, and then I make my way through his family before moving around to mine. Every so often, my eyes drift to his, watching him follow. We make our way to our seats. I'm at the head of the table, Summer on my left, Evan to my right.

"Thank you, everyone, for coming," I say, addressing all our friends and family. "It means so much to have you all here."

Evan squeezes my hand under the table; I pull my gaze to him, my heart swelling with affection. This isn't a simple dinner; this is a celebration surrounded by all the people I love.

"Happy Birthday, Shell."

I lean over to kiss him and murmur on his lips. "Thank you. This was the best birthday ever."

"I'm so happy I could make tonight special for you."

The waitress interrupts to deliver a large selection of dishes, including bruschetta with fresh tomatoes, creamy risotto, and an array of pasta that fills the air with tantalizing scents that make my mouth water and my stomach grumble.

In front of me is a glass of bubbly champagne. I take a sip between bites of food. During dinner, I can't help but steal glances at Evan, marveling at how easily he's slipped into my life. His interactions with my family and friends are effortless, as if we've been together much longer than we have. We're already building a life together, one I've always dreamed about.

After the main course, a chocolate sponge cake I recognise as Gram's with flickering candles is placed in front of me. Evan's amused eyes meet mine as he begins singing, "Happy Birthday," and the rest of the room joins. A blush creeps onto my cheeks at the attention on me. As the song finishes, Evan whispers in my ear, "Make a wish."

I close my eyes, reflecting on the past year, from heartache and pain to love and happiness. This year, I found Evan, and so when I blow out the candles, I wish for a future filled with Evan and our kids.

The End.

BONUS

EVAN

CHELSEA AND I HAVE come to our Connecticut house for the final walk-through. All the renovations have been completed. The house has been completely transformed. Our interior designer has meticulously finished adding the right blends of furniture and textures, as well as the carefully chosen colors and designs to reflect our taste.

We used the same designer from our other projects. Because she knows both of us and our styles, she was able to blend it.

"I'm nervous," Chelsea announces.

Walking hand in hand, my fingers intertwined with hers, we walk up the drive to the stairs. With a tender smile, I hand her the keys, urging her to take the lead.

"You open it, baby," I encourage, watching as her shaky hands unlock the door. A joyous squeal escapes her lips as she steps inside. Following suit, I close the door behind us, and my eyes widen in awe at the sight that unfolds within.

Our house.

The light wooden floors and the exposed wooden beams in the living room draw my attention, leading to a spacious white kitchen adorned with state-of-the-art appliances. As we move farther, the skylight in the center of the house bathes the space in natural light, accentuating its beauty.

"This is gorgeous," Chelsea exclaims, her words echoing my thoughts.

"It is," I reply.

Passing through the guest rooms, a den, and a mud room, we eventually reach our bedroom at the back of the house. Chelsea inhales sharply at the breathtaking views before her.

The floor-to-ceiling windows offer a picturesque view of the backyard, filled with flowers, a vegetable patch and, of course, my beloved oak tree with a tire swing and white gardenias.

I stand behind Chelsea, captivated not only by the vision outside but also by the woman standing before me. How did I get so lucky?

This moment as we stand in our house feels like the right time. I decide to seize it, stepping beside her and clearing my throat.

"Shell, baby," I say, taking her hands in mine. "I can't believe this is ours, and it's even better than I imagined."

I relish at how bright and vibrant she looks. Her hair is down and straight, with her bangs framing her face effortlessly. Her makeup is perfectly painted to accentuate her features. My gaze drops to her mouth.

Fuck, her lips.

I want to smash my own to them, but I need to wait. I need her to answer a question.

As my hands hold hers, I can't help but feel the warmth and sweat, hoping she doesn't notice my nerves.

"Since the first time I met you, when I held you in my arms——"

"You mean, I forced you to hug me." She giggles, but it's choked with tears. Her misty eyes make me wonder if she knows what I'm about to ask her.

"Truthfully, you've been my everything since that night. I'll give you anything to make you happy."

I kneel before her, removing my hands to get the ring out and hold it up to her as I gaze into her tear-filled eyes. "Chelsea, will you marry me?" I ask, anxiously awaiting her response.

With a quick nod, her hands fly up to her mouth covering her sobs, she whispers, "Yes," dropping her hand to allow me to slip the princess-cut diamond onto her finger. As she admires the ring, she grips my cheeks, leaning down to kiss me, her lips damp from tears.

Standing up, I hold her close, and we embrace as we gaze out into *our* yard. I can't help but wonder if she envisions our future children playing in the backyard, just as I do.

Two Years Later

Evan

"What did you say?" Evan's low voice shakes.

"You're having twins," the doctor repeats.

My heart beats wildly against my chest; I'm frozen, yet my eyes blink rapidly, trying to absorb the information. One kid, I was sweet with. Two kids at once... What the fuck am I going to do?

I run my hand over my mouth and turn to look at Chelsea. Her face is sprinkled with tears.

Mustering up the courage from somewhere inside me, I say, "We've got this."

"I know we do, I'm just worried..."

"Don't. I'll be fine. I just need a second——" I start.

"You have six months to adjust to the idea."

"Luckily, we have a big home."

The home we share in Connecticut is big enough for more than two kids, but I don't even want to think about that, or I might just throw up.

My nervousness must be showing in my expression because she wraps her arms around me, pulling me close. "We're going to be amazing parents. I can't wait for our kids to play in the yard."

I hold her tighter; our lives are about to change in the most incredible way, and I know I'll be fine with her by my side because I wholeheartedly trust her. "I love you, Shell. So fucking much."

ALSO BY

The Gentlemen Series
Accidental Neighbor
Bossy Mr. Ward
White Empire
The Christmas Agreement
Resisting Chase
Saffron and Secrets

Chicago Billionaire Doctors
Doctor Taylor
Doctor I DO
Doctor Gray
Doctor Spark

The Lincoln Brothers
Billion Dollar Mistake
Billion Dollar Revenge
Billion Dollar Dispute

ABOUT THE AUTHOR

Sharon Woods writes spicy, feel-good contemporary romance novels. Based in Melbourne, Australia, with her husband and two children. She drinks a lot of coffee, loves to workout, explore new places, and has an unhealthy addiction to reality TV.

Follow Sharon:
    Website: www.sharonwoodsauthor.com
    Newsletter